W9-CCX-585

A Billion Ways to Die

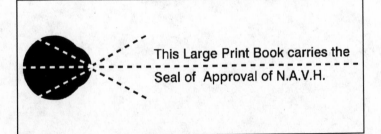

A BILLION WAYS TO DIE

CHRIS KNOPF

THORNDIKE PRESS

A part of Gale, Cengage Learning

GALE
CENGAGE Learning·

Farmington Hills, Mich • San Francisco • New York • Waterville, Maine
Meriden, Conn • Mason, Ohio • Chicago

GALE
CENGAGE Learning®

LIBRARY OF CONGRESS CATALOGING-IN-PUBLICATION DATA

Knopf, Chris.
    A billion ways to die / by Chris Knopf. — Large print edition.
      pages cm. — (Thorndike Press large print mystery)
    ISBN 978-1-4104-7680-7 (hardcover) — ISBN 1-4104-7680-4 (hardcover)
    1. Large type books. I. Title.
PS3611.N66B55 2014b
813'.6—dc23   2015004825

Published in 2015 by arrangement with The Permanent Press

Printed in Mexico
1 2 3 4 5 6 7 19 18 17 16 15

ACKNOWLEDGMENTS

Steve Pednault, forensic accountant, again taught me a lot about financial skullduggery, all in the service of fiction, of course. For the first time, I fully engaged my human resources staff, Kathy Rozsa, Nancy Dugan and Mary Farrell, who helped with corporate hiring and firing. Paige Goettel pitched in with Haitian graffiti interpretations. She and Al Hershner also lent veracity to sailing scenes in the Spanish Virgins.

Legal counsel Rich Orr, former Assistant United States Attorney, advised on federal law enforcement structure. Sean Cronin informed me on munitions and related military gear, as well as lending his keen editorial eye as one of my prized readers. Other readers, Bob Willemin, Randy Costello and Jill Fletcher, also greatly improved the first draft, with Randy correcting my pidgin Spanish. Assist here also from Amarilis Guerra. Thanks also to post-galley readers Mark Baronas and Elena Palermo (courtesy of Marjorie Drake), and, in particular, my sister, Leigh Knopf, who saved Omni from serious gender confusion.

Special thanks to Ian McAteer of Edinburgh ad agency The Union for providing proper Scottish nomenclature and choice of adult beverage, subjects on which he has impressive familiarity.

Bob Rooney, Mintz + Hoke IT samurai, added his usual excellent tech support.

Any inaccuracy or deviation from their knowledgeable advice is the fault of the author alone.

Thanks to cover designer Lon Kirschner, production artist Susan Ahlquist, and copy editor Barbara Anderson for their usual stellar work.

Deep gratitude to another reader, retired agent Mary Jack Wald, who's responsible for setting all this in motion twelve books ago. And to Marty and Judy Shepard, co-publishers of The Permanent Press, who continue to have faith in me and my expanding cast of characters.

And to Mary Farrell, who continues with her abiding patience and understanding.

CHAPTER 1

When you sleep at anchor you learn the language of waves against the hull of your boat. That night, the persistent flip-flip spoke of a steady breeze roughing up the tops of low-rolling swells, which a quick look at the wind direction and barometer promised to be our rocking cradle straight through to morning's first light.

This was hardly a remarkable event. It was the Caribbean, after all, a world where weather was both benevolent and predictable. Most of the time. Sometimes, it could ambush and kill, which is why you never stopped listening to the waves, even after falling asleep.

We were on our sailboat, *Detour,* in a familiar cove lined with palm trees and coarse, flowering bushes growing happily in the bleached blonde sand. The prevailing trades swept in from the hatch overhead, flicking strands of Natsumi's black hair as she slept curled in the forward berth. Moonlight turned the white bed sheet blue and made her skin, darkened by months in the near-equatorial sun, darker still.

I was on my back, my head propped up by the pillow, my mind decelerating to the merely overwound. For this, I had only my genetic code and a lifetime of mental frenzy to blame. Tropical paradise notwithstanding.

I was slowly approaching the moment when the cacophony in my head had quieted enough for the little bay waves to take over, the hypnotic lapping against the hull a welcome prelude to sleep.

Then I was suddenly awake. I opened my eyes, though my focus was on the sounds of the night. Sounds and the absence of sound.

The waves had stopped for about a half-dozen beats, then restarted. Though now there was a catch in the rhythm, an occasional random flip, barely audible, but incongruent.

I sat up, as if the higher elevation would improve my hearing. I slowed my breath and stilled my heart. The breeze freshened suddenly, causing a piece of rigging to clang rudely against the aluminum mast. The boat shimmered a brief moment and heeled so slightly to port. A puff and nothing more, I realized. I smiled at myself and lay back on the bed, inhaling a deep cleansing breath as the first step in regaining the calm of a few moments before.

It took barely minutes for the caress of the waves and the warm, freshly scented air flowing down into the berth to restore calm to my mind and luxurious weight to my limbs.

My eyes gave up the will to stay open and the first shreds of the coming dreamscape skittered into view. Wakefulness came and went a few more times, though I'd likely slipped all the way into slumber when I heard another alien sound. My eyes snapped open and my ears were now filled from the inside with sizzling alarm.

Through the open hatch above me I saw the black shape of a man wearing a helmet and an optical device over his face. He had a rifle pointed at my head.

"Permission to come aboard," came a voice from deep inside the other-worldly apparatus.

Natsumi woke up and made fearful little grunting sounds as she covered herself in a top sheet snatched from the bottom of the bed. I lay still, my hands raised from the bed. The man mumbled something into a device on his shoulder and we felt the boat rock, followed by the sound of heavy footfalls crossing the cockpit and descending into the boat through the companionway. Lights came on in the main living area. Doors to the other berths and the head opened and closed. The man above us nodded and said something else, and another man filled the narrow passage that led to our berth. He reached up to the dome light on the ceiling and flicked it on. He wore the same helmet and optical device. His rifle was slung over his shoulder and he held a handgun with a black barrel and yellow grip. It was pointed at Natsumi.

"Get dressed," the man above us said.

"My clothes are in the salon," said Natsumi.

The man in the passageway backed up. She slid off the bed and shuffled after him, using the sheet to form a makeshift kimono. I was in a pair of loose, flowered shorts. I grabbed a T-shirt left nearby and stepped into my flip-flops. In the salon, the man felt through a stack of Natsumi's clothes, then watched her put on underwear, shorts, bra and T-shirt. She tried to put on a pair of sneakers, but he shook his head and said, with a soft Spanish accent, "Nothing you can run in, baby."

He tossed her a pair of flip-flops that matched mine, forcing the recollection of when we'd bought them two months before, ashore on Tortola.

Then he frisked me, his hands large, strong and deft. Hands that said, "I will crush you if you even hint at resistance." He emptied my pockets of wallet, Chap-Stick and Swiss Army knife.

We were directed up the companionway to the cockpit, where we walked into a bright light. I looked down and saw scuffs on the cockpit floor. I remembered absurdly that I was nearly out of black skid remover. The light flicked off and in my near-blindness I counted the shapes of three men. One of them gripped my arm and moved me around the helm and down to the swim platform. Natsumi bumped into me from behind, so I knew she was still with us.

An inflatable boat was tied to the swim ladder. A fourth man was in the boat behind the wheel. He was in a wet suit, his face blacked out so only the whites of his eyes caught the beam from the flashlight as it slashed through the heavy night air.

I imagined him in the water, harnessed to the inflatable, using a slow, silent breast-stroke to pull the commando-filled boat

11

across the bay.

We were forced into the boat and placed side by side on a bench suspended between the pontoons. One of the men put a zip tie around my wrist, then looped another through a lifeline and cinched it tightly. They did the same with Natsumi. The inflatable rocked crazily as the men found their positions and released the tether from our boat. One of them slapped the helm and the man in the wet suit started the twin engines, nearly silent despite their impressive size.

The boat dug into the water as we spun away and motored out of the cove and into the moonlit ocean, bucking against the waves, causing an occasional burst of sea spray to douse our T-shirts. I held tight to the lifeline and tried to ignore the plastic zip tie cutting into my wrist.

I slipped my free arm around Natsumi's waist and she put hers around mine and we held firmly against the watery motion and the dread-filled darkness.

The motion of the boat as it rose and fell over flat, lazy swells told me we were well into the Caribbean when one of the men put a black hood over Natsumi's head, then one over mine.

Now the wave action became more keenly felt, and the sound of the pontoons slapping at the water and the deep hum of the twin outboards filled my mind. Natsumi pressed hard into me, her message, "I'm frightened, but I'm okay. I just need to know you're there next to me."

The men in the boat said nothing. I understood the futility of asking questions. No words of mine would change the fact that we were utterly in their power, and yet our own silence seemed to enforce a perverse equality. Emotional distance in defiance of physical helplessness.

My breath, trapped inside the cloth hood, smelled foul. It must be what fear smells like to dogs, I thought. A pungent, degraded smell.

After at least another hour, the boat suddenly slowed and changed direction. Now more perpendicular to the swells, we flopped over peak and trough. Then I felt fresh acceleration and another sharp turn. We were maneuvering.

The men started moving around, throwing random undulations into the natural pitch and roll. I heard a voice, speaking low, then a response. The motors dropped down to idle and the gear lever was slipped into neutral. We bumped into something immovable, knocking me into Natsumi. She breathed in sharply and her body tensed. A voice came from outside and above the boat. I heard the whirr of an electric winch, then felt a line weighted at the end smack into my shoulder. A hand gripped me for balance. The boat wobbled and bobbed, and banged steadily into a solid mass. I heard metallic clicks and one of the men shout, "Secured."

The boat performed one more loopy dance and we were suddenly free of the water. The winch whirred louder and a fresh breeze pushed us into the solid thing, which this time we slid against, causing a scraping sound.

I gripped Natsumi a little tighter.

Moments later, the upward movement reversed and I felt the boat move smoothly through the air. I braced for what I knew would follow.

Not necessary. The landing was firm, but gentle. The clicking sounds started again, the winch whirred once more, other softer sounds told of people moving quickly, but efficiently. Someone snipped the zip tie off my wrist and yanked me to my feet. Natsumi was pulled away from me. I heard her say a quiet little "Oh."

Two men helped me over the pontoon.

When I was standing on a solid, roughened surface, strong hands pulled my arms back behind me and another zip tie cinched both wrists together — unbreakable plastic handcuffs.

They took off the hood and I saw the topsides of an old metal vessel, with a center pilothouse, outriggers and cranes. Commercial fishing.

I didn't see Natsumi, or anyone other than two of our three abductors. They pushed my head down to get through a hatch at the top of a narrow stairwell. Supported from behind, I barely made it down the steep passage without falling forward. Light from a rusty bulkhead fixture filled my eyes when I reached the bottom. Everything was coated in layers of paint, white on the walls and ceiling, grey on the floor. Rust showed in spots and around the seams. It was damp and the air was soft and heavy, perfumed with stale salt water.

I was guided down the passage to a door less than ten feet away. At the door, I was shoved face forward against the bulkhead, held in place by a strong hand at the back of my neck. Other hands gripped my wrist and put a cool piece of metal to each of my fingertips. A moment later, I felt a sharp

15

pinprick in the crook of my arm. Taking blood.

Then one of the men cut off the zip tie and they gave me a gentle push into a bare room, closing and securing the door behind me. The room had a wooden bench against one wall, a big aluminum bucket about the size of a spaghetti pot in the opposite corner and a single, blazing light bulb inside a cage overhead. Plumbing and conduit ran across the ceiling. One of the water lines had a sprinkler head that looked new. A large drain was set in the middle of the floor.

That was it.

I sat on the bench and looked more carefully around the inside of the room. There was nothing to see but plain metal surfaces, textured by years of scraping and repainting the walls and building up the sand finish on the floor. The inside of the door was an uninterrupted plane — no latches, knobs or windows.

I looked around for another hour. Nothing changed. That was all there was. I lay down on the bench on my back with my knees up. The light bulb hurt my eyes, but closing them was little better. So I stared above me and studied the rows of randomly sized pipes attached with heavy metal fittings to the ceiling.

I traded this for time on my right side. Then my left. Then I sat up on the bench until that became unbearable, so I repeated the process. I sought other configurations but there was nothing that would make the room any better than painfully uncomfortable.

After a few hours of this, exhaustion began to war with my tattered nerves and sore eyes. I rolled on my right side, facing the wall, with my forearm across my eyes, shutting out the angry glare. Under the circumstances, I'd gained maximum comfort, and I think I slept for a short time.

Cramps drove me awake and onto my back again. I kept my arm over my face until stiffness in my shoulder forced it away. I sat up and swung my feet down to the floor. Head down, I opened my eyes and waited for my pupils to adjust.

I looked around the room again, but it had only become uglier and more forbidding. Of course, I told myself, that's what's supposed to happen. Anger started to creep up my throat, but I swallowed it down. That was supposed to happen as well, I thought. A loss of emotional control. That I wouldn't give them.

I stayed upright on the bench, leaning back against the wall. I experimented with keeping my eyes closed for ten minutes, then opening them for about the same length of time. For whatever reason, it became easier to gaze into the intensely lit room. I breathed evenly and calmed my mind down to near torpor.

With new cramps showing up in new places, I lay down again on my back, holding one hand up to shield against the light. I focused on the sprinkler head as the only thing in the room not covered with uneven globs of paint. I studied it, admiring the neatly soldered coupling in the water line, the symmetrical flower-shaped deflector, the shiny metallic bulb — designed to shatter under the heat of a fire and ignite the system — within the sturdy brass frame.

Shiny metallic bulb?

I turned my head away and rested my eyes, then looked again. I once did market research for a company that made fire suppression equipment. I'd seen plenty of red, blue and yellow bulbs, but never metallic. I glanced away, staring at another section of the ceiling for a few minutes before letting my eyes travel slowly back across the ceiling and onto the sprinkler head.

The bulb wasn't even shaped like a bulb, more of a cylinder. A cylinder that connected to the deflector, at the center of which was a tiny black dot.

I moved my eyes away and sat up again, concentrating on a new line of thought. My mind traveled from my flip-flops up my legs to the flimsy shorts and T-shirt. All soft material. I looked around the room for the hundredth time, coming to the same conclusion. There was very little there, and nothing detachable with bare hands. The wooden bench under me was four stout legs glued to a butcher-block slab. The bucket in the corner was just a bucket.

With a bucket handle.

I leaned back and rubbed my stomach, screwing up my face in discomfort. I bent forward, then back. I stood up and stretched to my full height, my palm against my midsection. I sat back down and tried to stay upright, but clearly was having trouble doing so.

I interrupted the routine for short periods, but then returned to worrying at my gut, burping and lying curled up on my side. After about an hour of this, I slid off the bench and went over to the opposite corner. I got on my hands and knees with my head over the bucket. My body jolted a few times and I shook my head, trying to cast off the sickness and pain. I sat back on my heels and held the bucket with two hands, pulling it up against my body.

Crimps at each end of the handle fit over raised rivets. The handle was strong, but flexible. The rivets were worn and only slightly bigger than the crimps that secured the handle. With my head drooping disconsolately, I studied how the relationship between the attachments shifted as the handle was raised and lowered a few inches. I tested the connections by jamming my thumbs between the handle and walls of the bucket. One side was sturdy, the other loosened by years of hard duty.

With no data upon which to estimate the odds, I decided they were fifty-fifty. Better than zero, less than a sure thing. Why not, I thought.

I took a few more deep breaths, composed myself and visualized the sequence of moves. My moves and the moves of others, impossible to predict.

I'm not a strong man, but I'm in reasonably good shape, and I know something about the destructive power of sudden, concentrated jolts, and the behavior of malleable material under uneven stress.

Or at least I convinced myself I did, as I grabbed the weak end of the handle, wrenched it free of the rivet, stood up with the bucket dangling by its good end, took two steps over to the bench and dragged it away from the wall. Then with as much force as I could gather, stood on the butcher-block slab and drove the crimped end of the bucket handle directly into the middle of the sprinkler head.

The miniature camera lens died with a little pop and the lightest spray of glass dusted the back of my hand. I stepped down off the bench, tossed the bucket into the corner, kicked the bench against the wall and sat back down.

"And fuck you," I told whoever was at the other end of the hidden mics, undoubtedly still operating somewhere in the room, though for how long was now an open question.

CHAPTER 2

I didn't have long to wait. Within minutes I heard the latches unlatch and saw the door swing open. An average-sized white man of early middle age, in a khaki shirt with the sleeves rolled up over thick biceps, olive drab slacks and hiking shoes, stepped over the raised threshold and into the little room.

His jaw was oversized, causing his lower bite to extend beyond his front teeth. With a high forehead and ski-jump nose, and buzz-cut brown hair, his face looked like a stern remark.

He was carrying a folding chair, which he flipped open so he could sit facing me. He pulled a small notebook out of his back pocket, held it for a moment as if considering what to do with it, then stuck it in his shirt.

"Touché," he said. "Very clever."

I said nothing.

He took the notebook back out, along

with a pen, which he uncapped with his mouth, holding it there like a tiny cigar.

"I have a replacement for the camera, and now you'll have to piss down the drain," he said.

He jotted something in his notebook.

"Thirsty?" he asked, looking up.

I didn't answer.

"You are. You haven't had anything to drink for over twenty-four hours. You'd be amazed how quickly you can die of thirst. Food, no big deal. People go weeks without eating. But we need water. You lose a little vapor with every breath."

He waited for me to speak. When I didn't, he said, "I know you can talk because I heard you tell me to go fuck myself."

"No I didn't. I said 'fuck you.' "

"A distinction without a difference. Are you thirsty?"

"Yes."

He looked down at his notebook again. Then still clutching it, folded his arms and looked me in the eyes.

"You never asked the men why you were being carried off. That's an odd lack of curiosity," he said.

"I'm curious about the volcanism that formed the Caribbean archipelago, but I don't bother interviewing the rocks."

"Rocks don't speak?"

"They may speak, but they probably don't know."

"You're referring to our Special Forces."

"They aren't Special Forces."

He tilted his head.

"Sez who?"

"They might have been at one time. Today they're mercenaries."

He smiled more through me than at me, as if recalling a private joke.

"And you know this?" he said.

"Their night vision equipment is a type commonly available, and more advanced than army issue, though it hasn't achieved Mil Spec due to unsatisfactory failure rate and per unit cost. Okay for a civilian hunter, no good for supply officers dispensing thousands in remote parts of the world."

He took out his pen and tapped it on his knee.

"But we did capture you. That should tell you something," he said.

"It does, but not enough. That's why I brought you here."

"You didn't bring," he started to say, then realized I had, in fact, brought him there.

"The camera was the only way to monitor what was going on inside this room," I said. "For all you knew, I was about to slash my wrists with the bucket handle. Somebody had to show up, and since it would take awhile to rig a new camera, you thought, what the heck, I'll start the interrogation now. A little ahead of schedule, I'm guessing, since I'm not yet dying of hunger and thirst or hallucinating from lack of sleep. Which tells me you're in a bit of a hurry."

His face was blank, though a stream of thought ran behind his eyes.

"Ready for that water now?" he asked.

"I am."

He left through the open door and returned seconds later holding a large bottle of water. I'd seen the brand in grocery stores around the Caribbean. French.

It wasn't until the cool water hit my lips that I realized how thirsty I really was. I drank half the bottle, then almost immediately had to pee.

"You're curious about your girlfriend, I imagine," he said.

"Very."

"What's her name?"

"What's mine?" I asked.

"You don't know?"

"I don't know what you know. This is the game. Meter out little bits and pieces of information over a long period of time. Deprive me of sleep and basic necessities in

25

order to wear me down, mentally and physically. Keep me guessing as long as possible in the hope I'll betray myself through sheer confusion. Keep me isolated and then win my trust by appealing to the instinctive need for human contact. Flatter me, frighten me, maybe drug and torture me. All to extract something I might eagerly provide if you simply ask."

He nodded, almost in disappointment, then referred to his notebook. The way he flicked randomly through the pages made me feel it was more of a prop than a legitimate tool.

"Her name is Natsumi Fitzgerald," he said. "There's a federal warrant out on her in connection with terrorist activities in the United States, Europe, the Caribbean and Latin America. She operates with a male Caucasian who goes by a series of aliases, among them David Reinhart, Alex Rimes, Kirk Tazman, and my favorite, El Timador. All these aliases, with the exception of El Timador, come complete with passports, driver's licenses, e-mail addresses, credit cards, bank accounts and so on, all acquired through identity theft. We have a video clip of this man, who happens to look a lot like you. How am I doing?"

I didn't answer. We waited each other out

for about five minutes, then he spoke.

"We have your fingerprints and DNA. Ergo, we know who you really are."

"Not yet. If you'd identified the prints and DNA, you'd tell me."

"It's only a matter of time," he said.

"Time won't help. If it's not there now it'll never be there."

"Quite the philosopher."

"Empiricist."

"Then you can see your situation is hopeless, empirically speaking."

"Nothing of the sort, though it is confusing. It would help if you told me what you wanted."

"You know what I want," he said, returning to his notebook and pen, as if ready to jot down my answer.

"No I don't. You're either giving me too much credit, or not enough. I can't tell."

"Where did you get the scar?" he asked, pointing toward my head with the butt of his pen.

"Car accident."

"Really. Looks like a bullet wound to me."

"That's what everybody says. But who survives a bullet wound to the head?"

"No one entirely," he said. "Some survive, but go crazy."

"You'd want to avoid those people."

"Do you know a man named Joselito Gor-rotxategi?"

I did. He was a financial expert and con-niver connected to a group of right-wing Basque extremists. He'd operated out of New York until the Basque operation took a bad turn. Now he was in federal prison, mostly because of me.

"No," I said.

"He knows you."

"Can't help that."

"He knows you as El Timador, but he thinks your real name is David Reinhart. We know it isn't."

"Better get word to Joselito."

"He said your technical skills are formi-dable. Apparently that's so."

"Everybody knows the old camera in the sprinkler trick."

"He says you're skillful in financial mat-ters as well."

"Then how come I'm not rich?" I asked.

"Who says you're not?"

"I'm not. But I have my health."

"Maybe not for long," he said.

I shifted around on the bench, knowing well it wasn't possible to find a comfortable position. I was tempted to say I'd make a full confession if he would only bring me one of his folding chairs. If I only knew what

28

to confess to.

"Could you just tell me what you want?" I asked.

"We need to know where it is," he said.

"What's 'it'?"

"You know."

I didn't. My knowledge of interrogation techniques came out of a book, though I guessed demanding someone tell you something he didn't know might be an effective tactic. To what end, who knew, though maybe I wasn't supposed to know that yet either.

I lay back down on the bench with my knees up and my hands clasped over my chest.

"Let me know when you're ready to talk," I said. "You know where to find me."

I half expected to be wrenched up off the bench and slammed into the wall, but after a few minutes, I heard him stand up, fold his chair and leave the room. The door closed again and the overhead light maintained its unblinking presence.

I got up and started searching for the hidden microphones.

About a half hour later the door opened again and this time a woman stepped into the room. She was older than the man, with severe, straight brown hair cut in bangs across her forehead and thick, plastic-framed glasses. Makeup free, she could have used some, especially on her shiny red nose. She wore simple cotton clothes and mannish shoes in need of polishing.

She brought her own chair, which she unfolded gracelessly before offering her hand.

"Alberta," she said.

"Victor," I said, shaking her hand.

"Of course," she said, settling into the chair like a stenographer about to take dictation, though instead of a notebook and pen, she held a digital recorder. She clicked it on and set it carefully on her lap.

"This shouldn't take long," she said, in delicately accented English. "I've already spoken to your lady friend Natsumi, who is quite delightful, by the way. She shared with me all sorts of lovely stories from her childhood, career as a blackjack dealer and studies of psychology. Lovely, but not very helpful."

"Better than the conversation I had with that other joker."

"I'm not a joker, Victor. That you should know," she said. I believed her.

"I believe you," I said.

"Good. So, first question. Are you frightened?"

"No. I'm terrified. I've been terrified since looking up the barrel of that combat weapon. I'm terrified for me, and for Natsumi. Do I want out of this? Yes. I really, really do. Am I willing to cooperate? Sure, but how can I cooperate if I don't know what it's about? I can try to guess, but I'm a data freak, and data-wise, I'm working with some pretty thin gruel."

"My colleague thinks you're feigning ignorance."

"Do you?"

She looked down at her recording device.

"Inconclusive," she said, looking up again.

"Voice stress analyzer?" I asked. "Who made it?"

She showed me.

"Good unit," I said, "but worthless on a subject you've already been stressing out for hours."

"I agree," she said, snapping off the device. She sat back in her chair and let out a frustrated little sigh. "You seem to know a great deal about clandestine technology."

"Everyone needs a hobby."

"We wonder how this knowledge came to you. There's no record of you working intelligence for any of our agencies."

I'd worked as a researcher for a half-dozen defense contractors trying to repurpose

31

military gear for domestic markets. Night vision goggles, hidden video cameras and voice stress analyzers were among the least sophisticated stuff I'd tested out in the field.

"Are you a US citizen or foreign national?" she asked. "According to your DNA, you're of mixed European ancestry, but that doesn't tell us much."

"I was hoping for something a little more exotic."

"With so many names, passports and driver's licenses, you must be in a constant identity crisis."

"Knowing thyself is way overrated."

"You're not the person described by your passport, of that I'm certain."

I'd used dozens of different identities to accomplish hundreds of tasks, so it was inevitable one would trip me up eventually.

"Only in a sense," I said.

"And your friend isn't Beverly."

"You'd have to ask her."

"She's Natsumi Fitzgerald. That's something we certainly know."

"You have more faith in certainty than I do."

"That was a neat trick you managed with the Basques," she said.

It wasn't a trick, I thought to myself, it was a series of highly intricate, interdependent dirty tricks. And I almost said that, before self-preservation trumped vanity.

"An ancient and honorable people," I said.

"We think we know how you did it, though there are gaps. I don't suppose you'll give us a thorough debriefing."

"Who's we?"

"Why should I tell you anything when you won't tell us anything at all?" she asked.

"Okay. Give me a chance. What do you want to know?"

"Where is it?" she asked.

I laughed an honest laugh.

"I read the book, you know," I said. "This whole approach didn't work any better on Joseph K."

She looked confused.

"Sorry, don't understand."

"You people keep asking me about 'it,' but you won't tell me what 'it' is. I think it's the first rule of interrogation. Tell the subject what you want to know."

"We're not interrogators," she said. "But we're not stupid. And we won't waste a lot of time playing games."

"Who's 'we'?"

She squinted at me from behind the thick glasses, as if seriously considering my question.

"We are either very dangerous enemies or

33

natural allies. It's for you to decide. This doesn't have to be adversarial. There's more than enough for everybody."

"Enough what?"

She leaned toward me with a look of earnest intent. I tried to stare into her eyes, but I couldn't make them out behind the thick glasses.

"My colleague doesn't think torturing you will work."

"There's a relief."

"But torturing Natsumi will. Not because of her, because of you. I'm inclined to agree."

Not knowing the right thing to say, I figured nothing was the best choice. Even with the voice stress analyzer in the off position.

"There's a drain in the room we have for her, just like this one," she said, pointing to the floor. "We can simply wash off the blood with a hose."

"You're right. I'll tell you anything."

This pleased her. She gave a little "atta-boy" gesture.

"I thought as much," she said.

"Just tell me what you want to know."

"Good," she said, actually slapping her knee, "where's the money?"

Ah, I thought. Of course. It always comes

back to the money.

My late wife had embezzled millions from her insurance agency for no apparent reason, given the agency's success and my wife's otherwise exemplary legal and ethical standing. I'd spent months, at great risk to life and limb, solving the puzzle and making whatever amends were possible.

Despite my best efforts, I knew there'd be loose ends, and it was inevitable others would catch wind of the scam. But at least now I had an explanation for our present circumstances, an immense relief.

"I don't have it anymore," I said.

Her excitement slid down a notch.

"Of course you have it."

"No. I gave it back to the rightful owners."

"That's impossible," she said.

"No, it's easy. Simple wire transfers. The hardest part was keeping the transactions from being traced back to me."

"We would have known."

That puzzled me.

"I have confirmation that all the funds made it to their rightful homes. Not 100 percent in all cases, but I think they were happy getting back what they didn't know they'd lost."

Now she looked puzzled.

"What you're suggesting is impossible," she repeated.

"Shuffling millions of dollars around these days is tough, but not impossible. For most of the people I was dealing with, ten million is a daily rounding error."

The woman blanched as if I'd given her a gentle slap.

"Ten million?"

"Give or take. I kept a little to cover expenses. Call it a recovery fee."

She jumped up so violently her chair toppled over and collapsed. She grabbed me by the shoulders and shook.

"Not funny mister," she said, enunciating every syllable. "I meant what I said about Natsumi. You can't even imagine."

"I don't understand," I said, as sincerely as I could.

"Ten *million*?" she said to me through her teeth. "Is that what you think will settle this? After we've come this far? Are you mental?"

She paced around the little room with her fists clenched to her side. I saw her as a child throwing a temper tantrum.

"I have other funds," I started to say, but she cut me off.

"*Billion*," she hissed at me. "With a *B*. That's the only thing I want to discuss with *you*." I shook my head and tried to convey my heartfelt confusion as I watched her leave the room, slamming the door behind her.

I was down a bucket, but I'd gained a folding chair, though before I could figure out what to do with it, the door opened and the original interrogator and three other men crammed into the room, shoving me back onto the bench. Two of the men pinned me against the wall and the third gripped my throat. The interrogator took a syringe out from behind his back, and without rolling up my sleeve, stuck it in my arm.

"*Buenas noches,*" said one of the men holding me, and before I could muster a response, my mouth filled with cotton, the little room lost all substance and I fell backward into the dark.

CHAPTER 3

A man in a short-sleeved shirt, shorts and sandals shook my leg. I looked at him through mist-filled eyes, wondering where he'd come from. As he shook my leg I heard him asking me questions. He was an island guy, speaking to me in accent-inflected tourist English.

"Talk to me, captain. Tell me you're okay," he said.

"I don't know."

My voice sounded distant and hollow, as if I were talking into a barrel. My eyes felt too big for my head, and my head too big for the rest of me. As I focused on the man, I saw his other hand shaking someone else's leg.

Natsumi.

I rolled over and looked at her sleeping face. I touched her cheek and she twitched, as if warding off a fly. I sat up, dragging my head along with me. The world wobbled for a moment, then settled back on its axis. The man was smiling at me.

"You had some kind of fun last night, eh captain?"

I recognized him. Clive Higgins, from the marina on Virgin Gorda, where we often put in for provisioning and a night or two at a sturdy dock.

"Hi, Clive. Where are we?"

He told me, naming a coral-lined cove on the northwest side of the island. The sun was high above the horizon, heating up the sand where we lay. *Detour* floated at anchor just outside the reef. I bent over Natsumi and brushed her hair back.

"Hello in there. Can you hear me? You okay?"

She opened her eyes in a squint, then shut them again. She rolled over on her back and put her forearm across her face.

"I might throw up," she said.

"That's okay," said Clive. "Good for the recovery."

She looked up at him.

"Easy for you to say."

Clive helped me to my feet and down to the sea where I scooped up some water and slapped it on my face and through my hair. I almost never drank alcohol and my only hangover was a distant teenhood memory, so I had no standing in claiming this to be the worst hangover in history, though it felt like it.

When we got back to Natsumi she was wiping her mouth with the bottom of her T-shirt. She told us to stay away from the other side of a nearby palm tree. I sat on the sand while Clive took her down to the water's edge. When they got back, she joined me on the beach.

"Did that just happen?" she asked.

"Yes."

"Good. I mean, good I wasn't on LSD."

"Too much rum make you think you are, ma'am," said Clive. "Though I never do those things myself."

"How did you know we were here?" I asked.

He pointed at *Detour*.

"Saw your boat. Got on board and nobody's home. Dinghy tied to the stern. Thought you might be dead bodies washed up on the reef. These things happen when parties get started."

"Some party," said Natsumi.

"That's unauthorized anchorin'," said Clive. "You're lucky the officials don't already tow you back to Road Town."

"So let's get the heck out of here," I said.

His open fishing boat had an aqua-colored

freeboard and a pair of eyes painted on the forward hull. He maneuvered through the reef with the confidence of long experience, then sprinted out to *Detour* as if British Virgin Islands maritime law enforcement was about to swarm the cove.

He wouldn't accept a tip.

"Just get somebody home some night who wouldn't be gettin' there himself and the bill's clear," he said. "And no more drunk swimmin'. Your luck there is all used up."

As we watched him glide away, Natsumi held on to me for a moment, then told me she needed a shower and some aspirin and then we could talk. When she went below, I raised the anchor and set a bearing for Saint Thomas, US Virgin Islands, where we'd left Omni the mutt at our home marina.

There was plenty of time to make plans and change course if that's what we decided. At that moment, I just wanted to move.

It had been nearly a year since we'd flown down from the States and joined the lazy flow of expats, idealists and escape artists that circulated continuously up and down the Caribbean Islands. After a short run of hotels and flats-by-the-week, we bought *Detour* from an iron miner who'd sailed her up from Australia and decided something more than a thirty-six-foot sloop made better sense for the trip back.

It was a year of recovery. Many months before, my wife, Florencia, and I had both been shot through the head. She died, I didn't, though the world was made to think I had. Crippled and brain damaged though I was, I'd used my status as a dead man to some effect, leading to an accounting with Florencia's killers.

But then there was the matter of Florencia's ill-gotten millions, which led to more months of deadly madness that proved the wages of obsessive frenzy and unrelenting fear were dearly paid.

Natsumi had been with me nearly throughout, through no fault of her own. I never required her to stay, though now the thought of her apart from me was beyond bearable.

So when she proposed that our next project involve a boat and a dog, the decision was easy.

I was still officially a dead man, though several unofficial versions of myself had racked up criminal records sufficient to put the corporeal me away for a very long time. We hadn't done Natsumi's legal standing any favors, either, so living as international fugitives had by necessity become our permanent status.

Fortunately, we were good at it. At least I thought we were, before the events of the last few days and nights.

"What happened?" Natsumi asked, after returning to the cockpit with a head full of wet black hair and two large mugs of coffee.

"We got caught."

"How?"

"I don't know. Best guess is the passports we used to clear customs on Jost Van Dyke are buggered," I said. "One or both. Had to happen some day."

"Those people weren't Brits," she said.

"I know. Americans. Though Alberta had a slight accent."

"So who were they?"

I gave her the same theory I'd given the first interrogator. Intelligence operatives or criminals. Assuming the difference mattered.

"Why'd they let us go?"

"I don't know."

"You really don't," she said.

"I really don't."

"I'd prefer it if you knew everything all the time."

"Sorry, darling."

"I was very frightened," she said.

"Me, too."

"Should I be now?"

43

"I don't know."

In the months we'd spent on the boat, concentrating on thick books, hearty food and obsessive exercise, our bodies had become lean and fit, our minds fresh and bright and our anxieties thoroughly repressed. Though not obliterated, at least not for me. Somewhere locked in a bitter chamber of existential fear, part of me was waiting for a reckoning. Maybe not the final test, but proof that idylls were the stuff of other people's dreams.

So when those nightmare mercs descended on our blissful refuge, I was aghast, but not surprised.

"Where are we going?" Natsumi asked.

"Back to Saint Thomas, but I want to discuss."

"We need to get Omni."

"And bring her where?"

"Wherever we go next."

"What if it's London? Put her on a jet in cargo? Then quarantined?"

She was quiet for a moment.

"You're saying she's safe and secure with Ellsworth on Saint Thomas," she said. "Leave her there till we sort this out."

"We have to assume everything on *Detour* is compromised. The computers, smartphones, nav equipment, documents, the

44

works. And since they know *Detour,* they know the marina in Red Hook. That's two identities blown."

"If they let us go, why do we care?"

I knew she already had her own theories, and the question was mostly rhetorical.

"Did they really let us go?" I said. "I don't know."

"But here we are. Back on our boat."

"I know. Doesn't make sense."

"So we shouldn't go back to Red Hook."

"No. Saint John. Right next door."

We had just enough time before nightfall to reach the mooring field off Caneel Bay, a short dinghy ride from Cruz Bay on Saint John's west coast, about five miles by water from Red Hook. Since we'd checked out of customs in the United States before entering BVI waters, we were supposed to check back in. Instead, we pulled together all the cash we could find — about eight hundred dollars — got in the dinghy and motored into town, leaving everything else on board, including the ID we'd used in the BVI.

At the first tourist joint, I gave the bartender twenty bucks to let me use the house phone to call Ellsworth Brinks, the owner of our home marina in Red Hook, Saint Thomas.

"Hey, folks, how's the cruisin'?" he asked.

"Truncated. How's the pup?"

"Enthusiastic. What's up?"

"We need to get back home in a hurry. We've got a lift to the airport. Can you come get the boat and hold on to Omni for a bit more?"

"Sure, man. Hope it's not trouble."

"No trouble. Just a thing we have to do."

"You're paid six months out, so no trouble for me."

I told him where to find *Detour*. He'd send one of his men over in the morning. We traded the types of banalities sailors usually trade, then I got off the phone. From there we went into the shopping district and bought all new clothes and soft bags in which to carry them.

We threw the old clothes in a dumpster behind the store and moved on to a very different kind of joint, a bit out of town and set like a bird's nest on a pile of rocks thrust into a neighboring bay. The light was crepuscular, the music declarative and the drinks dispensed and consumed with abandon. The patrons were uniformly weather-beaten and wiry, regardless of age, with swaggers in various states of compromise.

A wooden mast, complete with boom and a doused sail wrapped in its rigging, ran the length of the bar. Model sailboats on individual shelves covered the parts of the walls not laden with nets, portholes, framed charts, wooden ship wheels, barometers and other nautical totems.

Most importantly for us, on a wall between the men's and women's rooms was a white board where you could list the name of your vessel, its length, beam and sail plan, departure date, destination and the type of crew you hoped to recruit. Likewise, loose crew could post their credentials and preferred commissions, though most checked the box "Will consider anything."

There were two boats offering viable postings. I memorized the names and we moved off toward the next phase in the process: hanging around the bar, nursing drinks and asking if anyone knew our target cruisers.

It wasn't long before a bearded guy with thin, curly hair, and his wife, who looked identical from behind, latched on to us. They'd launched their trip two years before from Seattle and had traveled to the islands via the Panama Canal. The guy's name was Ed and he was joyfully drunk — for the first time, he claimed, since Catalina Island. His wife was reasonably sober, but didn't contradict him.

"We'd just come off a summer squall," she said. "Forty knot blow. Ten footers.

Confused seas. Heaved to and just rode it out. Ed had the helm for thirty straight hours. I thought I'd have to cut his fingers off the wheel."

"You'll be cuttin' my fingers offa this," he said, holding up a beer mug filled with something far more colorful than beer.

"We prefer our storms at anchor," said Natsumi.

"Smart woman," said Ed. He looked at me conspiratorially. "You get her in Bali Bali?"

"I got him, at a brothel in Kuala Lumpur," said Natsumi.

Ed's wife grinned.

"Give me the address," she said. "I might have a trade-in."

Ed felt that deserved a toast.

"We just need to get to Puerto Rico," I said. I asked them if they knew any boats headed that way.

"No, but *That's A Moray* goes back and forth all the time," said Ed. "You know Jersey and Dizzy?"

"Jersey and Desiree Mitchell," said his wife. "I saw them here earlier. Jersey's big," she held her hand about a foot over her head. "Frizzy hair like Ed's, what's left of it. I love him, he's a nut."

"She prefers frizzy haired nuts," said Ed.

"They own a furniture store on the island," said Ed's wife. "Do their own shipping and handling. How's your back?" she asked me.

Ed grabbed my shirtsleeve and started pulling me into the crowd. I let him, not knowing what else to do. Natsumi followed. A few minutes and some awkward tousling later, he deposited me in front of a tall woman with long, dirty blonde hair, a limp tank top, white shorts and a huge shell-festooned necklace.

"This is Dizzy," Ed said to me. "You gotta take it from here."

"Take it where?" asked Desiree.

"Puerto Rico, I hope," I said, introducing myself as Jonathan Cornwall, and Natsumi, when she came closer, as my wife, Natalia.

"Desiree," she said. "You looking to crew?"

"Absolutely," I said. "Whatever you need."

"Do you cook?" she asked.

That stumped me. I sure as hell didn't. Natsumi came to the rescue.

"I do," she said.

"Good. We need a cook for two passengers paying tourist fare. And a helmsman. You can do that can't you?" she asked me.

"You bet. How long's the boat?"

"Forty-eight feet. Custom cutter-rigged sloop."

She ran through all the crew requirements and I was fine with everything, even if I'd never wrangled two foresails, a cutter's distinctive feature.

We agreed to report at sunrise the day after next and be ready for anything from scrambling eggs to piloting the boat out of Cruz Bay and into the rolling Caribbean Sea. The pay was short, but so was the trip, and most importantly for us, it provided entry into Puerto Rico without the inconvenience of clearing customs.

We were about to drift back into the crowd when Jersey showed up. As stated, he was a big man, his collarless shirt unbuttoned to his navel, revealing some fleshiness around the middle. His hair was a kinky grey ball partially constrained by a woman's hair clip. A glaze of sweat reflected the bar light off skin baked a perpetual island brown. My hand felt like a child's when it disappeared into his grip.

"Most entirely excellent," he said, when Desiree introduced us as the week's crew. "It's the ultimate milk run. We only need crew because we'll have friends aboard. Their authentic Caribbean experience includes full-time attention from the captain. And first mate. Not that we mind. We're people people."

"Speak for yourself, Sammy Davis," said Desiree. "I was voted Miss Anthrope in high school. What about you?" she asked Natsumi. "What were you voted?"

"Most Likely to Attract Ethnic Insult."

"Oh," said Desiree.

Jersey grinned a crooked grin and nodded over the top of his beer.

"Ed tells me you have a furniture store," I said, trying to pull the attention back to me.

The two of them described running a custom design shop out of a loft in Soho through the eighties and nineties, burning out, getting drawn into the tropical haze, selling the loft for obscene money, moving down permanently and never looking back. They traded the story back and forth as they went, as if rehearsed, which it clearly was through hundreds of tellings. I couldn't decide if they completely bought their own myth, or so enjoyed how it sounded they may as well have. We honored them either way by lavishing envy.

"Maybe someday," I said, "maybe someday."

"Work kills," Jersey said. "I was in line for type two diabetes, coronary thrombosis, maybe a cerebral hemorrhage. All stress-related."

"He was dead man walking," said Desiree.

"Retail isn't exactly a cake walk," I said.

"The furniture gig was mine," said Desiree. "Jersey had a bigger issue."

"Government job," he said.

"Like having your soul sucked out through your nose," she said.

"Like getting pecked to death by ducks," said Jersey.

"What did you do?" asked Natsumi.

"FBI supporting the Assistant US Attorney," said Jersey. "New York Southern District. Rudy Giuliani's playground."

"Can't blame it on Rudy," said Desiree.

"I was a workaholic. Busting bad guys gets in your blood."

He gave a theatrical growl, which Desiree answered in kind. It felt like they'd done this before as well.

"Jersey liked the investigative part," said Desiree. "I used to call him Donnie Brasco."

He liked that, but said, "Never had the pleasure of doing undercover," he said. "Anyway, those guys keep a low profile. How would I do that?" he added, sweeping his hands up and down his oversized physique.

"Pretend you're a bear," said Desiree.

"But you gave it up," I said.

Jersey gave a long slow shrug, "Yeah, the bad guys aren't the problem. It's the bureaucracy that'll kill you."

"Do you stay in touch with the old crowd?" said Natsumi.

Jersey looked at her.

"Should I?" he asked.

"I would," she said, as if entranced by the idea. "Extreme coolness factor."

Jersey liked that enough to shift a little in Natsumi's direction. Desiree then shifted nearly imperceptively closer to her husband.

"Show how cool you really are and get these folks another round," she said to him. He took our orders and moved into the crowd, which instinctively opened up to give the big man a clear path to the bar.

While he was gone, Desiree described their boat's galley and what Natsumi could expect for provisions. Natsumi paid close attention, asking questions that seemed to solidify her standing as a bona fide ship's cook. Desiree reported that when Jersey came back with our beers. He gently grilled me on my nautical skills and experience, holding up his end of the screening process. I must have passed muster, because the conversation easily slid from there into a comparison of rum- versus vodka-based cocktails. I was actually far less qualified in that arena, though I held on well enough to take us to closing time.

Back out in the dark, Natsumi and I walked over to a park where street vendors ran their carts during the day and spent the night playing cards with cab drivers and other folks who had nowhere else to go. We stayed outside the social circle, but close enough to be sheltered within the gentle hubbub through the night and into the next day.

We managed another five hours of sleep out on the beach that day, and repeated the process over the next twenty-four hours. We had the money to pay for a hotel, but no identification. Cash payment would have probably obviated the need, but it wasn't worth the risk.

And it was good discipline. We hadn't talked about it, but those languid days and nights on the boat had taken the edge off the vigilance that had kept us alive through months of relentless peril and pursuit across half the globe. The capture and interrogation had dragged us painfully back to our exclusive reality.

"Why did they let us go?" Natsumi asked, not for the first time, as we walked stiffly through the predawn light on the way to

"I still don't know," I said.

She bumped into me as we walked.

"Come on, theories."

"They wanted information from us. Information we didn't have."

"Or didn't know we had," she said. "Doesn't explain why they let us go."

"Unless we gave it to them after all."

"How could that be?"

"Drugs. Sodium Pentothal, or some other truth serum," I said.

"Does that stuff work?"

"Not really. If it did, we wouldn't have a debate on torturing terrorists. We'd just give them a shot and sit back with a notepad."

"Say they didn't get what they wanted. Why let us go?"

"They aren't killers."

"Do you believe that?"

"No," I said. "There's another reason."

"They want us out here?" she asked.

I looked over at her in the fresh light coming up from just below the horizon. Her long black hair was in a ponytail forced through the back of a yellow baseball cap. In shorts, running shoes, tank top and lightweight windbreaker, she looked to all the world like a jogger about to go a few miles before her commute down to Wall Street.

"That's my best guess," I said.

"But we're out of their control."

"Not if they keep track of us."

"Tough to do unless they shot GPS monitors up our butts."

"Technically, subcutaneous beacons. Those things don't work either."

"So I still don't get it."

"They found us once. They think they can do it again," I said.

"Oh."

CHAPTER 4

That's A Moray wasn't the newest boat in Cruz Bay, but it looked plenty shipshape. The white hull was polished and the teak brightwork sparkled with fresh varnish. Jersey was directing a pair of island guys loading boxes into an aft hold. I ran up and pitched in. No one spoke a word to me until we'd cleared the docks. Jersey paid the men, then gave me a paper chart that was stuck in a cup holder at the helm.

"Plot a course to San Juan by way of Dewey," he told me. "With waypoints."

I went below to the nav table where I could lay out the chart and access the onboard GPS chart plotter, marine forecasts and whatever guide books Jersey had lying around. Like all experienced Caribbean captains, he had plenty of reference material, and it took less than an hour to work out a sail plan. It would have taken even less if I hadn't been distracted by Natsumi and Desiree swirling around the galley, stowing provisions, tossing things in sizzling fry pans and speaking over each other.

I went back up topside and found Jersey greeting a plump guy in his sixties, with the soft blond hair of a much younger man, in a logo-less polo shirt and ironed khakis. His wife looked like she'd been plucked from a different matched set, considerably younger and darker, thin, fit and a few inches taller courtesy of treacherously high mules.

She stood back as the men exchanged pleasantries that seemed to go beyond casual familiarity. When Jersey saw me, he also backed away, dropping the other man's hand.

"Mr. Cornwall, meet Angus and Angela."

"Sounds like a duet," said Angus, offering his hand. "We should take it on the road."

Angus was an actual Scot, so he pronounced road with an extra "r." His grip was forthright, with a hint of challenge in it. Angela cocked her hips before offering her own hand, as if stabilizing her footing, not unwisely. Her handshake was a warm and fluid thing, as if searching for the proper purchase.

"I'm sure," she said, with a contemporary American accent.

I took their duffle bags and slung them

over my shoulder. Angela handed me her pocketbook, then her inappropriate shoes. Her bare feet were long and sinewy, almost arboreal, which she put to good use crossing the gangplank from the dock and into the cockpit. She reached out her hand to me, and I took it, though there was little need. Angus followed less steadily, though under his own control.

I stowed their stuff in the V berth, a large enough accommodation to be called a stateroom. I noticed for no good reason that his bag was nearly twice as heavy as hers.

The motor was running when I got back to the cockpit. Jersey had partially released the dock lines, manually held to the cleats until I could get behind the wheel. On my nod he twirled the bow line free and tossed it up to Desiree. I dropped the gear changer into forward and held the boat into the dock until he could stow the gangplank and give us a good shove out of the slip. He walked the stern line down the dock, and at the last rational moment, jumped onto the swim ladder.

"Ease her out of the bay, Mr. Cornwall, and make for the first waypoint after we're clear of the ferries," he said, scrambling up into the cockpit.

"Aye, Cap," I said, and a thoroughly

satisfying thing it was to say.

The morning mist had cleared quickly, brushed away by the trades barreling down from the northeast. Outside the bay, the swells rolled by in good order, the low sun lighting the wave tips, painting silver accents on the cerulean sea.

On Jersey's signal, I bore up into the wind and he raised the mainsail with a power winch, watching carefully as the halyard slid across the cabin top. I felt the big sail trying to catch the wind, conspiring with the wave action to shove our bow off course. But *That's A Moray* was a heavy boat with a deep keel and her engine a muscular Cummins throbbing beneath my feet, and we held our bearing until Jersey dropped his hand like a hatchet through the wind and held it, pointing the way. I fell off the wind and felt the forty-eight footer heeling hard to port, digging into the water and finding her true nature as a boat under sail.

A female down below, I assumed Angela, had let out a startled whoop when we first lurched over on our side. I hoped not because she hadn't been briefed on a sailboat's tipping behaviors.

I killed the motor and watched the speedometer climb quickly up to seven knots. Jersey had left about 20 percent of the sail still gathered on top of the boom, and likewise, kept a reef in the genoa, the parachute-like sail that ballooned out above the bow.

With the raising of the second headsail, we were fully underway, and I felt through the wheel the force of the wind against the countervailing keel and rudder, and the ease with which the heavy displacement hull cut through the waves. Though less immediately responsive than our thirty-six footer, *That's A Moray* was a mannerly vessel, secure to the hand and true to the helmsman's commands.

"You're enjoying yourself," said Natsumi, before she was halfway up the companionway with a banana and a mug of coffee.

Her hair flew in all directions, forcing her to twist it into a loose ponytail that she stuck under her windbreaker.

"How're the passengers?" I asked.

"You'll know as soon as Jersey gives permission for us to come topside."

I caught him looking back at us from where he stood near the mast, his hands gripping the fixed rigging, his hair as ill behaved in the wind as Natsumi's. Interpreting our faces, he gave a thumbs-up. His face was alight with the joy of the moment, this Puerto Rican milk run holding all of us in its thrall.

When we were clear of local traffic and outside the smaller islands that lined the northern boundaries of the US Virgin Islands, he told me to sail past the waypoint and set a new course to the northwest.

"At this rate, we'll get there too quickly," he said. "Let's give the passengers a bit more of a sail."

By then, Angus and Angela were in the cockpit sipping coffee and noshing from a bowl of fresh fruit. Angus was in shorts and penny loafers, Angela in just enough to offer a pretense of modesty. Somewhat understandably, given that her body belonged to a woman half her age.

Jersey shared the plan to sail in a big V, eventually reaching Dewey on the island of Culebra, the eastern outpost of Puerto Rico, in time to get settled on a mooring for the night.

The rest of the day involved a lot of eating and lounging by Angus and Angela, and general boat operations by the rest of us. Jersey offered to spell me at the helm, but I never felt the need. The big boat was stable on all points of sail, requiring little in the way of pushing and pulling on the wheel. And I fell gladly into the hypnotic effects, a balm to nerves ignited by the capture and rough handling a few days before.

In all my life, I never felt the need for conventional entertainment. Learning and research was my work and my play, all consuming. My late wife, Florencia, took it well enough, only occasionally complaining how hard it was for us to go to the movies.

"All that noise in your head drowns out the dialogue," she'd say.

It wasn't until Natsumi introduced me to sailing that I understood how an experience could decouple the senses from the mind, quelling nettlesome emotions and subduing the frantic deliberations that filled my every waking minute.

Thus occupied, it was as if waking from a dream when we finally doused the sails, started the motor and crept up to a mooring in the harbor outside Dewey. Only after Jersey signaled that we were secure did I let go of the wheel and return to the realm of the conscious and preoccupied.

That night was consumed by alcohol. Beginning with gin and tonics and hors d'oeuvres, then bottles of wine over dinner followed by various rum concoctions and straight up whisky Natsumi and I brought up from the galley, our four companions managed to ingest a titanic volume of booze.

63

Desiree and Angela were the first to succumb. After a fair amount of hugging and protestations of deep affection, along with surprise that these feelings could arise over so short a time together, they both passed out and were carried below by Jersey, the steadier and stronger of the two survivors.

Now on their own in the cockpit, Jersey and Angus carried on with the conversation, loud but remarkably lucid. Natsumi and I stayed below in the galley sipping straight tonic water. The talk topside mostly involved asking after old friends and professional acquaintances, so it seemed easy enough for Natsumi and me to drift into a desultory conversation of our own. Until we heard Angus say:

"Hey galley slaves, come on up and have a drink with management."

"Not required, kids," said Jersey. "Unless you want to, of course."

Natsumi made the decision for us by grabbing a half bottle of wine and climbing up through the companionway. I followed with my tonic water.

"There's a right girl," said Angus. "I'm sick of this boring old Yank. Tell us how you ended up in paradise."

Custom among the transients and escape artists in the Caribbean frowned on this kind of direct intrusion on personal history. It made Jersey uncomfortable, even though he'd gladly shared his own narrative the night before in the bar. Natsumi came to his rescue.

"Jonathan's writing a book. I'm recovering from my psychotherapy practice," she said. "I wish it was more romantic than that, but there you are."

"Nothing of the sort," said Angus. "What's more romantic than writing a book? Could never do it myself. No self-discipline. What's the topic?"

"Safe computing," I said. "For small business."

During my career as a market researcher, I'd gained mastery over dozens of arcane disciplines, but after recent years of digital cat and mouse with various organizations — public, private and clandestine — cybersecurity was a subject on which I'd become painfully current. It became my favorite cover story, thus far unchallenged.

"So you're in luck," said Jersey. "That's what Angus does."

"Good gracious, please, no shop talk," said Angus. "Unless Natalia wants to tell us about nutters. With Jersey's permission, as the daftest one on the boat."

"Everyone's a little nuts, sir," said Nat-sumi.

"Is that your clinical opinion? And call me Angus."

"Yes it is, Angus. For all we know, you're battier than a March hare. But if I find you out, I promise to be discreet."

"And what do you think of Nanoscreen?" he asked me, whipping his head in my direction, his voice full of challenge.

"Tighter than a gnat's butt, as the name implies, so it's effective if you don't mind what it does to load times," I said. "The cryptography isn't all that different from what the Unix guys developed thirty years ago. Just a lot of numbers to the right of the decimal. Breakable by brute force."

"Agreed. What about quantum key distribution?"

"Fine for Bob and Alice as long as Ted and Carol aren't eavesdropping," I said, physics code for commentary that would fill a shelf of textbooks. "We all know what happens with those kinds of entanglements."

Angus looked at me over the rim of a glass filled with the Bruichladdich whisky, half of which disappeared as he took a long pull.

"Pretty fancy stuff for a small business, though, wouldn't you say?" he said. "Not too relevant for readers like yours."

"Command of the irrelevant is one of Jonathan's strong suits," said Natsumi.

"Angus has a PhD in computer technology," said Jersey. "Thinks women find it attractive."

"Why else would Angela fuck my brains out?"

"Therapists never answer rhetorical questions," said Natsumi.

"Where did you find these two?" Angus asked Jersey.

"In a bar. Where else?"

"Jersey and I did our bar time in the day," said Angus.

"Still serving. I think it's twenty years to life," said Jersey.

"Show me a sober spook and I'll give you a thousand pounds."

Jersey didn't like that.

"Angus thinks busting junior stockbrokers for buying on a tip from Uncle Billy makes you a spook."

"Right. I always get Uncle Billy mixed up with Uncle Osama," said Angus.

"I understand burnout's pretty high for therapists," Jersey said to Natsumi, still trying to change the subject.

Natsumi never actually had a psychotherapy practice, unless you count her years running a blackjack table. Patient outcomes weren't trackable, but it did help her learn the trade.

"We don't burn out. We simply examine our options, reorder our priorities and then make appropriate life choices."

"I choose to have another single malt, thank you," said Angus.

"Everyone has stress," said Jersey. "The only difference is how you handle it."

"You're a good man, Jersey, that was the difference with you," said Angus. "You have to be a heartless sot like me to enjoy putting people away."

"You're not supposed to enjoy that part," said Jersey, though without censure.

"Like I said. Too good a man."

Jersey went below to check on Desiree and retrieve outerwear against the cooling night. Angus waited until he was out of earshot to half whisper, half slur, "Putting people away means putting them away." He used his hand to mimic firing a gun. "Permanent withdrawal from the field of action."

"You're kidding," said Natsumi. "What the hell did you guys do?"

"Of course I'm kidding. No one kills anyone anymore over something as silly as national security. Anyway, Jersey's retired. I'm the one still in harness. Can't afford to give it up. Angela's Pilates alone threatens bankruptcy."

"But a good investment," said Natsumi. "From your brain's perspective."

Angus looked at me.

"What did she specialize in, clever girls therapy?"

"Clever boys," said Natsumi.

Jersey came topside with a handful of sweatshirts. Only Angus felt the need to grab one. Jersey dropped into his seat as if shoved there by an invisible hand and exhaled a cloud of vaporized rum.

"Fuck, the seas are runnin' high tonight," he said.

"Should I be puttin' out the Mayday, Cap'n?" Angus asked.

"I could make coffee," Natsumi said.

They looked like she'd offered them a bowl of live insects.

Jersey held up his drink, a favorite in the Caribbean known as a painkiller. "Don't be ruining the painkilling properties," he said. "Which reminds me, I need another."

He tried to stand again, but Natsumi told him to stay put. I stood watch while she went below to rustle up another round for the two of them. Their level of consumption was a dubious achievement, though I couldn't help being a little impressed. Were it me, I'd be on life support.

"I get the feeling you guys saw a lot of action back in the day," I said.

"Don't believe anything Angus tells you," said Jersey. "Bullshit is the Scottish national pastime."

"Second only to shaggin' Yanks."

Jersey responded in like terms and the back and forth escalated accordingly. Natsumi and I sat back and waited it out. Jersey was the first to run out of fuel, sliding effortlessly from fluent insult to a snore reminiscent of the cranky chain saw I once used in Connecticut.

"Doesn't sound safe, now does it?" Angus asked.

"I'm wondering how we get him below," said Natsumi. "He outweighs all three of us combined."

"Good of you to include me in that, lassie. But for movin' Jersey, *dinnae* bother. He's slept off more a good night's drinking in the cockpit than anywhere else. Lord knows Desiree'll be happier for it."

While Natsumi went below to get our cabin in order I dug up a safety tether to join Jersey's sturdy leather belt to the helm. Three feet was enough play to let him roll around the cockpit without pitching himself over the coaming and into the sea.

Angus endorsed the idea.

"That's thinkin', Cornwall. Wouldn't want the lad's drownin' to plague my conscience."

Angus himself was another matter. He made it to the stairway mostly on his own power, but the angle proved daunting. He asked for another tether, but instead I went below and offered support for the trip down. He took it and all went well, even though the stateroom seemed a formidable distance away in the V of the bow.

Angus allowed me to help him to the head where I left him seated on the toilet lid, teetering but optimistic about prospects from there.

He gripped my sleeve before I could withdraw.

"Are you really writing a book on cybersecurity for small business?"

"Have you really put people away?" I asked.

He leaned back from me, as if trying to get my face in better focus.

"Yes. As it turns out."

"Me, too."

He let go of me and I was able to escape to our tiny berth for the minimum night's sleep.

The next day Natsumi and I were able to perform our respective functions with distinction, a feat admired by our companions, for whom sprawled lounging seemed to be the only viable pursuit. I was just as glad, as I followed a leisurely, but fairly direct course around the top of the island and into San Juan, where a berth awaited *That's A Moray*.

We spent another night on board, then collected our belongings and two days' pay, and gave our farewells. We walked out of the marina and back into the netherworld we'd inhabited before our fanciful diversion on the shimmering tropical seas.

CHAPTER 5

It wasn't the first time I had to start from scratch. In the twenty-first century, the only way to live off the grid is to be dead. If you really want to live and move about, and not simply hide in a cave or a motel room somewhere deep in the Rockies, you need a real identity, and dead people are the best source of that.

An American only needed two keys to establish a modern identity. Only two, both difficult to obtain: a driver's license and a Social Security number.

Popular myth would have you think such things are easy to get on the open criminal market. That's partly true if your only purpose is to snag cash or consumer goods with a stolen credit card. My ambitions ran deeper than that. We needed to be flesh and blood people, not just strings of misbegotten numbers. We needed to be people you could talk to, do business with, be thoroughly deceived by.

For that, we needed to be dead people. Not just any dead people, but ones with identities unencumbered by a history that would attract the interest of pervasive and unblinking digital surveillance.

The process began with an Internet café. I paid cash, picked out a remote spot, and went to work. What once took me a few days, I could now manage in about four hours. Going directly to familiar databases, I was able to assemble a decent list of people fitting our general ethnic and morphological descriptions who'd had the misfortune of a recent and untimely departure from this earth.

Thus equipped, I bought a disposable cell phone and parked myself on a bench in a quiet corner of the Castillo San Felipe del Morro. The scam from there was a simple one. I was from the IRS in the orphan payables department. I was charged with uncovering the family members of people who had never cashed prior tax refunds. If mom, or dad, or husband, wife, brother, sister, whoever, could simply provide the correct Social Security number, I would gladly forward the abandoned funds.

The trick wasn't necessarily in the credibility of the story, it was the delivery. After logging thousands of phone interviews, the vast majority being legal efforts to extract information from often unwilling respondents, this was something I was particularly good at doing. Good enough to have a half-dozen solid names and Social Security numbers for Natsumi and me before the sun set over the ancient fortification.

We used cash again for a "used" laptop offered by an eager young entrepreneur on a corner in Puerto de Tierro. Then, before the night hardened into more forbidding hours, we used false, though unchallenged, names in the registry at a desperately crummy little hotel around the corner.

The next day, I foraged farther afield, securing a fresh hard drive for the laptop and a toolkit to make the necessary modifications. I gave the red-eyed desk clerk at our hotel a hundred dollars to hold our mail and spent the rest of the day and most of the night setting up accounts in various banks around the country. Into these I flowed operating funds uncompromised by the busted identities left behind in the Virgins. I hoped.

From there all we could do was wait and avoid getting mugged until collecting the incoming mail with credit and debit cards, and subsequently improved financial circumstances.

It felt a little like a rebirth.

Once back in the black, we flew to Miami. After the quick plane flight, a cab delivered us to a boutique hotel in the Art Deco district in South Beach. In addition to the allure of luxury accommodations after days in captivity, at sea, in the barrio and traveling from Puerto Rico, the eclectic American, Asian and European guest population offered fair camouflage, and the concierge services convenient logistical support.

On the way into the city, we stopped at one of the retail outlets of a national transport service that was holding a package of mine. I told the guy at the desk that my driver's license had been stolen in Puerto Rico, but perhaps a pair of hundred dollar bills would be enough to satisfy ID requirements. He thought that would do fine.

Inside the package were a driver's license, birth certificate and five years of tax returns confirming the bona fide existence of an entirely made-up person.

For the rest of the week, Natsumi committed herself to lying on the windy beach while I hid away in the room assembling documents to support a new identity for her, mostly secured through legitimate channels, a few forged.

I used some of that time to move money around. While I had given all of Florencia's embezzled funds back to her insurance company victims, I still had plenty left over from selling the agency itself, along with whatever assets we owned together before she died. As a further backstop, I had a warehouse in Connecticut full of vintage guitars. With a ready market, I could peddle individual guitars as needed, providing a foolproof source of untraceable, tax-free liquidity.

Every financial action comes with risk. But the biggest risk was being too static. The cyber bloodhounds who paid attention to these things looked for too much activity or too little. It was best to convey the appearance of normal day-to-day commerce. Whether I'd followed a wise strategy, or success thus far had been a lucky illusion, I still had most of the money I'd accumulated since slipping into a shadow world of my own making.

We were going to need it.

"What are you thinking?" Natsumi asked when she opened her eyes and saw me staring at the ceiling.

"Our captors gave us a priceless lesson in

asymmetrical conflict."

"Which is?"

"The more powerful always win. You can't hide from them forever. We're tricky and resourceful, but their capabilities are overwhelming. Partly because they can do things we can't even know and probably never will."

"That's bleak."

"There's good news. They confirmed that my dead guy status is still intact. For now."

"Which is why you're worried?" she asked.

"They have my fingerprints, DNA and crystal clear photos. It's only dumb luck the fingerprints and DNA have never found their way into anyone's database. As for the photos, I might think I look a lot different from how I used to look, but not to a computer loaded with facial recognition software."

"You're saying they have all the dots, they just haven't connected them to Arthur Cathcart," she said.

"And when they do, it'll lead directly to fraud, embezzlement, extortion, international terrorism and murder."

"That's all you're worried about?"

The open hotel window looked out over the broad beach and light green ocean beyond. Hot, dry, salt-soaked air blew in and mussed up the gauzy curtains. I had come to an agreeable accommodation with warm climates, at odds with a lifetime in cold, cranky places like Connecticut, Boston and Philadelphia. Being aware of any kind of weather — searing sun, mists, winds and willful cloudbursts — was a new thing for me, a person whose attention was once rarely diverted from the printed page, the computer screen or a legal pad covered with equations.

I'd loved that world of the abstract and remote, the feast of facts, oceans of knowledge too vast ever to be entirely known. I hadn't chosen to leave it; the impetus was a bullet passing through the outer neighborhoods of my brain's frontal and parietal lobes. Somewhat mangled, I still managed to live, something the neurologists at the time said was incredibly lucky, a word I still had a hard time reconciling with the actual experience.

Unless it was this newfound ability to notice the outdoors. To possess, however fleetingly, a Buddhist's mindfulness in lieu of a state in which one is merely full of one's own mind.

But I knew life in the virtual world was no guarantee of survival in the material. And looking over at Natsumi, with the sheet pulled up to just below her eyes and waves of jet black hair spread out across the pillow, I also knew that simple survival was in itself a form of death sentence.

"I want to go back," I said. "All the way."

"To Connecticut?"

"To being Arthur. My own name, with my own face and my own passport."

"What about your girl?"

"With her, too."

"She was never in that world. She's only of this one. The fake one."

"Not a problem. I'll introduce you around. You and Omni."

"What you want is impossible," she said.

"I know."

"But you're going to try anyway."

I sat up so that I could look her full in the face.

"There's no choice. That's the lesson. We'll never be truly safe until we're truly free."

"You can't be both. You know that. They'll put you away forever," she said.

"The only way out is through."

"Uh?"

"Robert Frost. Big with Vietnam vets and recovering addicts."

"And recovering fugitives?"

"Right."

■ ■ ■ ■

The first thing I did that morning was e-mail a ninety-nine-year-old man. Raul Preciado-Cotto was professor emeritus of European history at the *Universidad Complutense* in Madrid. His command of twentieth-century history was enhanced by having seen most of it, as an undercover investigator, journalist and intellectual bon vivant. His specialty was Spanish political movements and all things expressed with a Spanish accent.

"I know nothing about Latin American mercenaries," he wrote back in response to my inquiry. "But I know a person who may."

I thanked him and promised to provide the vintage French brandy as requisite compensation. He demurred, citing a new regimen of healthy consumption and regular aerobic exercise.

"I've been advised you're never too young to attend to your physical fitness," he wrote.

In the time it took Natsumi and me to eat breakfast on the narrow balcony above the Atlantic glare, he'd made the connection and written back.

"I am told the person most likely to know the people you seek frequents the *Tocororo*

81

Loco in Hialeah. I am further advised that only gringos with faint regard for personal safety would venture there. *Tenga cuidado.*"

With the rest of the day to spend before heading for the mercenary saloon, I started up the computer and began charting out the next digital passage. Natsumi had other plans.

"You're wearing a bikini," I said.

"We're in Miami. What else should I wear?"

"Does this mean you're going to the beach?"

"It's right outside the door. You should come with me."

"To do what?"

I grew up not far from the public beaches of Stamford, Connecticut, though I'd never sat on the sand. Having seen people from a distance lounging, passed out and pretending to enjoy the temperature shock from abrupt immersion in the icy Long Island Sound, I could merely surmise the purpose. My parents were too harried by the need to earn money in an expensive place with few marketable skills to attend to their children's recreational needs. Fortunately, my sister and I needed nothing more than access to the Stamford public library and the astonishing freedom made possible by our parents' benign neglect.

"You could read a book," said Natsumi. "Or examine the local fauna and flora."

She really didn't expect me to go, so I surprised her by printing out a stack of reading material, dressing up in appropriate beach-going apparel and sticking a rolled-up bath towel under my arm.

"Into the fray," I said to her.

I survived the day reasonably well. It occurred to me, as I tried to read through the loose printouts fluttering in the wind, that Natsumi wanted to keep me close without appearing to. She was worried about the *Tocororo Loco*.

That was confirmed when we got back to the room, sunbaked and windblown.

"I'm concerned about tonight," she said.

"Me, too."

"You should have backup."

"No time to set that up. I'll have my smartphone ready to ping you at a tap on the screen."

"To do what?"

"I don't know yet."

"Swell."

She knew the truth. There was nothing we could do if things went wrong. All I could do was stay alert and all she could do was stay in the hotel and worry.

As the day drifted into dinnertime, I dressed in khakis and a simple guayabera shirt, and put on a Miami Marlins baseball cap. I brought along the driver's license that matched the name on our hotel registration, Frascuelo Rana, and a roll of cash. As promised, I had my smartphone preset to three options: A speed dial to her phone that meant call the cops. An e-mail that said, "Everything A-Okay." And a text that read, "Run like hell."

I kissed her on the lips and took a cab over to Hialeah. As we drove, I practiced my Spanish with the cabdriver. He'd been an orthopedic surgeon in Havana before an indiscreet blog posting had prompted a midnight boat trip to Port-au-Prince and subsequent slide into Miami, so he had little trouble with my fancy Castilian syntax and word choice. I'd taught myself Spanish before meeting Florencia, something that greatly helped to cement the relationship, but I was never able to conform to her native-born vernacular.

Consequently, it was clear I'd go about as unnoticed at *Tocororo Loco* as Sir Laurence Olivier riding one of Gilley's mechanical bulls.

The cabby noted as much when we pulled up to the curb.

"I can show you other restaurants where you might be more comfortable," he said, helpfully.

"Can I call you when I'm ready to leave?" I asked.

He looked noncommittal, but gave me his card and said, "Sure. Call and we'll see what we can do."

Inside, *Tocororo Loco* looked like it had been assembled from a collection of disparate parts. Near the storefront window was a long counter, like you find in any mid-twentieth-century American greasy spoon, though with freshly upholstered swivel stools, paintings of Cuban street scenes on the wall and a gigantic espresso machine towering in the rear corner. A few old men were at the counter crouched over plates of rice, beans and chicken, *cortaditos* coffee and ashtrays emitting smoke plumes. Jazz was on the jukebox and a scrawny woman with dyed hair tied at the top of her head held the command position behind the counter. She saw me come in and without hesitation pointed to a double door at the back of the place that opened into a dark bar. I didn't know whether to take this as a good sign or bad, but walked through the doors anyway.

This section was much darker, filled with

rattan tables and chairs and younger, far noisier people. There was a small service bar in one corner, though the principal purpose here was eating from large plates filled with *pan con bistec* and *ropa vieja.* There were only two stools set up at the bar. I sat in one.

"I was told there was another bar here," I said in Spanish. "Perhaps I'm mistaken."

"Mistakes happen," said the bartender. "But I am certain I can help with your thirst."

He was a tall man with cool, blue eyes, receding silver hairline and thin, delicate hands. He reminded me more of a priest than a bartender, though to many that's a slight distinction. He showed me a Hatuey from a cooler behind the bar and I nodded.

"Do you need a table?" he asked.

"Maybe later. I'm still wondering about that other bar."

He put both hands on the bar, one holding a wet rag.

"We have a special dining area in the back. You must mean that."

"Probably."

"What part of Spain are you from, if you don't mind me asking," he said, burying any pretense I had about disguising my pretentious accent.

"Madrid. Though I've lived in America for many years. It rubs off."

"Of course."

"I'm traveling here on business. An associate told me I had to visit *Tocororo Loco.*"

"They have excellent taste. They surely mentioned our *moros y cristianos*? People from Miami prefer it to their own."

"It sounds delicious, but my taste runs more toward *armas y balas.*" Guns and bullets.

"A very dangerous diet," he said. "Is your doctor aware?"

"Yes. In fact, he sent me here to fill a prescription. Although perhaps you have limited supplies."

He might have smiled, though I might have imagined it. He made another superfluous wipe across the bar, dropped a menu in front of me, then left through a door behind the bar. I drank the Hatuey and pretended to read the menu. Fifteen minutes later he stuck his head through the door.

"I might have the medicine you ordered, if you don't mind following me," he said, opening the door a bit more. I got up off my barstool, came around and followed him through the door into a dimly lit room barely the size of a walk-in closet. The door closed behind me and once again I was the helpless object of muscular hands.

It was easy to imagine they were the same people who manhandled us in the Caribbean. They had the same irresistible strength and professional finesse. But this time a brief frisking was followed by an all-out strip search.

"Whoa," I said. "How 'bout it?"

No one answered while they peeled off my shirt, patting around my exposed torso, then shucked my sandals one at a time, followed by my pants. In no time I was naked as a baby and feeling no less helpless.

They were thorough if nothing else. I joked that few people had examined me that closely without asking for a copayment, but no one laughed. Or spoke, in any language, until I was given my clothes and had a chance to get dressed again.

"You travel light, Señor Rana," said the bartender, handing back my license and roll of bills.

"Less to lose."

"I don't suppose you'll tell us who suggested you visit our humble establishment."

"Does it matter?" I asked.

"Not really," he said, taking my arm and guiding me through another door out to a courtyard restaurant decorated in a style several socioeconomic strata above the storefront canteen that fronted the place. Palm trees and giant flowering shrubs were up lit from a hundred small lamps, as was a fountain in the center of the patio that would have made a good birdbath for condors. The tables were draped in woven fabric, topped with glass and surrounded by oversized wicker chairs heaped with pillows. We walked across the rough-tiled floor to a distant table where a large young man in a white shirt with the sleeves rolled up over thick forearms sat with a blonde woman, also in white, wearing tiny sunglasses and smoking a pencil-shaped cigar.

They stood as the bartender brought me up to the table.

"*Siéntate, Norberto. No formalidades necesarias,*" the bartender told him. Sit down. No need to be formal.

"*Si, general. Lo que usted quieras,*" said the young man, pulling the woman down with him.

That marked the first time a general had served me a beer. He also pulled out a chair for me. Before sitting, I shook hands with the sturdy Norberto and his date, Fernanda. No last names.

A waiter appeared seconds later and a round of Cuba Libres was ordered for the table. A whiff of panic hit me as I pondered the effects of a rum cocktail on my feeble capacity. I asked the water to bring me a hunk of bread with the drink.

"Haven't eaten all day," I said to the table.

"I thought you only ate guns and bullets," said the general.

"Mostly. *Con mercenarios.*"

"Ah," said the general.

Norberto looked sideways at the older man. Fernanda took a long pull on her sleek *cigarro* and sighed out the smoke. Gloria Esteban started singing something from speakers hidden in the foliage. No one said much until the Cuba Libres showed up along with a long loaf of hot bread wrapped in a cotton napkin.

"Such strange appetites, eh Norberto?" said the general, toasting the table.

"We hear strange things every day, general. Can't take them all seriously."

"Of course not," I said. "Being professional is a serious business."

The general reached over and took my right hand in both of his. He turned it over and ran his fingers across my palm. He paused to rub the meaty calluses that had built up over months raising, dousing and adjusting *Detour*'s restless sails.

"Not all professionals live behind desks,

am I right Señor Rana?"

"There are many ways to earn money in this world," I said.

The general sat back and used his long, thin fingers to turn his Cuba Libre by the lip of the glass.

"How do you earn yours, Señor Rana?" he asked.

"I buy and sell something we all want."

"Love?" said Fernanda, surprising everyone, most of all Norberto.

"Information," I said to her. "Not as sweet, but more valuable."

"Not to me," she said, tossing a false smile at Norberto in a challenge he chose to ignore.

The general reached across the table and gripped Fernanda's wrist. She sat back in her chair and flicked an ash off the end of her *cigarro*. Message received.

I took a sip of the Cuba Libre, wondering why you'd want to louse up the flavor of a perfectly good soft drink with that sour rum.

"What happened to your head?" the general asked.

"Accident."

"Same one that put a bullet in your leg?"

"Yes."

"You should be more careful, especially with a diet like yours."

"Some diet," said Fernanda. "The guy's a bean."

The general told Norberto in French that she better be a good fuck. See for yourself, Norberto answered. Any time.

"You won't be surprised to learn that I am frequently approached by people wishing to claim my attention," said the general. "The legitimate ones I listen to. The others I turn over to Norberto who is charged with discouraging further inquiry."

Norberto shrugged as if apologizing in advance for carrying out this responsibility. Fernanda moved closer and stroked his meaty arm. I wondered if she liked to watch him at his work.

"Understood," I said. I slipped the cocktail napkin out from under my Cuba Libre and took out a pen. "Go to your bank, or any bank, and open an account with a minimum balance. Use this e-mail address to send me the account number and the bank's routing number, and I will deposit five thousand dollars as a show of good faith." I wrote the address on the napkin. "Once you have the money secured, I will ask for the courtesy of a meeting where we can discuss the project I have in mind."

I dropped the napkin in front of him and stood up, gratefully leaving half my Cuba

Libre undisturbed. The general ignored it, keeping his eyes locked on mine.

"Do I know you?" he asked.

"Not before tonight," I said. "But you don't have to."

"That's right. It doesn't matter."

Norberto was also on his feet at this point, looking at his boss for the signal to stop me from leaving. He didn't get it, so I left through the proper doorway to the inside restaurant and then through the tired little storefront joint and out into the night air, suddenly damp and heavy, too far away to catch an errant breeze from the sleepless Atlantic Ocean.

CHAPTER 6

It took me three cab rides and a trip through the kitchen of another aromatic Cuban restaurant to shake the tails. Inconvenience aside, it was a fine showing of the general's bona fides, a welcome assurance before dropping five grand into a wildly speculative venture. I shared that with Natsumi when I got back to the hotel room.

"You have to start somewhere," she said.

Before we went to bed I checked my e-mail where the general had left a message moments before. It included the routing and account numbers, and evidence that bona fides were established on both sides of the pending transaction: "Nicely done, Sr. Rana," he wrote. "You've embarrassed my team, a healthy antidote to overconfidence. And by the way, add another fifteen thousand. We'll take it from there."

Natsumi went to bed alone, recognizing that sleep for me at this point was impossible. For my part, I went shopping.

There are people in the world who stockpile illicitly acquired information the way others horde material things, whether mere trash or valuable collectibles. It isn't so much the intrinsic value of their possessions, it's the possessing itself that drives the behavior. So it's possible you could read about some gross breach of security at a credit card company, wherein thousands of card numbers had been stolen, and yet not a single piece of merchandise was illegally purchased with the ill-gotten information.

These hoarders worked alone, hacking the card companies themselves, or trading with others in their cohort. While common hackers were nearly always caught by counter-forces at the banks or in government, collectors were more likely to be betrayed by their compulsions, or the irresistible urge to brag about their exploits.

So they were people I generally avoided, for that exact reason. I could ill afford the possibility of getting swept up in some other outlaw's clumsy transaction. There was one, however, who had been in operation as long as I'd been researching credit card fraud as a component of identity theft, which I was hired to do nearly ten years before.

I once traded with him when I had something worth trading for. Now, I didn't have much in the way of leverage but for the simple fact that I knew how to find him, and that was likely the most potent leverage of all.

It wasn't an easy or immediate form of communication. I couldn't just type in an e-mail address and that was that. It started with a search of websites and discussion groups focused on the wildly perilous pursuit of stolen credit card data. These sites were always somewhere between formation, obliteration and reconstitution. So there was spadework even in identifying the authentic gathering places.

Next I had to search through long rows of comments, using an application to isolate key words or phrases my target frequently used. It wasn't inconceivable that another commentator, on either side of the law, had intentionally adopted his signature style as a way to entice or entrap data trollers. For that I hoped my usual precautions were good to the task, but there was no way to be sure.

Even with the software assist, I had to read hundreds of lines of commentary, most coarse or banal, at best, before I thought I had a match. It was a feeling, a gut reaction no algorithm had yet learned to emulate.

The commentator's handle was Strider, further support for the hunch. The Tolkien character was a brave loner, a seeker of the key that could thwart the evil power. It fit my amateur psych-op of the elusive, arrogant data thief.

Things went much faster after that. I merely had to find a site where Strider was engaged in an active discussion. I took off as fast as the keyboard and mouse would let me. If search programs were bloodhounds, I would have been baying down the trail.

An hour later I saw a comment from Strider appear in close to real time. I jumped on the response: "I know where you are," I wrote, signing on as Spanky, a handle he would likely remember.

A few minutes later, he wrote, "Same box?"

He meant the message service we'd used in past transactions, one that claimed to destroy all record of your exchange five seconds after it was concluded. Again, no way to know if that was really true, or if my address hadn't been compromised along the way. I had to risk it, and I hoped Strider felt the same way.

"Yes," I wrote, and switched over to the service. Ten minutes later he was there.

"What the hell does that mean?"

"I need something," I wrote, and waited through the two minutes delay.

"Don't we all. You want pro quo, I need a few quid. You want tit, I need a little tat. I love writing that."

"We dealt successfully in the past. And honorably."

"Yeah, yeah, true enough."

"I need a doorway," I wrote. "Just one and I'll leave you alone."

I sent him the routing number for the general's bank. Strider would know what that meant.

"That's a pretty big ask. A lot of disruption."

"I'm not going for a big haul. Just one account. Precision strike."

"Okay, let's talk compensation."

"You don't want to know how I located you?" I asked.

"I'm pretending that isn't a threat."

"Consider it a security analysis."

I sent him the general's account and bank routing numbers. He took longer than usual to respond. I was ready to hit the end conversation button when he wrote, "That's too hot for this box. Await instructions."

"How so?"

"You'll know."

■ ■ ■ ■

I stayed off the beach the next day. And the day after that. The only thing I had to do was wait, and waiting was the thing I least liked to do. Especially when I could do nothing to hurry the process along. So I distracted myself the only way I knew how. I did research.

Back in my old life, another side business was tracking down missing persons. I had one client, a law firm who paid me to uncover the recipients of class action settlements who were unaware of their windfall. It was great work, since it often involved travel, carried the romance of detective work, and no one was unhappy to be found.

So with some relish, I started chasing a few of our more recent acquaintances. People like Alberta, Angus and Angela, and Jersey and Desiree Mitchell.

Not surprisingly, after several hours I located no one named Alberta whose description fit the woman who'd interrogated me on the fishing boat. It didn't mean I hadn't found her, just that not all the Albertas were photographed or adequately described. I compiled a list of about a hundred candidate Albertas and stuck it away.

The same was true for a married couple named Angus and Angela. We had good clear photos taken on the sly with our smartphones. Angus was a computer scientist, and a Scot, and Angela an American, so they should have been much easier to pin down, but I had little luck.

"I don't think they're married," said Natsumi, when I drew her into the hunt. "At least not to each other."

"Why's that?"

"Wedding rings didn't match."

"Very good," I said.

"And she asked me if I thought he was cute. Married women rarely seek that kind of validation. Usually the opposite."

"Opposite?"

" 'Don't you think he's an idiot?' " she said, mimicking another woman.

"What did you tell her?"

"I said, absolutely, cute as all get-out."

"And no idiot."

Jersey Mitchell wasn't even a challenge. Real name Lucien, born and raised in Jersey City, New Jersey, undergrad and law degree from Columbia, spent most of his career as an FBI agent attached to the US Attorney's Office in New York City, etc. Everything he gladly told us. He had hundreds of Facebook, LinkedIn and Twitter contacts and not a one named Angus. Nor anyone who looked like Angus, or Angela.

I was about to dive into more sophisticated search programs when a ping from one of my mailboxes alerted me the general had transferred the money I'd deposited, completing that portion of the transaction. He told me to wait at a corner in Hialeah later that afternoon and he'd take it from there.

"Just like that?" Natsumi asked.

"Same drill," I said. We went over the codes I'd use if I ran into trouble — the type of trouble, whether things were fine, whether to come get me, or run for her life. These I would deliver by smartphone, if I could call. If I didn't call by a certain time, we picked a place for her to go and what she should do next.

It should have been a comfort to have this down to a routine, but it only reminded us of the anxieties and terrors of the past.

And so it was that I stood there, dressed more or less like a native, packing my smartphone, fake ID and a few hundred dollars in cash. Natsumi was in a coffee shop across the street to see me off. She had a long-lens camera to capture what she could. We chatted through our Bluetooth earbuds while we waited, which was a comfort.

A big SUV stopped in front of me and the

rear door opened. I stepped in without hesitation and the truck sped off. The interior smelled new and it was appointed like a luxury car. The driver was a pale Anglo guy with a buzz cut and sunglasses. The guy in the passenger seat was thin, Hispanic, with long unkempt hair and an oily pretense of a beard. Also in sunglasses.

No one spoke.

Back in the coffee shop, Natsumi followed our progress on her iPad, linked up with the GPS in my smartphone. In her camera was a clear enough image of the SUV to make out the license plate. Nothing on the men, since the windows were tinted and highly reflective of the brilliant Floridian day.

Not long after we pulled into an alley. The Hispanic man got out and walked away, fast. I stayed in the backseat as we continued on. The driver was cautious and deliberate, his eyes constantly scanning the environments we moved through. In the face of the larger peril, it made me feel secure.

We crossed a bridge, drove into an affluent enclave and stopped at an iron gate. The driver punched a code into the keypad and the gate opened for us. The home inside the walls was all glass and steel. The driver frisked me with exceptional thoroughness, though I got to keep my clothes on. Then he brought me to a side entry that opened into a large space with twelve-foot, floor-to-ceiling window walls, an intimate seating area and a grand piano.

At the piano the general was improvising around a Duke Ellington classic. Quite artfully. The driver left me standing there to wait out the performance. I spent the time looking out the giant windows at the sailboats sliding across the blue water and the row of South Beach hotels rising like a citadel above the opposite shore.

He reached a logical break point in the song and turned to me.

"Do you play?" he asked, in English.

"Not a note."

"The piano kept me alive when I first got here from Cuba. I stay in practice, just in case."

"Seems prudent."

He wore a collarless black linen shirt with the sleeves cut off at the shoulders, white linen pants tied at the waist and bare feet. His two-day growth of beard was silvery white, matching his hair. He stood up and pointed to a pair of love seats, the only seating in the room. We sat across from each other, the general with his feet tucked up beneath him in a modified Lotus position, mine firmly on the ground.

"Do you have a back-up plan?" he asked. "Should your career buying and selling information turn sour?"

"I crewed on a sailboat for a couple days recently. That could work."

"My brother and I paddled here in a canoe. Destroyed any desire to be out on the open water."

"Does he work with you?"

"He's dead. The result of working with me."

"I'm sorry," I said.

"Me, too. Most of what I do is perfectly legal, depending on how you read the law. Unfortunately, every country seems to have a different interpretation. Applied according to the interests of the moment."

"I need to locate a Latino mercenary who was part of a specific operation on a specific date and time. I don't know if it was legal."

"That's what you want to learn?"

"No. That's important, to some degree, but I need more basic information."

"Such as?" he asked.

"Who the mercenary was working for."

"To what end?"

"That's a private matter," I said.

He put his fingertips together in a prayerful gesture, gazing off to the side, as if to better hear his internal dialogue. Though physically robust — slender and clear-eyed — he looked weary, as if warding off an irresistible lassitude.

"Of course," he said. "Tell me what you know of this Latino mercenary, and I'll see what I can learn."

I described our capture and interrogation, including as much detail as I could remember, not knowing which particular would be the most useful in his search. I left out the substance of my conversations with Alberta and her colleague, which he surely noticed, but had the good form to ignore.

He listened carefully to the end, nodding along to show he was following the narrative. When I was finished, he sat back in the love seat, even more languidly composed.

"This is not difficult," he said, "though you leave me curious. Not only about your tormentors, but about you. Why don't I know who you are?"

"I can't answer that," I said. "But I can tell you, honoring my privacy will make me an ideal customer."

He nodded, not necessarily in response to my comment.

"Do you know what I miss the most?" he asked me, after a long pause.

"About what?"

"The loss of innocence. What becomes of us after so many years of experience."

"Trust," I said. "You regret the assumption of betrayal."

He nodded again, this time directly to me.

"Yes, Señor Rana. Precisely put."

"Regrettable, but necessary," I said, "when engaged in pursuits other than piano playing and Caribbean cruising."

"How do I communicate?" he asked.

I asked if I could take something out of my shirt pocket. He said yes.

"My phone number," I said, putting a slip of paper next to me on the love seat. "It's good for a week. Then we'll have to make other arrangements."

"Your e-mail?"

"Already shut down."

"Of course."

We both stood up and he reached out his hand.

"Keep your phone within reach," he said.

A door opened and the driver came into the room. I shook the general's hand and turned to leave. He called to me before I cleared the door.

"Señor Rana," he said. "You didn't ask what happened to my brother."

"I didn't think it polite."

"I killed him," he said. "For betraying my trust."

I shrugged, turned on my heel and followed the muscular gait of the driver through the house and out to his SUV where we once again rode in silence through the sultry streets of Miami.

CHAPTER 7

I was on the phone with Natsumi after an evasive zigzag trip back to our hotel, so I barely noticed the slim shape in a long summer raincoat and black Mary Janes fall in behind me. In the elevator, I saw it was a woman with straight brown hair nearly covering her face, much of which was also obscured by a Toronto Blue Jays hat. On her back was a lightweight leather backpack. She pushed my floor number then leaned up against the rear wall. I signed off with Natsumi before leaving the elevator.

The woman followed me. I walked past our room to the end of the hall, then turned to walk back, almost running into the woman who was following close behind. She stood back to let me pass, then fell in behind again. I ignored our room a second time and returned to the bank of elevators.

The woman waited with me at the elevators. She had her hands in her pockets and rocked back and forth, letting her toes lift off the floor. She rode the elevator with me to the lobby. I got out and went into the small bar that served the hotel and a restaurant that opened out onto the sidewalk. I sat down at the bar and she sat next to me, pulling off the backpack and setting it on her lap.

When the bartender approached, I said, "I'll have whatever she's having," nodding my head toward the young woman.

"Give me a hurricane," she said. "With bitters."

I balked at that and ordered a beer. The woman turned on her stool and faced me, her arms wrapped around her backpack.

"I expected more in the adventurous department, Spanky," she said.

"Strider?" I asked.

"You found me, sort of. So I found you. Like, for real."

"Crap."

"It's not that hard anymore. You should know that."

"I suppose I should."

"I guessed at the visual ID. I had two false hits, if that makes you feel any better."

The hurricane looked too big for her hands — fragile and white, with chipped fingernails and nicotine stains. She held up the glass and drank a third of it through the straw.

"I've been up for almost two days," she said, wiping her mouth with the sleeve of her raincoat. "So it's not, like, automatic, but the tools are getting so fast. It's the banks. They got billions to spend on this shit and you just can't keep up."

"You're probably not going to tell me how you did it."

She shook her head.

"It won't do you any good," she said. "Everything changes too fast. As soon as you think you're an expert, an hour later you'll be wrong."

I didn't want to think that. It was too frightening, too apocalyptic. I said as much.

"You're fucked," she said. "I'm fucked, too. We're all fucked. Get used to it. It's the ineluctable modality of the calculable. Warps folded into warps. Syncopated algorithms. I'm only sitting here because they haven't gotten around to killing me yet." She finished off the drink and set it down gently on the bar. "Wow, I better eat something. If you're still buying."

While she ordered a meal and another hurricane, I texted Natsumi that I was delayed, not to worry, but to stay away from the hotel bar and keep the phone handy.

"Girlfriend? Boyfriend? Wife?" Strider asked me, glancing down at my phone.

"Spiritual adviser."

She took off her raincoat and dropped it at her feet. Underneath was a white T-shirt with the words "Starship Hijacker" in a bold, blocky font written across her surprisingly prominent breasts.

"It's my favorite," she said, following my eyes. "My lucky traveling shirt."

She looked down and pulled out the fabric, as if trying to read the familiar words. I caught a whiff of body odor.

"Should I forget about getting my backdoor?" I asked.

She shook her head.

"I didn't say that. I just didn't want you to think extortion works on me. And I wanted to meet you. You're so fucking polite. I'm not surprised you're bald. It's a compensation thing."

Her shoulders were narrow, but her posture almost unnaturally erect as she used both hands to consume her cheeseburger. I was relieved to see her dab her face frequently with the cloth napkin, staying ahead of errant globs of catsup and relish juice.

"Do you actually think people want to kill you?" I asked.

She nodded and pulled her hair back away

from her face, trying to keep the thin strands from brushing against her burger.

"Oh, yeah. What's the worst they can do to me for data theft? A few years in jail? Banishment from the Internet? I've got a photographic memory. I could just do this," she made a writing motion in the air, "to unlock the vaults of half the banks in the world."

"You implied you were losing the hacker arms race."

She frowned into her drink and shook her little balled fists.

"Don't get all debatey on me, Spanky. You know what I mean."

"I do. Sorry."

"The thing is, there's no such thing as money anymore. It's all data. Bits and bytes. It only becomes what we used to think of as money when you have a chunk of cash in your hand. There are physicists who think nothing is real unless it's observed. It's like that with money. It doesn't exist until you hit the ATM machine. Not even then, if you want to talk gold standard and all that currency crap. But you get the idea."

"I do."

"So, if you fuck around with their data, you're essentially running your hands through their money, like Scrooge McDuck in his vault swimming around in dollar bills. They can't let that happen. And they can't stop addicts like me forever, so the only way to deal with us is to purge the gene pool. Makes me want to have a baby. Almost."

I watched her finish her meal, including a giant order of french fries. Throughout, she worried at her backpack, occasionally adjusting where she supported it on her thighs.

"I still hope you're wrong," I added.

"Rationalization and denial are excellent survival mechanisms," she said. "Until they get you killed. But then you don't care, right?"

"Your loved ones care."

"I'm done with that crap since my parents died. Except for my cat, and he'd love anyone who fed him."

"Sorry."

She rolled her eyes like an annoyed teenager.

"Oh Christ, that wasn't a pity play. Not interested in the lovey-dovey thing. Don't like all that genital entanglement. It's not an abuse thing, no matter what the shrinks tell you. Why am I telling you all this? You're not a shrink are you?"

"No, but people like to tell me things."

"I'll bet they do."

"I only steal when I have to," I said. "And

never for money."

"And junkies do heroin to get those cool needle marks."

She opened her backpack and pulled out a slip of yellow paper covered with a pencil scrawl of alphanumeric code. She handed it to me.

"I hate it when people try to take from me something I'd gladly give away if they'd just ask," she said. "But here it is anyway. Just don't threaten me again. I want to like you."

When I went to take the paper, she gripped my hand, kneading it like a piece of dough. Then she used her other hand to pat around my face, like you'd do with wet modeling clay.

"Real is still real," she said, before zipping up the backpack, sliding off the bar stool, slipping on her raincoat, and disappearing out the door, her back straight, her feet in a slight shuffle, the backpack nearly dragging on the floor.

I called Natsumi.

"It's you," she said, answering the phone.

"It is. Real is still real," I said.

The general called me the next day and told me to meet him at the lifeguard stand on the beach at the north end of Ocean Drive.

He told me to come in a bathing suit and nothing else.

"No reason for modesty," he said. "I already know what your prick looks like."

When I told Natsumi the plan, she offered to come along and try to get his photo.

"He'll have spotters posted all around the beach. They might see you."

"I'm feeling superfluous," she said.

"I need to know you're safe."

"You're more cautious since they grabbed us off the boat."

"I am?"

"You once told me inaction was the most dangerous thing we could do."

"Why did I say that?"

"If I leave now, I'll be an hour ahead. Time to get comfy and see if I can spot the spotters."

She changed into a bathing suit over which she slipped a beach dress in a loud floral pattern. She put the SLR camera with the longest lens in the bottom of a canvas beach bag. I stayed silent as I watched her leave the hotel room.

I used the intervening time on the computer, cruising around nearly aimlessly as if that would help me feel less anxious. It didn't.

I left the room and walked north from our

hotel through the tan haze of sand-blown Miami Beach. It was a warm wind, with a threat of rain, the tropical kind that came and went like the sweep of a broom, cleaning the air. When I reached the assigned beach, I stripped down to my bathing suit and left the little pile of clothes under a palm tree. I resisted the impulse to seek out Natsumi as I walked across the beach, instead fixing my eyes on the big purple, green and yellow lifeguard stand.

When I got there, the general was sitting nearby in a beach chair. His body was lean and ropy, a greying mat of hair almost concealing a scar across his right breast. He pointed to an identical beach chair to his left. I sat down.

"I understand the attraction of sitting by the ocean," he said. "The primordial pull. I just don't get doing it all day. The time investment."

"Agreed," I said, brushing sand off my lower legs.

"It's good to have common ground between business partners," he said.

"I appreciate your help."

He took a smartphone from his lap and tapped around on the screen.

"I appreciate the twenty thousand," he

said. "You won't mind if I move it to a safer place?"

"Not at all."

"I can do this while sunning myself on the beach," he said, working the phone's screen. "Most think such things commonplace. Me, I still have the wonder of *un joven Cubano.*"

"A young brain is good for survival."

"Agreed on that as well."

"So, any luck with my *mercenario?*"

He squinted at the phone for another moment, then nodded and put it back on his lap.

"Si. It happens I know the man well. Someone I have respect for. We were able to speak with candor, which saved a lot of time, effort and money. So much I'm almost embarrassed taking your twenty thousand. Almost."

He rummaged around in a beach bag and came up with a pad of paper and a pen. He wrote down the name and handed it to me.

"Rolando Mosqueda," I read out loud.

"I asked him point blank about the operation you described. He just laughed."

"Laughed?"

"I don't know why. I gave him your e-mail address and left it up to him if he wants to contact you. No guarantees there."

"What if he doesn't? How can I get word

to him?"

"Not my problem, Señor Rana. You asked about a certain Latino mercenary on a certain operation, I give you this name. Be thankful I give this much."

"There're probably a lot of Rolando Mosquedas in the world," I said.

"At least one's a soldier of fortune. That should narrow the field." Two young women wearing suits in tenuous conformance with South Beach decency standards walked by us on the way back from the ocean, their eyes cast furtively toward the rambling guard stand. "On the other hand," he said, taking up a prior conversational thread.

"How about an address," I said.

When he looked over at me I saw my face reflected in his oversized sunglasses. Then, another shape flashed across. I turned and saw Norberto unfolding another beach chair. He sat down next to me so I was sandwiched between the two men.

"Hola," he said to me as he reached in a woven beach bag. He pulled out a can of beer. "Too early for you?"

"No thanks," I said, as did the general.

Norberto shrugged and dove back into the bag, this time pulling out a towel. He pulled a piece of it away to show me the tip of a silencer. He grinned, and I grinned back.

"Just in case we run into any beach banditos," he said.

I turned my head back to the general, who was gazing out at the sea.

"I need more than just a name. I can't afford the research time," I said, honestly.

"What's the hurry, young man?" said the general. "With your whole life ahead of you?"

"This wasn't the deal."

"You must be unaware of the organizational chart," said the general. He put one hand above the other. "I'm here, you're there. Your responsibility is to thank me for such high quality information for such a reasonable price. My job is to go back to my piano and away from all this primordial pulling. You can keep the chair," he added, as both he and Norberto stood up to leave.

"Did you check your investment account?" I asked.

"I'm sorry, what did you say?"

"Have you checked your investment account, the one at the bank? First off, I wouldn't trust a banker with my investments; secondly, you have way too much in growth stocks and too little in solid, dividend-yielding blue chips. So I rebalanced everything. You don't have to thank me."

The general unfolded his chair and sat back down, this time facing me. Norberto stayed standing. The general took out his smartphone and poked at it for a few minutes before looking up at me.

"You did this?" he asked.

"It's all still there. You can move it back if you want. I don't recommend it, but it's your money. For now, anyway."

"You're a dead man," he said in Spanish.

Norberto held the towel in both hands, the muzzle of the silencer sticking out in plain view.

"That dopey money market thing they talked you into," I said. "Way too much cash sitting on the sidelines, if you ask me."

"You know I can't let this stand," he said. "Norberto, if you would."

Norberto squatted down in front of me and took a deep breath, letting the air out slowly.

"I promise your money will go to a good cause," I said.

The general put his hand up. Norberto lowered the gun. The general held up his smartphone.

"My money is here," he said.

I held up my own.

"If I don't send an all-clear signal in five

minutes, it will all be withdrawn. Permanently."

Norberto started to raise his gun again, but the general stuck his foot out and lightly kicked the other man's calf. "*Bastante.* How did you do this?" he asked me.

"What's Rolando's address?"

"I don't know." I sat there and stared at him through my own impenetrable sunglasses. "Palm Beach," he said, finally. "I don't remember the exact address. Gated community. I have his phone number."

He played around with the smartphone for a few moments, then took out the pad of paper to write on.

"You knew I wouldn't give you what you wanted," he said, handing me the paper. "You were ready."

"Like you, I wish I could be more trustful."

"Am I going to have to worry about this forever?" he asked. "Are we about to have a war?"

"No war. I have other things to do." I stood up and adjusted my hat and sunglasses. "You can keep the chair. And the twenty K, but remember, it always feels better to give something freely than to have it taken away."

I kept my eyes toward the street as I

walked across the beach, my attention un-diverted by thoughts of Norberto's sup-pressed firearm and *otros jovenes Cubanos* lurking among the umbrellas or the pull of subterranean forces, primordial or other-wise.

CHAPTER 8

The trip up the coast from Miami to Palm Beach is less than a hundred miles, but it felt longer because of our chosen route, hard up against the ocean and away from Interstate 95 where sensible people drove. I'd rented a convertible to gain a greater feeling of connectedness as we made our way along trackless strip development and through the occasional neighborhood, some poor, some ensconced behind thick shrubbery, stone walls and metal gates.

It was behind such fortifications that we found Rolando's house, though not immediately, since that would have taken either the proper access card or an M1 Abrams tank. I knew we had the right neighborhood, however, so now it was just a matter of getting inside the gates.

"How're we going to do that?" Natsumi asked.

"Where there's broadband, there's a way."

Which we found quickly enough at the neighborhood Starbucks. I commandeered a corner seating area while Natsumi provisioned at the counter. We'd left Miami so abruptly, I hadn't had a chance to note more than Rolando's address, though I'd recorded a related list of URLs for further inquiry. It only took a few moments to get what I most wanted at that point. A photo.

It was taken at the Palm Beach Rotary Club luncheon. He was standing at a podium, speaking to the group on the subject, "Financial Planning in the Age of the Underwater House." He held a snorkel and face mask up to the microphone. He was smiling broadly. I could easily imagine the opening remarks.

With dark black hair, goatee and wire-rim glasses, his topic could have been far more academic and he'd look the part. His skin was pale white and his wide smile showed a row of perfect teeth, and even under the suit you could detect the broad shoulders. A meaty fist gripped the snorkeling gear.

I recognized the face, and still felt those large hands gripping my arms and pulling my wrists together, the rock hard body beneath the black Special Ops uniforms as the mercs jostled us in and out of the inflatable boat.

"What do you think?" Natsumi asked.

"The general could have used his help. Do a trade out."

"So we don't have to storm the gates?" she asked.

"Just the office suite. About two miles from here."

I showed it to her on the smartphone's GPS.

"So let's go," she said.

"We can't do that," I said, a faint panic rising in my throat.

"Why not?"

I thought a moment.

"I don't know," I said.

Natsumi sat back in her overstuffed Starbucks couch and smiled at me with her eyes, a talent that seemed uniquely her own.

"That happened too quickly," she said. "You're not ready."

"I'm not."

"The curse of the analytic mind. You haven't crunched the numbers. Weighed the odds. Analyzed the regressions."

"I'm unarmed. I've got nothing."

"Yes you do. You've got me."

She stood up and left the Starbucks. I followed, slightly unnerved. She got in the driver's seat.

"You navigate," she said.

Which I did, not knowing what else to do. As promised, we were there in a few minutes. It was a new office building made of phony brownstone and reflective blue windows. The sign out front suggested a warren of small operations, though we quickly spotted Rolando Mosqueda, Certified Financial Planner, *Hablamos Español*.

Natsumi parked near the exit, facing out. She shut off the car and turned to me.

"Sometimes it's better not to think so much," she said.

"Thinking keeps us alive."

"There's different kinds of thinking. You never heard of Gestalt?"

"They wouldn't let mathematicians into psych courses."

She opened the car door.

"Come on," she said, "before the moment's lost."

I followed her into the building and up the elevator to Rolando's office. Inside was a tight reception area with a pink-faced young guy manning the desk. He had thinning red hair and a scar that started in the center of his cheek and sliced straight back through the ear. I forced my eyes away, but it wasn't necessary. All his attention was on Natsumi.

"We're here to see Señor Mosqueda," she

said before the guy's "Can I help you?" was halfway out. He looked down at something on his desk.

"No, we don't have an appointment," said Natsumi. "Tell him what we look like. He'll see us."

The guy stood up and went through the door behind his desk. Natsumi watched him go from where she was leaning forward, both hands flat on the desk. We didn't have long to wait. The door opened and out walked Rolando, looking just as handsome as he did in the Rotary photo, only three inches taller and that much broader across the chest. His sleeves were rolled up over thick forearms and he had an old-fashioned pencil in one of his hands.

He didn't offer to shake and neither did we.

"The general has some explaining to do," he said.

"Not as much as you," said Natsumi.

He used both hands to twirl the pencil. His face seemed under the strain of careful thought. The red-haired scar face looked like he wanted to squeeze back into the reception area. Rolando stood aside and waved to us to follow him. We went back into another open area off of which were three enclosed offices and a conference room, into which he guided us. It was well lit by a bank of windows. A coffee machine was in the corner and a white board covered in figures and acronyms filled the other wall.

"Sit," he said. "Please. Can I get you anything?" he added, then immediately said, "No, of course not."

He sat across from us.

"Do they know what you really do?" Natsumi asked. "Your colleagues? Your family?"

He touched his wedding ring.

"This is what I really do," he said, and then, "What do you want?"

"Information," she said.

He nodded, looking down at the table.

"I may not be able to do that," he said. "Not because I don't want to." He looked up again. "I only know what I know."

"What do you know?" she asked.

"That the world is a dangerous place. That it isn't what people think it is. That sometimes it's better to just let things be. To walk away while you still can."

"We can't," said Natsumi.

Something akin to a smile lightened his face.

"I'm not surprised. You two are a handful."

He sat back in the office chair, which surprised him by tipping back even farther.

He caught the edge of the table and pulled himself back up, Latin dignity slightly akilter.

"We're not here to threaten you, or expose your extracurricular activities," said Natsumi. "All we want are answers."

"That's good, because threats don't work so well with me."

"Who hired you?" I asked.

He looked at me, his gentle amusement deepening.

"So, he talks. Not so easy for people to get you to do, from what I remember."

"What else do you remember?" asked Natsumi.

He looked out the windows as if to assist his memory.

"Bush league. The contact had clearance. Our team leader had worked for him before. But some other dick from the same outfit met us at the dock before shipping out. Civilian puke. No operational sense. Our team leader had to run the thing."

"What thing?" asked Natsumi.

"The snatch. You two."

We let the silence sit there so long it nearly crowded us out of the room. He finally relented.

"All we had were the coordinates of a boat at anchor and a description of the two targets. The job was to bring you in undamaged and to provide security on the ship."

"The fishing scow," said Natsumi.

"That's what it looked like, yeah. I don't know why they wanted you and I don't care. Not part of my contract. So I don't know what went on in the interrogation rooms, what you said or didn't say. I just know the civilians were very unhappy with the results."

"How do you know that?" she asked.

"Screaming and cursing? Unprofessional, as I said. Usually clients never let you see them sweat."

"Who was your contact?" I asked.

That irritated him, though he tried not to show it.

"You don't know who's fighting our wars these days? You never read the paper?"

"You said they worked for the same outfit. What outfit?" Natsumi asked.

"You know, one of you is supposed to be the good cop. I learned that in interrogation school."

"You don't have to tell us anything, I know that," I said. "In fact, I'm a little surprised you're telling us anything at all. We don't have much in the way of leverage. We could make your life unpleasant for a while, probably, but not without great risk to ourselves. And to be honest, I don't have another fight in me right now. So I'm asking you, please, just tell us whatever you can about the people who hired you to do this to us. And then we'll go away and you'll never hear from us again."

I realized he still held the pencil when he started tapping it on the conference room table. He stopped when he saw me look, as if unaware himself.

"The Société Commerciale Fontaine," he said. "Big engineering company, originally. Now expanded to a general services contractor for our nation-building-happy federal government. Provides everything from road construction to desalinization plants to delivering yogurt and hometown papers to the officers' mess. Got into trouble when their security people mistook a family outing for an insurgents' attack, how I don't know, but the bad PR lost them that contract. Officially. Still all tangled up in black ops, which won't come as a surprise. These things take infrastructure that's too hard to hide inside the regular military."

"They hired you," I said.

He shook his head.

"The contact came through e-mail. Then this civilian appears. Nonconventional, but he shows us the money. Literally. Cash up

131

front, bonus at the end. What the hell. So, no, I'm not really sure he was Fontaine, but that's what he said."

"There was a woman," said Natsumi.

"The screamer," he said. "Scary *chica,* if you pardon me for saying."

"I pardon you," said Natsumi.

"They were working together, but she wasn't working for him, I don't think. I heard her refer to Fontaine as 'your people.' Not always in a complimentary way."

"You never heard what they wanted to learn from us," I said.

"I tried, but even these *imbéciles* knew better than to talk too much in front of us."

"You said your job was to capture us, then provide security during the interrogation," said Natsumi. "What about after?"

He caught himself tapping the pencil again. Annoyed, he tossed it into a nearby trash can with a quick flip of the wrist. Then he leaned forward on his elbows, his hands clasped almost prayerfully.

"There was no after. Not for you. They told our team leader to snap your necks on the way back to your boat, which we were ordered to burn at anchor with you in it."

Another silence gathered in the spare conference room. Rolando sat there and looked at us and we looked back at him.

Then, as before, he answered the question hanging in the air.

"No way were we doing that," he said. "What, do they think we're murderers? It's insulting."

"You towed our boat to Virgin Gorda and dropped us on the beach," I said, "to make sure no one fell overboard in a drug-induced haze."

"Our team leader was a little embarrassed for getting us into this shit operation, though we all got paid pretty well at the end of the day. And you can be as mad at me as you want, but we did save your lives."

"So the Fontaine people think we're dead," said Natsumi.

"Sure," said Rolando. "That's how we got the bonus. Felt good to stick it to those amateurs. Feels good to talk about it."

After a few more probing questions, it was clear he was finished sharing, and there wasn't much left to share. Natsumi also looked ready to let it go, so like a pair of reasonably satisfied financial clients, we stood up from the table and this time shook his hand, thanking him for his time and candor. He gave a little bow when he thanked us in return for understanding that business was business, and offered his apologies for any inconvenience.

We just returned the bow and headed for the door, though on the way I had one more question.

"You didn't happen to get their names, did you?" I asked him. "The Fontaine guy and the woman?"

"They called themselves Chuck and Alberta, but that doesn't mean anything," he said. "But, when they weren't looking, I did snap their pictures."

He thumbed around his smartphone, then held it up. On the screen was a clear image of the two of them in conversation.

"I have some good individual shots, too," he said. "You want them?"

Back out in the parking lot, I forwarded the photos from my text mailbox to a secure e-mail address. I checked the time. We'd been in Rolando's office for less than an hour, yet it felt like months had passed.

"Often," said Natsumi, "if you simply ask someone for something, they'll just give it to you."

CHAPTER 9

We were back in our hotel room in South Beach. Natsumi was in the bathtub. I sat on a desk chair dragged in from the bedroom. The bathroom was all white and she was beneath a white-bubble quilt. In fact, the prevailing whiteness of the scene turned the red wine in the glass a bloody red.

The air in the bathroom was not unlike the Miami air outside — hot and humid. I slumped down in the rolling chair and put my feet up on the edge of the tub.

"Score one for Gestalt."

"Gestalt's not a person. It's a thing."

"You knew the mercenaries had let us go," I said.

She shook her head.

"No. I knew we needed to talk to him right away. That we'd learn something important. I didn't know what."

"What are you thinking now?" I asked.

"That Rolando or the general will drop a

135

dime on us."

"Not a chance. They're not that mercenary."

"What do we do now?" she asked.

"You keep soaking. I'll go deliberate."

"Check on me once in a while. I could drown in here."

I left her for my computer, waiting in the other room, untethered and eager to fly.

After hours of fruitless searching using every legal and extra-legal people-finder program I had, I stumbled over Angus the computer scientist. As it turned out, he was neither a computer scientist nor a guy named Angus, though he was a PhD in particle physics with credentials in a branch of mathematics favored by the makers and breakers of exotic code.

I found him at a science fiction writers' conference where he'd delivered a talk on the future of cryptography. He was dressed up like Ray Bradbury at an end-of-the-conference party. I only knew he was playing Ray Bradbury because a caption under the photo said he was. I knew it was Angus because it looked just like him, and his real name, according to the caption, was Ian MacPhail, and if that wasn't Scottish, I didn't know what the hell was.

I was on the site looking around for Strider the Data Thief, who once told me she wrote science fiction and frequented writers conferences as her only social engagement. In the photo, MacPhail was chatting with a Jawa trader from the planet Tatooine, who for all I knew was Strider herself. Armed with the right search parameters, I also learned that MacPhail was a Harvard professor married to a woman named Joann, with a daughter and a son who'd contributed three grandchildren to the family. His prior work experience included consulting for the FBI in their New York City office and extensive work in private enterprise.

Joann was Angela's opposite. Round faced and pale, with short, light brown hair and glasses. And a ready smile, if the two images I found of her were any indication.

"I would have rather been wrong," said Natsumi, thoroughly sodden from the bubble bath and half-buzzed, now reading on the bed behind me. I'd held the computer up for her to see.

"I know."

"So what do we do with him?"

"He's speaking again this Monday at another conference. This time at Harvard in front of the American Academy of Physicists. That gives us time to get up to Cambridge with a stop in Connecticut along the way. I can pack while you book the flight. Do you think you'll need the bikini?" I added, already dropping clothes into our carry-ons.

"It's the end of March."

"Right. So we rent something with four-wheel drive. We can buy warm clothes at the airport."

"We could get a hotel with an indoor pool," she said.

"Excellent idea," I said, stuffing the bikini into a one-inch-square space in the suitcase.

"I'm still not sure what you want with Angus."

"Ian."

I brought the computer all the way over to where she lay on top of the bed. I tapped on his LinkedIn page and scrolled down to his experience and turned the computer around so she could see. It was there between the end of his FBI career in New York City and his appointment as associate professor at Harvard:

Senior Project Director, Cybersecurity, The Société Commerciale Fontaine
■ Lead Task Force Charged with International Security Protocol Co-

ordination
- Oversee Enterprise-wide Digital Security Policies
- Liaison with Appropriate Government Agencies
- As Directed by The Société Commerciale Fontaine CEO

"Oh," said Natsumi, putting the computer on her lap and clicking on her favorite travel site.

CHAPTER 10

As we rode the shuttle bus from the arrival gates at JFK to the car rental area it felt like God had sapped all the warmth and color from the world and replaced it with a permanent cloak of chilly grey gauze. The bus smelled of wet wool and illicit cigarettes and our fellow passengers wore the hollow expressions of the already damned and long ago consigned to the rocking, lumbering box van for all eternity.

The only sounds came from the tires cutting through mounded curbs of grit-encrusted slush and the occasional incoherent bark from the driver's radio. Outside, jets taking off and landing in close proximity produced a rolling thunder both heard and felt through the exhausted nylon-upholstered seats.

It wasn't until we were in the cushioned embrace of a Jeep Cherokee, inhaling the new-car fumes and fiddling the climate control into perfection, that our spirits began to lift. After some minor navigational confusion, we cleared the snarled confines of Queens and crossed the Throgs Neck Bridge on our way to New England.

"We lived here, right?" said Natsumi.

"Born and raised."

"I was born in Japan, though I was little when we left."

"What do you remember?"

"The traffic."

The Jeep took well to the twisty Hutchinson Parkway that soon merged into the Merritt, equally blessed with hill and curve, which crossed the line into Connecticut. We took a detour into Stamford to buy more clothing and rugged footwear, and to startle my sister by sitting down across from her in the cafeteria at the hospital where she practiced cardiology.

"You've got to be kidding me," she said, clearly stunned, a cheeseburger halfway to her mouth.

"I thought heart doctors only ate tofu and sprouts."

"You're not dead," she said, or rather breathed in relief.

"Depends on your definition."

"Hello, Natsumi," she said.

"Hello, Evelyn. I told him we should call

141

ahead," she added, aware and sympathetic over the shock we'd caused.

"Phones aren't safe," I said.

"You call this safe?" asked Evelyn.

"Nobody's watching," I said. "Not at the moment."

"The last I heard you were in Europe," said Evelyn. "According to Shelly."

Shelly Gross was a former FBI agent who'd spent his recent retirement years tangled up in severe approach-avoidance. It was my fault — I'd drawn him back into service when I needed a connection inside serious law enforcement. Though it was a little like coaxing a poisonous snake to be your proxy in a snake fight. One wrong move and you're the one with the fangs in your throat.

Still, he'd helped me when he didn't have to, and kept quiet about me when he could have burnished an already illustrious career with a high-profile collar. It made it easier to forgive his declared desire that I spend the rest of my life in jail.

"How is the old stiff?" I asked.

"Still sore at you, but said I shouldn't suffer because of that."

"I need to talk to him," I said.

She looked down and realized she was still holding her half-raised burger. She took a bite and wiped her face with the napkin.

"So it's not over yet," she said.

"Far from it," I said.

"The world's a dangerous place," said Natsumi, "and not what people think it is."

"How bad is it?" Evelyn asked.

"I'm not sure," I said. "I thought we were more or less in the clear. In exile, but comfortably so. But apparently we'd stumbled over something in the past that caught up to us."

"And you don't know what?"

"No. It has something to do with money, an imprisoned financial security consultant named Joselito Gorrotxategi and people connected to The Société Commerciale Fontaine, the big engineering firm working for the State Department."

"That doesn't sound that serious," said Evelyn.

"They kidnapped us in the middle of the night, put us through psychological torture and threatened to make it physical. Then they tried to kill us," said Natsumi.

"Oh."

"It's possible we could be in even worse trouble than before, we just didn't realize it," I said.

"What do the French have to do with all this?" Evelyn asked.

"Fontaine is only nominally French," I told her. "They rolled up a bunch of American engineering and defense contractors. Enough to clear domestic political hurdles. Besides building oil refineries and petrochemical plants, they specialize in big public works following disasters, natural and manmade. And they're also woven into the international security community, which means everything deep, dark and nasty anywhere in the world."

"I might have read that."

"You read about them losing the security part of the contract with the State Department. Apparently, not really."

"Then who is the Spanish guy with the unpronounceable name?" Evelyn asked.

"Joselito Gorrotxategi. He's a forensic accountant who worked IT security for lots of big organizations, public and private, including the Guardia Civil, the national police force of Spain, and relevant to us, a Guardia spin-off group of vigilantes who were after Florencia's embezzled money."

"Which they didn't get," said Evelyn.

"Suffice it to say, Arthur upset their plans," said Natsumi.

"Badly enough that Joselito is now in federal prison. What really put him there wasn't just playing footsie with the vigilan-

144

tes. He'd also managed to get inside the FBI's international operations and caused enough mischief to attract the full wrath of our country's counterterrorism forces."

"That's where Shelly came in," said Natsumi.

"Who thought the problems inside the FBI had been corrected," I said. "But now I'm not so sure. Shelly got around resistance inside the bureau by going directly to Stephen Holt, the assistant director in charge of international operations. At great risk to his retirement standing, along with his pension."

"And now you want Shelly's help again," said Evelyn.

"I do. I can't say he's a friend, but he's the only honest guy I know in the federal government. And what's with the first-name basis?"

Evelyn would have blushed if she'd possessed the requisite physiological equipment.

"He's been taking me out to dinner."

"No way," said Natsumi.

I laughed, a solid laugh from deep in the belly. A scowl or a curse might have been easier for Evelyn to hear.

"He's a widower. We go to a restaurant and talk about horticulture and breeding honey bees. Sometimes a little bioscience or predictive meteorology. Never about you or his job or any of that. It's innocent."

I imagined that the dryness of that discourse was enough to desiccate neighboring restaurant-goers.

I also thought to myself, "So Evelyn, you're also keeping your own occasional obstruction of justice, accessory to murder and insurance fraud off the topic list?" But I didn't say it, because I loved my sister and was happy enough she was actually dating, a thing I'd rarely known her to do.

"Please don't tell him we're in town," I said. "We need to be careful here. Maintain some reasonable separation."

"Like church and state," said Natsumi.

"More like nitro and glycerin."

Evelyn put both hands in the air.

"I'm not saying anything."

We caught up on some mundane family business, which Natsumi patiently waited through. Before we left I gave Evelyn a disposable phone and a number she could call in an emergency. Otherwise, I told her radio silence would probably have to prevail for the foreseeable future.

"You need to figure a way out of this, Arthur," Evelyn said. "It's no way to live."

I hoped there was a way to live, I thought

as we walked out of the hospital, because there sure seemed to be plenty of ways to die.

CHAPTER 11

There was a time when I could have written out the equations for Einstein's General Theory of Relativity from memory and been able to discuss the more subtle nuances of the great work with a fellow mathematician. The portion of my brain designed to handle that task was now pulpy, though current neuroscience doctrine and my own experience indicated slight remediation of my dyscalculia as the brain established new wiring, compensating for the loss of parietal lobe function.

I didn't need the language of math, however, to appreciate the interwoven nature of space and time. Sitting with Natsumi in the Jeep parked across the street from the house I'd shared with Florencia, I felt myself filling a space that time had warped out of recognition.

It wasn't just the passage of time, it was what had occurred in the nearly four years from when a man in a baggy trench coat had sat in our living room and complimented my wife on her decorating talents, had her write down a few things on a slip of paper, then shot us both through the head.

I wasn't looking at my old house to contemplate the magnitude of the changes I'd experienced, nor mourn the loss of my past life, now as foreign and remote as any distant place we'd traveled through, often pursued, while in constant pursuit ourselves of salvation. Rather, I needed a visual to orient my perceptions. I had to see that the house still existed. I had to share the proximate air with the place where the course of my life had made a violent pivot away from the benighted bliss in which I once dwelled into another region, formerly unknown and vastly more dark and complex.

There was no point in wanting to go home again, because home as I knew it no longer existed. Even if it did, I didn't want it back. Looking at the house in Stamford, I was now sure of that. What I wanted was something that was still to be decided upon. I wanted the privilege of discovering what time might further conceive for me, but not while so furtive and constrained.

Our capture and confinement, however brief, had taught me a lesson as potent and powerful as the one bestowed by the man in the trench coat. I didn't know where it would all end up, but I knew one thing for certain: I'd rather be truly dead than go back to that room on Chuck and Alberta's fishing scow — caged, degraded and alone.

The house in Stamford was about an hour from Shelly Gross's subdivision in Rocky Hill. It was built in the early sixties, though decades of weekend toil by earnest and determined homeowners had overcome the neighborhood's innate suburban dullness. Shelly's house itself, prim and contained as its owner, was a triumph of domestic artistry.

Even in early spring, there were things to admire about the place, which must have distracted my attention from Shelly pulling out of his driveway in a Toyota Prius the color of the overcast sky.

The plan, still formative, called for a quick drive-by, followed by a carefully plotted surprise encounter, the particulars of which had yet to be worked out. Colliding with the target wasn't part of the concept.

"Son of a bitch," I said, veering away from Shelly's rear fender and trying to look invisible. I suggested Natsumi do the same.

"I'm wearing a baseball cap. That's the

best I can do for now," she said.

Aside from an angry honk of the horn, Shelly seemed to take little notice of the event, to my relief. I was able to drive at a normal, even unhurried pace around the block and still be able to fall in behind the Prius when he pulled out onto the strip highway that anchored this swath of Central Connecticut.

I'd followed Shelly before. He was considered the most skillful and experienced federal agent in the state, retired or otherwise. I'd learned this reputation had been built partly on a preternatural ability to focus on the objective at hand, clearing from his vision any surrounding distraction. It made him a great agent and an easy guy to sneak up on.

Nevertheless, I wasn't about to push it, assuming I'd have to turn off before even Shelly's blunted suspicions were roused. Instead, he quickly arrived at his destination, pulling through two stone pillars into a parking lot. The sign on one of the pillars read "Jason P. Fellingham Academy of the Military Arts." We rolled by and I caught a glimpse of a sturdy old brick mansion of the type whose ultimate state was either an office complex or a museum or a mountain of used brick in the salvage yard.

At the next chance, we turned into another parking lot, this one serving a shabby row of low-slung storefronts. I parked the Jeep and asked Natsumi how she thought we ought to proceed.

"Through the front door," she said.

"You really like the frontal assault."

"Only when called for."

"Shelly is not to be trifled with."

She brushed that off.

"He's sleeping with your sister."

"He's dating her."

"He had plenty of opportunities before that to turn us in. He never did it. He really doesn't want to. And now, he really can't. Let's enjoy a little normalcy and only worry about the things we need to worry about, which is a lot."

I almost started lecturing on the benefits of paranoia in the pursuit of personal security, which she would have listened to patiently and with great understanding. But I knew she was right. If you try to stay on maximum alert all the time, it begins to erode, becoming less available when you really need it.

"I'll follow you," I said, as I watched her slip out of the Jeep.

The entrance to the museum was a cramped foyer with a desk behind which sat a woman who looked too large to ever rise from the seat again. Her smile was wide and friendly and she held two tickets in both hands as if prepared to make an offering.

"Ten dollars for the two of you unless you're members. Then it's free. Except for the membership dues, which is a bargain in my opinion."

While Natsumi paid, I picked a slim museum guide off a stack on the woman's desk which I leafed through until I came to a list of volunteer docents. As suspected, Shelly was on the list. I asked about him.

"Colonel Gross, retired army reserves, is usually in the document room for part of the morning. Captain Wolfson, also retired, should be here momentarily. He can take you around."

"We'll be fine," said Natsumi, slipping her arm through mine and moving me through the foyer.

Just inside was another room, in the center of which stood a blue-coated infantryman from the American Revolution. He was well equipped with a sturdy musket and turned out nicely in his uniform, his gaze appropriately steely, though with a touch of uncertainty about the whole thing. I started to read the explanatory placard, but Natsumi gently moved me along. In the subsequent rooms we breezed past glass cases filled with maps, weapons and accoutrements from the dismal march of armed conflicts through the centuries. It wasn't until we'd surveyed most of the collection that we came to a large room reinforced with artillery where a small World War I field piece guarded a door with a sign that said, "Archives."

Natsumi tried the door and it opened. I followed her.

The walls were lined with deep shelves and file cabinets, neatly arranged and carefully labeled. In the center of the room was a big metal worktable at which Shelly sat looking through a jewelers' magnifier light at a ragged-edged sheet of paper.

He still had his full head of close-cropped white hair, clear pink face and erect posture. When he looked over the top of the light his expression stayed in neutral.

"We have video surveillance," he said. "They'll be here in about a minute."

"Can you take a coffee break?" I asked.

"You're still alive," he said.

"So far," I said. "I hope we can talk."

"It's better if you sit down," he said, nodding toward the chairs facing him. As soon as we settled down, the door opened behind us and a young man in a khaki shirt and blue jeans walked in. Blue eyes set in a dark-skinned face lent him an air of cautious alert.

"Stand down, sergeant," said Shelly. "These are associates."

The young man backed out again and closed the door.

"You look well," I said.

"I was well," he said. "Now I'm feeling slightly ill."

"Is the room bugged?" Natsumi asked.

"We're not that nuts," said Shelly, without humor. Then he added, "That was quite a mess you left for our people."

"You took in Joselito," I said, more a question.

"The FBI took him in. I'm permanently persona non grata. I only know because one of my last remaining friends in the bureau risked his career to tell me."

"They should be giving you medals," said Natsumi.

"That's not how it works. My reward is I get to keep my pension. Orders are to stay retired this time. They mean it."

"Can we tell you our story?" Natsumi asked.

He nodded slowly, reluctantly. So we did, leaving out details unessential to the narrative. He listened carefully, still holding the document we'd interrupted him examining. He asked no questions and showed no affect, even when we ended with our visit to Evelyn in the hospital.

"You're blown," he said.

"We were blown. Now we're back in business," I said. "For now."

He shrugged, allowing the point.

"The world isn't the same," he said. "I don't know anything anymore, and I really don't want to know. After 9/11, everybody screamed about the operational firewalls between intelligence services. So they poked them full of holes, and now they got the Wild West. As bad as you think it is, it's worse."

"How could Fontaine know our passports were fraudulent when we cleared through the BVI?" Natsumi asked.

He shrugged again.

"Like I said, Wild West. Everybody thinks information is all tidily secured by these official bastards in blue suits and epaulets. It's not. What we can do with data has gotten way ahead of anyone's ability to control it. The best they can do is pretend they can. It'll be at least a generation before they get it all cleaned up. I'll be dead by then. Probably you'll be, too. Sorry, but that's the truth."

I wished he'd looked sorrier.

"We need to speak to Joselito."

"Good luck with that. They got him on a big list of terrorist activities. Maximum-security federal pen, secret location, protective custody. For all I know he's in Gitmo."

"He must have been a very bad boy," said Natsumi.

"A foreign national, cybersecurity expert, in the service of terror groups," said Shelly, ticking off the points on his fingers. "He's never getting out."

"So he's not playing on his computer," I said.

"No. And he never will again, even in his wildest dreams."

He finally put down the yellowing paper he was holding. It was covered in the beautiful, flowing handwritten script of prior centuries, eighteenth or nineteenth, it was hard to tell from across the table. Shelly saw me look and said, "Captain Oliver Perry trying to convince his superior officers that he'd in fact conquered Lake Erie during the War of 1812. Even then the boneheads in Washington had a talent for fucking up from afar."

"We want to come in from the cold," I said, "metaphorically. It's actually been pretty warm for us lately."

"Won't happen. The best you can hope for is to enter custody with enough visibility that they can't risk taking you out."

"That's not good enough," I said.

Shelly balled his fists, but drew them into his body, as if to gain greater control of himself.

"You've got a remarkable brain and it's gotten you farther than anyone could have predicted. But it doesn't mean the rules of the world don't apply to you. The smartest thing you did was to avoid drawing attention to yourself. It's a lot easier to stay hidden when no one is looking for you. But that's over. They don't need your given name and Social Security number. They have your profile, a bunch of your aliases, your patterns, your modus operandi. So they think those mercs dumped you in the Caribbean. Big deal. As soon as some analytical software somewhere spots one of your tell tales, the alerts will fire, the wonks will send reports, operational control will click on orders and the hounds of hell will be racing down your trail. The only thing left to decide is how you end it. Bloody or not, it's over, Arthur. You're done."

He'd long ago guessed, then undoubtedly confirmed in his own mind, who I really was. But this was the first time I heard him use my real name. It was no slip of the tongue.

"No reason to soft-pedal it," said Natsumi. "We're all adults here."

He glowered at her.

"I gave you a chance to save yourself," he said to her. "That deal's gone forever."

The quiet in the museum's archives room rivaled the inside of a tomb, which in many ways, it was. We let it collect around us for a moment, then I said, "Okay, now that that's out of the way, can you do us a favor?"

He shoved himself back in his chair and put his hands in his lap.

"Jesus Christ, I hate talking to myself," he said.

"Since you're spent goods, we need someone else with tentacles into the FBI, who can connect with an honest man high up on the food chain."

"Honest person," said Natsumi.

"Right. They don't have to do anything. We'll do all the work. We just need some place safe to go with it."

"What makes you think any place is safe?" Shelly asked. "The higher you go, the uglier it gets."

"You mentioned the rules of the world. There are other rules that exist no matter what the current state of human affairs.

159

Take probability. It's impossible that an entire institution the size and historical significance of the FBI is utterly and thoroughly corrupt. Somewhere, in positions of power, are people for whom fairness, decency, and legality are not alien concepts. Who will take at least half a second to consider the greater principle over the political, organizational expedient."

Shelly grinned. Maybe underpinned with disenchantment and cynicism, but still a grin. He held up a faded photo of Oliver Perry, the focus of his research.

"If such a person exists, and I can find him. Let's call him Captain Perry," he said. "But don't count on it. And don't be too disappointed when you learn the most cynical guy in the room is overly optimistic."

He went back to studying the old document, moving the magnifying lamp into place in a deliberate gesture of dismissal. So we left.

When we were back in the Jeep and nearly clear of the strip development jumble of Rocky Hill, Natsumi said, "I wonder if he knows you really believe what you said."

It was late in the day by the time we got to Cambridge. The early darkness of March had relieved the season's pallid gloom, leaving Harvard Square lit up with fast-moving, brilliant kids crowding the sidewalks with those there to teach or exploit, all besotted by the intensity of their unrestrained ambition. Foolish, maybe, all that unbridled optimism. Or maybe not.

CHAPTER 12

After years of living under false pretenses, drenched in deception and masquerade, consorting with murderous gangsters, fanatics and sociopathic opportunists, I was finally poised to sneak into one of the few gatherings where I naturally belonged.

An academic conference.

When I shared these thoughts with Natsumi, she said, "Doesn't seem that much different to me."

My only regret was having given away my old clothes. I'd lost about sixty pounds after spending a few months in a coma, and dumping all my former belongings at Goodwill bolstered my status as a dead man.

"Don't worry. This is Cambridge, Massachusetts," said Natsumi. "I think there's an Effete and Pretentious Menswear right on Harvard Square."

The occasion also called for an actual disguise, my least favorite thing, though necessity had made us both fairly proficient makeup artists. On the ride up from Connecticut I ordered what I needed from a theatrical supply company, which came the next day. I opted for a big ball of loosely curled hair and a droopy moustache.

"You look like Kurt Vonnegut," said Natsumi. "Or maybe Saddam Hussein."

We decided this would be a solo mission for me, acknowledging silently, for the hundredth time, that a Caucasian man with an Asian woman was the first thing hostile forces would be looking for. It was unseasonably warm, so I walked the mile or so to the university. MacPhail's bit was scheduled to cap off the first day of the conference, right before a cocktail reception. So the timing was good. The only issue was crashing a room filled with the smartest people in the world.

"Strictly book smart," Natsumi had assured me. "Einstein couldn't even find his socks."

The GPS in my smartphone got me to the right campus, but not the specific red brick building. For that I had the help of a chubby, but sprightly, coed who literally took me by the arm and brought me to the front door. She obviously shared Natsumi's view of physicists' practical skills.

Inside was a gate-crasher's dream — a long table with a number of unclaimed name badges. I picked up Israel Finestein's and told the lady behind the table that they'd spelled it wrong. She handed me a Sharpie and an unmarked sticker on which I wrote "Glen Carlson" and stuck it on my new tweed jacket.

I sat in the back as Ian MacPhail walked up to the podium. A striped shirt covered an ample gut shoved well past the opening of his blue blazer. A bow tie and worn Topsiders completed the look of a preppy yachtsman long gone to seed.

I might have followed his talk if I hadn't been shot in the head, since it was mostly a tour of long mathematical formulas that somehow described a strategy for tying a super computer into calculational knots. Though it was easy to glean his central premise, which he summarized often throughout the presentation: the weird probabilities underlying quantum physics are the key to unbreakable cryptography. You just have to get used to being less than 100 percent sure you've properly interpreted any given code.

"It's not called the Heisenberg Sure Thing Principle," he said, his Scottish brogue thickening for added emphasis. "Yet only in approximation can we ever gain a true understanding of fundamental truths."

With that he rapped the top of the podium, sharpening the attention of any whose attention might have drifted, and stalked off the stage. The applause was generous, though probably less than hoped for. I followed him and the rest of the physicists out to the large hallway where the bar and obligatory cheese table were set up. First served, Ian found a corner to receive the few from the audience who wished to continue the discussion.

I stood in the little pack and listened, waiting for the others to weary of Ian's self-referential commentary and drift away, as they eventually did. I fixed him in place with another open-ended question regarding quantum code, occupying him until we were alone. Then I said, "And you still don't see the relevance to small business?"

"Small business?"

"And I was wondering how the Pilates were going."

"Beg pardon?"

"Pilates. Angela's Pilates."

He cocked his head and squinted at me.

"I don't know any Angela."

"Might not be her name, but you know her, Angus."

A deeper red flooded his already florid face.

"You're not that guy. No way." He snapped his fingers in the air. "The writer with the Japanese bird."

"I am that guy. I need a conversation," I told him.

"Bloody fucking hell."

"I just need some information."

"You're one of ours?" he nearly whispered, not really a question.

"I'm serious, if that's what you mean."

"Don't tell me Jersey gave me up."

"No."

"Can you tell me what you want?"

"I told you. I want to talk," I said. "And now would be a good time."

I touched his arm as if preparing to haul him physically from the room, which got him going. I followed him to the coat check, and stayed with him when he went to the restroom. I pissed in the next urinal. He told a guy at the front door that he had an urgent consult, with apologies for leaving early, though the guy didn't seem to care. I guided him out of the campus and onto Cambridge Street, where I'd spied a tavern on the way in. I let him lead the way into the small, dark, beery place and also let him choose an uncomfortable wooden booth.

He ordered a double Glenfiddich. I got club soda with a twist of lime.

"So I take it you're here to fuck up my life," he said, after downing half the drink.

"That's up to you."

"I won't betray my country," he said, though not with the conviction you'd think the words warranted.

"Which country is that?" I asked.

"The UK," he said, as if I were an idiot not to know that.

"Okay. Who are you willing to betray?"

He downed the rest of the drink and rocked back and forth in his seat.

"Just give it to me," he said. "Give me a chance to settle it in my mind."

"I need a name. An employee of The Société Commerciale Fontaine." I showed him the photo of Chuck taken by the mercenary Rolando. "About fifty. Flat Midwestern American accent, corporate business casual clothes. Went by the name Chuck. Had a female colleague who called herself Alberta. They had the juice to hire a band of top mercs and charter a commercial fishing boat. But neither was operationally experienced. My guess is desk people doing a little field duty, not willingly. I need to know who they are. Names and contact info. Tell me and I go away."

He moved the picture closer and used his fingertips to stroke the image, as if conjuring an accurate ID. He shook his head.

"Fontaine employs thousands of people. I've been gone for ten years. No chance."

"You're a global expert in cybersecurity. You know every back door, side door, trapdoor in every program in the world. You designed and installed Fontaine's firewall. You can't get all modest now. I heard your speech."

"Modesty's never been an issue for me. It's more the matter of arrest and ruin. Bright lights, third degree from the filth, professional banishment, academic disgrace, that sort of thing."

"Joann looks like a nice person."

"She does. She isn't."

"How's the 401(k)?" I asked.

"Insufficient."

"You're on the lecture circuit."

"Not the A list. Maybe C plus. So yes, I'd be buggered by a divorce, if that's what you're getting at."

"I am," I said.

"That's pretty harsh."

"Depends on your perspective. What would Joann think?"

"Are you going to take this bloke out?" he asked.

"I don't know."

"Honest answer," he said. "I hope."

"He tried to kill me and the Japanese woman. We're not dealing with children here."

"Children can be very cruel."

"My offer has a shelf life," I said.

"Your offer?"

"It's due to run out in about thirty seconds."

He got up from the booth and snagged the waitress. Moments later she brought over another double whisky. He took a sip.

"If this is a setup," he said, placing the glass unsteadily on the table, "a test of my loyalty, or willingness to allow a foreign power to extort information out of me, I could be making the stupidest mistake of my life. If it's the real thing, I could be committing treason. Or, I could be saving my arse by taking a practical step that hurts no one but some *eejit* in desperate need of getting hurt. Does that sum it up?"

"It does."

"Fucking hell."

"I called a cab," I said, bringing my smartphone up above the table. "He's going to take us back to my hotel. I've got a computer set up for you to use. I'll be right there with you. You do this, and zip-zip, you're back home before Joann hardly knows you're late. Then you pretend it never happened, and everything is back to the way it was before."

"But it never is, is it?"

"No. But you can convince yourself it is, and that's just as good."

I don't think he entirely believed he was in the situation he was in until he was all the way up the elevator and standing in front of my hotel room door. It might have been the six double whiskies since leaving the faculty auditorium, or just the shock of the occasion, but something awoke in him when I slid the card reader through the door lock.

"You're not shootin' me in there, are you, lad?" he asked, a touch of sadness in his voice.

I opened the door and Natsumi stood there ready to receive.

"No," I said, "though we might poison you with coffee."

"I have hazelnut," said Natsumi. "Do you take cream?"

We took our time getting him set up in front of the computer. With a mug of black coffee at hand and an invisible, but all too real, gun at his temple. He started to tap the keys.

I sat next to him to fortify his resolve, not to watch his hacker moves. For that I had software that would record every keystroke. He probably knew that, so there was little point in staring over his shoulder.

"You're far too clever a lass to be mixed up with this lot," he said to Natsumi.

"Thank you," she said.

In about an hour he had a row of six head shots lined up across the screen. Some were formal portraits, others were decent candids taken at company events. We looked at about fifty sets before Natsumi stuck a forefinger on the screen, in the middle of one of the guys' foreheads.

"Him," she said.

Ian looked over at me and I nodded. He called up the supporting data.

"Shite," he said, looking back at the screen. "Don't know him personally, but you're right about the Chuck bit. Charles Andalusky. Senior Vice President, Global Operations, Economic and Cultural Development Department. BS, Mechanical Engineering, Caltech. Winner, Simon Wasserman Achievement in Science Award, 2002. Westchester County Rotary."

"Fuck him," said Natsumi.

"That's not my department," said Ian.

"Let's save it all," I said, reaching over his

171

hands and doing it myself.

We spent another hour searching for Albertas, and came up with nothing. We agreed looking at every face of every Fontaine employee would take weeks. So I said the hell with it.

"So now what?" Ian asked.

"We call a cab and I wait with you in the lobby."

"That's it?"

"We can't entertain you all night," said Natsumi. "We've got a busy day tomorrow."

I gripped him by his two fleshy shoulders and gently encouraged him to stand. I marched him back to the bank of elevators and went down to the lobby. He was silent until we were at the curb waiting for the cab.

"How do I know you won't come back for more?" he asked.

"You don't."

"I'm not a bad man," he said.

"Me neither," I said.

"You won't hurt Jersey."

"I don't want to hurt Jersey," I said. "I want to crew on his boat."

"He's a good man."

"So you've said."

"Oh no, he is. Saved my miserable life. You either love or hate a man who does that.

'Course, I've known him nearly my whole life."

One of the tricks of market research is to put yourself in the place of the person you're interviewing, establishing empathy, not unlike a psychotherapist or interrogator. You ask much better questions and get much closer to the bone. So when I thought about Ian's comment, I tried to connect, but couldn't. I didn't have the experience.

"I don't have any lifelong friends," I said. "Hardly any friends at all, when I think about it."

"I'm sorry for you," he said, briefly touching my back.

An expression of unambiguous kindness over one of my life's failings, rarely recognized much less expressed, from a man whom I was cruelly extorting, who not an hour before thought I was going to put a bullet in his head.

"Thanks, Ian. Life's complicated, isn't it."

"Aye, 'tis that."

I put him in the cab, gave the cabbie directions and two twenty dollar bills with strict admonishments regarding his fare's well-being and safe delivery to his chosen destination.

"No problem here, sir," said the cabbie. "Forty dollars guarantees everything but armed escort."

"Fucking hell," said Ian, as I shut the car door.

CHAPTER 13

Natsumi had already downloaded all the publicly accessible data on Chuck Andalusky when I got back to the room. So as not to break her flow, I used the iPad to boot up a few other applications handy for tracking people, none public and not all entirely legal. I lay down on the bed and composed myself after the rigors of nabbing and coercing Ian MacPhail.

"He only has one testicle," she told me about an hour later.

"How do you know that?"

"He had to confess an embarrassing fact as part of his initiation into a college fraternity. He lost it in a gymnastics accident in high school."

"What else do you know?"

"His home and business address, office and cell phone numbers and those of his wife, Okayo Alphonsine. She's Haitian. And a dermatologist."

"So he definitely works for Fontaine?"

"Senior Vice President, Offshore Operations, Principal Contract Director for Economic Development and Assistance. I think I know what that means, but I'm not sure."

"It's a big company," I said.

"Fontaine's fundamentally an engineering outfit, but when the State Department is handing out grants to foreign governments, there's often a social welfare component. You build a dam, but you also build a few schools or open a malaria clinic. Since Fontaine's already sitting at the table, it's easy to subcontract that sort of stuff to them along with the heavy engineering. And they can do anything, or at least claim they can."

Chuck and Okayo had a home in Rye, New York, an expensive suburb that wrapped around the western frontiers of Fairfield County, Connecticut, not far from my hometown of Stamford. According to Google Maps, it was in a wooded tract in the northern part of the town, on about two acres. A real estate website thought you could buy it for $1.2 million.

Okayo was part of a dermatology practice in White Plains. They'd married three years before in Washington, DC. There were no kids.

"I wonder if one ball has to work twice as

hard," said Natsumi.

We spent another hour downloading as much information on Andalusky as we could, which I also saved on a flash drive I kept in my pocket. Natsumi went to sleep after that, and I sat up and diddled, knowing that sleep would be elusive until exhaustion had thoroughly bludgeoned my nervous system into submission.

So it was about one in the morning and I was still awake when we heard a knock. Natsumi bolted upright. I put on my shoes and walked to the door.

"Who's there?" I asked.

"Mr. Cornwall?" a man asked.

"Not me," I said.

"I think it is."

"What do you want?"

"We need to talk to you."

"Who are you?"

"FBI."

Natsumi was powering into her clothes. I put a jacket over my T-shirt and checked my pants for my wallet and keys.

"I'll need to see identification," I said.

"Open the door and we'll show you."

"We need to get some clothes on," I said.

"Do it fast."

I went to the window. It was our habit to get a room as close to the ground as possible. This one was about a story above the roof that covered the main entrance. Undoubtedly it was being covered by other agents, but being trapped in the room was a sure thing. I wrapped the laptop and external hard drive in some clothes and stuffed it into one of our two duffle bags. Natsumi was shoving other things into the second.

Another knock at the door.

"We can make this easy or hard," said the man. "Ten seconds to open up."

I tossed the duffles onto the roof below and then opened the door the few inches allowed by the safety hardware. I saw a man and a woman in suits and heavy overcoats. They looked at me closely through the crack of the door.

"ID," I said.

They held up what looked like official ID cards, though, of course, who knows what they really look like. Though they seemed undeterred when I took photos of the IDs, and their faces, with my smartphone.

"We have a few questions," said the woman.

"Okay," I said. "My wife just needs another minute. She was asleep."

"A minute," said the woman.

I shut the door, turned around and saw Natsumi with one leg already out the win-

178

dow, prepared to squeeze through the narrow opening. She looked at me for the high sign, and I pointed to the right. Without hesitation, she dragged her other leg through and disappeared. I heard the sound of her hitting the gravel-covered roof and running across to the right.

I was right behind her. Neither my spatial orientation nor basic agility could match Natsumi's, so I hit hard, crumpling into a ragged heap. One ankle lit up in pain, but it took weight as I scooped up the duffle bag and ran across the roof and dropped to my stomach, looking over the brink. Natsumi was down in the bushes with the other duffle bag waving to me. I swiveled my legs around and dropped again, this time landing on my feet.

"Hold it there," said a woman's voice to my left. I swung the duffle bag in the direction of the voice and felt the laptop inside crunch down on something hard. The woman made a startled little yelp, but that's all we heard as we ran as quickly as my lousy ankle would let us behind a row of cars, around the hotel and down an embankment toward the Charles River.

Natsumi didn't hold me up so much as guide my progress, making little corrective shoves and pulls to keep me on my feet.

This wasn't the first time we'd done this, so we both knew what was required.

We ran through a narrow park, then between beeping traffic across the four-lane Memorial Drive, which follows the curves of the Charles, then down nearly to the water's edge, where we sat up against the east side of a boathouse behind some ragged rhododendrons and worked on catching our breath.

"You're hurt?" Natsumi whispered.

"A little. Ankle."

I didn't tell her about the burning sting coming from my knees and elbows, since that hurt, too, but wouldn't debilitate.

"Can you keep moving?" she asked.

"Yes."

"Stay here."

She scrambled on all fours along the side of the building and disappeared around the other side. I waited and listened, rewarded soon after by a metallic bang. Natsumi came back on two feet and helped me get on mine.

"Follow me."

We went around to a big ramp the rowers used to slide their practice sculls into the water. A side door had been padlocked, which Natsumi took care of with a big rock dragged up from the river's edge. We went inside and found a light.

It was a storage area filled with oars, ways to clean and sand the oars, tank tops, gym bags, shoes, sweatshirts, and all the other detritus of an active sporting club. Natsumi started pulling things out of her duffle bag, including some of the makeup gear we'd recently acquired. She tucked her long hair up into a baseball cap and applied a small black moustache. She handed me a wig made of long, straight blond hair and a pair of heavy-framed glasses. We helped ourselves to some of the rowers' shirts and hoodies, and one unfortunate guy's backpack. I dumped out the contents and left fifty dollars in its place. The laptop housing was badly cracked, with one corner thoroughly crushed in, but it fit in the backpack along with the external hard drive and related cords and chargers, which all looked fine.

We checked ourselves out in a full-length mirror.

"Effeminate punks?" I offered.

"Not the same people who were in that hotel."

We left the boat house and walked along a path that followed the river bank up to a brick wall, forcing us to go back up to the streets. We made for Massachusetts Avenue, hoping to catch a cab.

What we got instead was a patrol car. It pulled up to the curb several feet ahead of us. Nothing happened, so we kept walking till we passed the car. Twenty feet down the street I gave in and looked back. One cop was on the sidewalk, the other in the passenger seat with the door open. They were talking to a big white guy in a jumpsuit and work boots. Maybe a utility worker. They didn't look at us. We kept walking until a cab slowed at the curb. We took it.

I asked the cabbie to drive us to the nearest car rental place. He looked it up on his smartphone, then took off with the usual Boston cabdriver abandon, which is to say somewhere just shy of suicidal.

We had to wait until we were in the rented Honda headed west before we could speak freely.

"What do we know?" I asked.

"They called you Mr. Cornwall. The name we used with Jersey and Angus/Ian."

"Ian dropped a dime on us," I said.

"Not afraid of losing his wife?"

"Not afraid we'd actually follow through on our threat. He got to know us. Established empathetic connections. Did his psyche-ops. He knew we wouldn't do it."

"We wouldn't?"

"Not sure."

"Were they real FBI?" she asked.

"Not sure there either. Very little backup. The Cambridge cops would have had us in five minutes."

"What does that mean?"

"I don't know."

I pondered the damage to our supplies and felt some satisfaction we'd gotten out of there with everything that really mattered. I was happy with myself and with Natsumi. For better or worse, we were becoming highly adept at spontaneous operations, with no words spoken and very little overlap in assumed responsibilities.

Despite what I feared, we hadn't grown soft during those blessed months afloat in the Caribbean. In fact, our survival instincts had settled in, becoming woven into our natural way in the world.

When we reached Greenwich, the sun was all the way up and the crackle of busy commerce was already well underway. We found a diner with wireless access — an obvious necessity for any establishment in that town — and settled in a booth with eggs, ham and toast on the way.

"We need to be more careful," I said, after the coffee arrived.

"We do. It's my fault. I let myself get angry with that Latino mercenary."

"Anger is human."

"Fear and anger make you stupid," she said. "All your life energy flows out of your brain and into your extremities. This so you can better knock someone on the head or run like hell. Nothing left for subtle cognition."

"We should think more about our physical disposition. Not much room to maneuver on a sailboat or in a hotel room."

"So let's get a house," she said.

I nodded and Natsumi started working on her iPad. Before we finished our meal she'd secured a year's lease on a four-bedroom custom-built home a few miles from the Andaluskys. It was in the neighboring town of Pound Ridge and also in the woods, though much more remote, being adjacent to both a country club and a wildlife preserve.

"You'll need to sign the papers and pick up the keys," said Natsumi. "I say go as the blond hippie."

I took her suggestion, tempering the look by pulling the fake hair into a ponytail. For no good reason, since the guy at the real estate office barely looked at me. He tossed the keys and rental agreement on the counter and returned my "thank you" with a "yeah." As so often happened, our ability to slip unnoticed through the world was well served by the bored and resentful.

The house was at the end of a long driveway, and thus invisible from the road, even with the trees stripped down for the winter. It had a three-car attached garage that led into the basement. This at least gave a powerful illusion of security as we brought our bags into the finished basement rec room, complete with a huge couch, TV set, pool table, banners from the last decade's Super Bowls and a bar. Most importantly for me, it also had two big tables with task lights and power strips. A craft area, I guessed, but ideally suited to a bank of computers and attendant gadgets.

"Shall we check out the rest of the house?" Natsumi asked.

"You go ahead. I'll be staying here."

"I'm taking a shower."

While she was gone I used a cell card and my laptop to get online and begin to resupply. Before shopping, I ran a routine checkup on my liquid assets — bank accounts scattered around the country attached to credit and debit cards used for regular and extraordinary expenses. I had about two hundred thousand dollars distributed across these accounts. This was my working capital, fed by much larger amounts tucked away in secure, revenue-generating investments. The checkup was so habitual I could do it half asleep, which I was until a little window popped up on the sign-in screen for one of the accounts declaring, "Access Denied."

Assuming I'd hit a wrong key, I signed in again and got the same response. I went to reset my user name and password and another message said, "Sorry, Incorrect Information. Please Try Again." Which I did, to no avail.

So I was forced to take another approach, rarely employed. I called the bank.

The automated voice asked me to enter the account number followed by the PIN number that went with the account. I punched it all in and got another apology and request that I try again. After a second failure, I ran the gauntlet of automated phone support until I reached a living person. I gave her the name and address I'd used to open the account, and the account number.

"I'm sorry, sir. The name and address are incorrect."

I stared at the Word document where I kept user names and passwords in a code only I could possibly know, since it relied heavily on certain distinct and highly personal memories.

"Maybe the account number is wrong," I told her.

"There is a checking account with that number. It isn't under the name you've provided."

"What is?" I asked.

"Nothing, sir. You don't appear to be a customer."

"I've been using this account for months. I'm definitely a customer."

She went silent for a few moments, then came back.

"I'm sorry. Are you sure you have the right bank?"

I didn't need the cheat sheet to remember what I had in that account. Twenty-three thousand dollars. A modest percentage of the whole, but real money.

I hung up the phone and spent the next hour sitting quietly in front of the computer in the basement of the big suburban house, listening for the silent sounds of existential threat.

"What does this mean?" asked Natsumi, when she returned from her shower.

"I don't know."

"What do you think it *might* mean?"

"The account has been compromised or I've lost my mind," I told her.

"I feel like we're sprinting through a minefield."

"So what do we do? Stop running?"

"Run faster."

It took about an hour to restore a secure connection with Strider, the girl hacker. She didn't seem surprised.

"I thought I'd hear from you again," she wrote.

"I need another favor."

"That's why I thought I'd hear from you."

"One of my bank accounts has been hijacked," I wrote.

"Really? Not good."

"It's troubling."

"Send the details and stay away from the bank. I'll need a clear path."

"I owe you again," I wrote.

"And you'll pay me back."

The fear instilled by a sudden loss of money seemed to amplify the shopping impulse. I double-checked the other accounts, then went to town.

First I bought a pair of cars: A silver Toyota Camry and a black Jeep Cherokee.

Then I bought two more laptops, a pair of terabyte external hard drives, a printer, a scanner and wireless router. And a complete video security array that would augment the home security system that came with the house. After hacking a gun shop I knew in Connecticut to secure their FFL (allowing me to ship across state lines), I bought fully automatic M16s, military grade M9 Beretta pistols, Kevlar body armor, black fatigues, white fatigues, carrier vests, night vision, side arms with matching muzzle suppressors, military-grade GPS, and personal communications including radios and headsets.

I was putting the finishing touches on that order when Natsumi came up behind me smelling like soap and moisturizing lotion.

"You shouldn't go to the grocery store when you're hungry," she said.

"Huh?"

"Your feelings of vulnerability are expressing themselves through your credit card."

I kept reviewing the order.

"Apparently you can't buy grenades on the open market."

"Do you actually know how to shoot an assault rifle?"

"No. But you can learn online."

"Don't forget food. We'll need some of that, too."

The last thing I did that night was send

the names and images of the FBI people who knocked on our door in Cambridge to Shelly Gross. I didn't know if Shelly would help us, protective as he was toward his former employer, no matter what they did to him. Though I knew these feelings were complicated and emotionally convoluted, thus worth testing.

Natsumi talked me into getting a few hours sleep before we went to drop off the rental and pick up the new cars. Since the house had no bedding, we slept on the couch in the basement, the electric heat turned up to compensate for the lack of blankets. Neither of us cared. In fact, we nearly slept through the next day and had to hustle to get our vehicles sorted out and home supplies secured before all the stores closed.

That night we slept in a master bedroom that was bigger than the apartment I grew up in over the storefront in Stamford. It actually echoed. But we were too tired to move and quickly fell into about nine hours of oblivion.

Chapter 14

It took the better part of two days to install the video array around the property, load the software and set up the monitors, including an alarm app on my smartphone. In between, I checked on our bank accounts and searched for Alberta using applications that hummed away in the background. We also took a short road trip up to Danbury to pick up our survival gear.

Given the nature of the shipment, having it delivered to the logistics company added an attractive layer of security. It reduced unwanted attention on our new rental and the people who worked there were so robotic the boxes could have been labeled "Parts for Quick Assembly Thermonuclear Device" without raising much curiosity.

I'd contracted with the place during the first few months off the grid, using an exclusive identity now the oldest in my repertoire. In one of their temperature- and humidity-controlled warehouses I'd stored several hundred thousand dollars worth of vintage guitars — my untraceable, easily liquidated source of backup funding. I left the cache undisturbed on that trip, though I made a mental note to establish current value by checking the inventory against advertised comparables. I did learn, how-ever, when thinking out loud about this, that Natsumi knew how to play acoustic guitar.

"Not like a professional or anything, but I can get through *Alice's Restaurant* and most of the John Fahey oeuvre," she said.

"I don't play a note, though I studied the math behind intervals and harmonics in high school."

"Of course you did."

We filled the Jeep to capacity and then some, having to strap several boxes to the roof rack, supporting Natsumi's claim that I'd overbought.

"You know the old story," I said, "for want of a nail . . ."

"Let's drive really carefully."

The oversized finished basement of the house was ideal for uncrating and assem-bling the equipment. We stored everything in a locked closet in the utility room next door, except a black jumpsuit and a set of night vision goggles that I used that evening to case the Andalusky residence.

It was part of a development of like homes, sited on a large property, but easily visible from the street. Natsumi was behind the wheel. We made one slow pass, then turned around and went back the other way, stopping at the edge of the woods across from the house. I got out of the Jeep and walked a few steps into the woods, where I placed a fake pine tree with a video camera and transmitter hidden inside. The camera, used by scientists to track wild animals, only flicked on when detecting movement, like a passing coyote or automobile.

Before heading back to the rental, I checked the video app on my smartphone and felt reasonably happy with the camera's placement. Software would store and organize the recordings, with a resolution high enough to ascertain Chuck's shaving skills.

The next morning I had the license plate numbers for Chuck's Lexus sedan and his wife's Prius. We drove our own Toyota over to where Okayo practiced dermatology and stuck a GPS tracker to her car's chassis. Chuck was a bigger challenge, since Fontaine's offices were in a huge suburban complex outside White Plains. We drove over to reconnoiter the location, determining there were only two entrances and exits, neither guarded. There also were a hell of a lot of cars.

What followed were five days tailing him with both the Jeep and the Toyota, picking up the trail at different points along the route as we learned it. On the fifth day, I used another rented Honda to pick him up less than a mile to the complex, and then follow him into the parking garage. It was a staggering expense of time and tedious effort, but the information gained was invaluable.

Also, partway through that tedium we got an e-mail from Captain Perry. It was sent from a Gmail account, and simply said, "They're ours," obviously referring to the photos of the FBI agents who'd chased us out of Cambridge.

"Shelly's last friend?" Natsumi asked.

"Most likely."

"How traceable is our address?"

"That one's pretty elusive, even for the FBI. It travels through thousands of IPs every hour. Even if they crack the provider, who's in Kazakhstan, they're still light years from connecting to us."

"Can we trust Captain Perry?" she asked.

"No way to tell. For now, I'm assuming yes, at least on the reported facts."

"So MacPhail had a line into the FBI. He

could have also warned Andalusky."

"We have to assume he did," I said. "Though where's the precaution? I don't see it."

"Maybe they're watching him," she said.

"Or watching us watch him."

"Kafka lived too early."

We settled in and became familiarized with the Andaluskys' routines. Of greatest potential were their gym memberships, in two different gyms. That was an easy division of labor.

"You'll need a good disguise," said Natsumi. "He got a long, close look at you."

"At you, too. Don't let Okayo snap your photo."

The characters of our missions were also different. Natsumi would try to connect with Okayo, perhaps establish a social relationship. And steal her cell phone so we could load in monitoring software. My only job was to get to Chuck's phone as quickly as possible and leave it at that.

In my old life, the last thing I considered doing was voluntary exercise, and I'd had the bulging gut to show for it. And with the exception of a one-year membership I used for a single day at Shelly's gym, for the sole purpose of having a chat, I'd never been inside one. So I was unprepared for what I

195

found at the Universal Health and Fitness Club of Pound Ridge.

The lobby was twice the size of Shelly's gym, with an assortment of seating areas with fine leather couches, off of which were juice bars, broadband kiosks, a delicatessen, three different types of massage, a clothing store and an actual bar serving what any other bar would serve. At least it didn't open until four in the afternoon. Might be tough to work off a few martinis in the middle of the day.

The membership lady's fitness was well displayed by her formfitting exercise wear — which for some might encourage a type of exercise not explicitly offered by the club. I was lucky, it turned out, that she could provide a week's free trial if I agreed to sign up for three months.

"How's that first week free, then?" I asked. "Or for that matter, a trial?"

"You only pay for twelve weeks. *And,* after that you can retire your membership with zero penalty."

"Otherwise?"

"It's a year. *Plus,* we offer direct withdrawal from the bank account of your choice."

"At least I get to choose," I said.

I took my gym bag and fresh membership

card into the locker room where I fiddled around changing into shorts and T-shirt, examining my face — with the fake nose and eyebrows, and full head of dark hair — in the mirror, checking my smartphone and generally wasting time until Chuck showed up right on schedule.

Though prepared with my appearance, I was totally unprepared to be in close proximity with a person who had essentially tortured me, then tried to have me killed. It made me a little dizzy, so I sat down while I sneaked looks at him changing clothes and securing his belongings with a combination lock.

It isn't often you see a person in the nude who ordered you killed. Andalusky looked in good shape, with maybe ten extra pounds around his waist and another ten distributed elsewhere. His gym clothes looked well-worn, in particular his shoes. A true gym rat.

I followed him out to a small herd of stationary bikes and took one behind him. I had to get one of the club's young staff to show me how to work the thing. He suggested I start out on a weak setting and I gave no argument.

Thus only moderately taxed, I was able to watch Andalusky ride his fixed bike with focused intensity, his whole body seemingly engaged in moving the pedals. I also saw him pause once to take his smartphone out of a pocket in his shorts and check the screen. Within feet of me, yet as remote as Mars.

Barely breaking a sweat after half an hour, Andalusky finally dismounted and went back into the locker room. I waited what I hoped was an unnoticeable stretch of time, then followed. He was already stripped down, his gym clothes piled on the bench. Three lockers down from me, I could think of no way to snag the phone undetected.

I spotted a scale several feet past Andalusky's locker. I took off my shoes and walked toward it, dropping my towel on his pile of clothes as I went by. I was on the scale moving the weights around when he came up to me and said, "Excuse me, sir, you dropped your towel."

"Oh, geez, thanks."

"No prob."

Brilliant, I thought, on my way back to my locker. By now Andalusky was in the shower and all his stuff either in the locker or his gym bag. Men were moving around as they busied themselves stripping, dressing, toweling off or preening in the rough, offhand way men do around other men.

I willed myself to stop thinking about the phone and went to the showers, giving up for the day. And thus a routine started, repeated throughout the week. Natsumi had no better luck.

"Okayo is very much unto herself," she said. "Indifferent to my social entreaties, if you can believe that. Though she does have the most beautiful skin I've ever seen."

"I wish there was a better way, but I have to have physical possession of Chuck's phone for at least five minutes," I said.

"I don't suppose you could simply ask him for it."

Back in the gym the next day, I walked up to where he was riding the stationary bike and said, "Excuse me, I was wondering what you thought of your phone. It looks like the latest release."

"What are you on?" he asked.

I told him the version, three behind his.

"Oh, yeah, this is a big improvement. Lots faster, better interface."

"Mind if I look?" I asked. He handed it to me. "The biggest thing for me is browser speed. You don't mind if I test that out? Take a minute."

"All I'm doing is running my butt into the ground," he said, increasing pedal speed to emphasize the point.

"Thanks," I said, as I called up the monitoring software, hit download and watched, occasionally moving my finger over the screen as if working the controls. As promised by the developer, the download took about three minutes, and if their other claims were true, left no trace of the infection. I handed him back the phone.

"You're right. I'm getting one."

"You might wait another month," he said. "An even better version's on the way, if you believe the bullshit."

"Sure. I'm a sucker for better bullshit."

We nodded knowingly, grizzled veterans of the digital age. I left him and took a shower, got dressed and beat it out of there. I hoped for the last time.

At home, I shared the good news with Natsumi.

"How did you do it?"

"I asked him for it."

"Brilliant."

While every call, e-mail, text message and Internet connection Andalusky made on his cell phone was being recorded and analyzed, I was busy breaking into his house. Natsumi waited in the Toyota with our sneaky GPS monitors displayed on an iPad, assuring that Okayo was at work, and Chuck as well, assuming his phone was in his pocket and his car in the company garage. I approached the house from the woods and went straight to a rear porch, which was open, leading to a back door, which was locked.

Aside from wearing a pair of surgical gloves, I decided there was no advantage in making this an invisible B&E, given the vastly more complicated requirements. In fact, I talked myself into thinking a break-in might help the cause by putting a little stress on the family dynamic. So instead of carefully picking the lock, I used a cordless drill with a carbide bit to put a big hole in the dead bolt. I'd seen no evidence of a dog or an alarm system, though there was still a chance of either. So after I opened the door, I held a can of pepper spray while studying the doorjamb and searching for a keypad, finding nothing.

The house was a little smaller than our rental, and older, maybe by twenty years. It was cool inside, the result of a timer on the thermostat. The décor was a balanced mix of contemporary American, Caribbean and African motifs. The rooms were clean, but you wouldn't call the Andaluskys neat freaks.

I searched for computers and found a

desktop in a home office on the second floor. The appointments in the office indicated the computer was most likely Chuck's. I turned it on just long enough to install another monitoring application, this one powerful enough to collect every scrap of data and control all functions, including keystrokes, which was the simplest way to capture user names and passwords.

Now, aside from strapping a heart monitor to his chest and jacking an fMRI directly into his brain, there wasn't much more I could do to open a window onto Chuck Andalusky's intimate daily existence. In real time.

In fact, I'd decided against bugging his landlines or sticking surveillance cameras around the inside of the house. I hardly cared about their privacy; I'd learned in other situations the danger of clogging up the analytical software with too much inconsequential information.

I searched his desk and found only a few paper files, seemingly innocent in their corporate blandness, though I knew too little to tell either way. I left it all.

On the way out, I took some of Okayo's jewelry and a Blu-Ray player, and cut an important-looking oil painting out of the frame, rolled it up and stuck it in my bag. I portrayed a pretty unambitious thief, admittedly, but it was enough to lay down a crude cover.

I walked back through the woods, signaling Natsumi along the way. She picked me up when I reached the road. I sat in the car, took off my rubber boots and tossed them by the side of the road. I could almost feel the cop's excitement when he or she discovered the clue.

We went back to the rental where Natsumi continued to turn the arid suburban ark into something resembling a home and I hunkered down for my study of Charles Andalusky, husband, corporate economic development professional, torturer and killer.

One of my great loves is the iterative nature of research. Starting with minimum information, nibbling around the edges, poking the data with a stick, stacking up knowns in place of unknowns, until patterns begin to emerge. As ignorance clears before careful search and discovery, knowledge accumulates in waves, building exponentially. Facts organize into systems of information and concepts either disintegrate or coalesce into solid learning.

The picture that formed of Andalusky was

of an intelligent man whose public congeniality was well supported by his private correspondence. He eschewed typical sins of character and morality, confining his private web searches to car enthusiast and outdoorsman websites. No porn, gambling or even computer games. He hated golf, apparently, while extolling a nearly poetical love of fly-fishing.

He was nuts about Okayo, whom he'd met in the wake of the Haitian earthquake, him in his official duties as Fontaine's development lead, her as a board member of a nongovernmental organization called The People Project, committed to providing microloans to individuals in developing countries, notably Haiti.

He pushed his company hard, just within the boundaries of propriety, to fund various social welfare projects in his wife's native country, despite Fontaine's minimal business interests there. So the Haitian operations received a large measure of Fontaine's corporate largesse, though relatively insignificant compared to its global investments. It still resulted in a grateful group of NGOs, an equally grateful wife, and good works for people in constant, desperate need.

As Andalusky tirelessly acknowledged, Fontaine's core enterprise was building things. Big things — petrochemical plants, refineries, gas pipelines, automated manufacturing, roads, bridges, dams, airports and casino resort hotels. Projects on this scale could only happen in cooperation with governments, national and local, official, ostensible and covert. For this, Fontaine needed a way to sweeten deals, provide political cover to local officials and grease the gears with the US State Department, which was another inevitable player in every project and transaction.

That corrupt practices managed to occur regularly within such a sprawling and complex global enterprise was inevitable. Yet the penalties for getting caught in that kind of hanky-panky were extremely harsh and unflinching. It could ruin an individual. For Fontaine as a corporate entity, in a highly visible and competitive environment, it was a matter of existential consequence. The result was a far more honestly run enterprise than the casual observer, fed a daily news fare about rampant corruption, might imagine.

In this, Chuck Andalusky was not only a paragon, he was the lead corporate officer in carrying out Fontaine's fiduciary responsibility for hundreds of millions of dollars of US government investment in foreign economies.

No one took this role more seriously than Chuck himself, to the extent that much of his e-mail commentary involved nearly peevish complaints about how others grossly undervalued the importance of the task, and the need for relentless diligence.

Likewise, no matter how cynical or calculating his upper management (I read more than once, "The only good I care about is what's good for the business."), Andalusky himself expressed unabashed pride in the positive achievements his operation produced, constant concern for the people it was meant to help, and tireless promotion of the very concept of foreign aid and international economic development.

While this zeal might have alienated the callous plutocrats at the top of the company, there was no evidence of that. His yearly reviews were filled with glittering assessments, raises and bonuses on a steady upward arc, and the tone of his incoming e-mails was uniformly complimentary and appreciative. In others' eyes, Andalusky was a man of high principle, who got things done for the good of humanity, without compromising his company's financial goals or undermining loyalty to its capitalist mission.

"If we didn't know better, you'd think the guy was a mensch," said Natsumi.

"If we didn't know better."

Soon after, maybe a few days, Natsumi invited me up from the basement to the cavernous living room, where she had a fire raging, candles on every horizontal surface, chamber music on the stereo and a rolling cart heaped with tasty meats, cheeses and slimy green things in a pool of liquid that I ate despite my better judgment.

"I need to feel like a girl who lives in the world," she said. "For just a little bit."

"I think the boy might benefit from this as well."

"I hope so. I meant to bring dripping washcloths to bathe your tired eyes and exotic oils with which to massage your weary, computer-tormented shoulders, but I ran out of time. So here's a beer."

I took the cold, tall bottle in hand and used it to salute her.

"Thanks for this. I appreciate it."

"I know. How's your work coming?"

"I'm learning things, but likely fruitless," I said.

"How so?"

"It feels like knowledge for knowledge's sake. Don't know what to do with it."

She uncurled from her seat on the couch and leaned over to gather up a plateful of hors d'oeuvres from the rolling cart. She poured a glass of red wine before dropping back into the overstuffed upholstery.

"I was thinking along similar lines," she said, wiggling her butt deeper into the folds of cushioned fabric. "We're too distant."

"What would be closer?"

"Face-to-face."

"I could get away with that?"

"You could."

"You think if he could recognize me he would have done so at the gym," I said.

"There have been loads of studies on facial recognition and visual memory, most of which show that people suck at remembering the faces of anyone but dear loved ones, or those we see every day. Simply adding hair and a phony nose changed your appearance, to Chuck, completely."

"So what else are you thinking?" I asked.

"I looked at the job postings at The Société Commerciale Fontaine. There's an open position for a data analytics professional at their White Plains Office. Among other duties, to support the international economic development division run by Charles Andalusky."

"I should apply for the job."

"That's what I was thinking."

She took out her iPad and called up the ad.

"They want someone with at least ten years experience collecting, compiling and analyzing data from multiple sources, quantitative and qualitative, who has a close familiarity with standard- and custom-search algorithms and the ability to create real-time dashboards utilized in tracking and redirecting front-end input," said Natsumi. "What's so hard about that?"

"I'm not as good as I used to be. Since the bullet in the brain."

"Okay, how about Marketing Specialist. Develop and propagate content in support of product management and sales objectives. Familiarity with web formats, social media and cause marketing/social welfare affinity groups a plus."

"I know nothing about that."

"You're a quick study."

"I'm better off with the research position. As long as I can use a calculator. I'll also need a fake résumé, college and graduate degrees, work history and references," I said.

"Half of Congress can tell you how to do that."

"And business casual clothes."

"Sounds like an oxymoron."

■ ■ ■ ■

I invested about a day plotting a counterfeit résumé before realizing inventing something from scratch would be prohibitively difficult and time-consuming. So I reverted to a strategy I'd already proven effective. I stole it.

Unlike my usual victims, it was preferable this guy be alive, avoiding the inconvenience of a death notice. When Human Resources checked a person's professional past — education, work history, awards — it happened confidentially, and was a simple matter of confirming the facts. For anything beyond that, to get any subjective commentary about a person, you had to connect with references. That was the key to this game.

"You want me to do what?" Evelyn asked over the phone.

"Pretend to be one of my former employers. I'll give you a script and Q&A. Along with how to answer the unanswerable."

"That would be every question."

"Just pretend you think I'm the best man for the job."

"I wouldn't be pretending. I'm a cardiologist, not a researcher."

"In this case you'll be something like head of research and strategic planning."

"Arthur, this is nuts."

"You'll do great."

Natsumi was an easier sell.

"Should I mention that I'm sleeping with you?" she asked.

"I don't know. Play it by ear."

The third reference was the biggest challenge. The only other person I could trust with the mission was a Bosnian gangster named Little Boy Boyanov, a former arborist most recently employed in freelance weapons smuggling, prostitution and marketing tractor trailers full of stolen cigarettes.

"Hey, Mr. G. Long time no hear," he said, using the only name he'd known me by. "You're still alive."

"Despite some people's best efforts."

"You want me to shoot them?"

It was a fair question, since that was a task he'd accomplished for me on two recent occasions.

"This situation's a little different."

I explained what I wanted him to do. He was game.

"You sure come up with some crazy shit, Mr. G."

"I'll send you the phone and a basic

outline of your story. It has to make sense, but I don't want to cramp your style."

"What business am I in?" he asked.

"What do you want?"

"The tree business. I still have dreams."

"Okay. I'll just have to find a forestry outfit with a former executive from Bosnia."

"Make sure the guy's a PhD. I'll need the credibility."

"I'll put something together and see how you like it."

"How's Mrs. G?"

"Well, thanks. She sends her regards."

"I like that girl. Hard to rattle her."

"She does roll with the punches."

"More importantly, punches back."

We exchanged more news on family and mutual acquaintances before signing off. I was glad to talk to him. In years past, I wouldn't have imagined the flowering of this particular relationship, but recent times had borne the fruits of the unimaginable.

Not knowing when Fontaine would fill the job I was hoping for, I felt some urgency, but forced myself to be as deliberate and calculating as possible. This was strange new territory, with lots of unknown risks. So when I thought I might be ready, about a week into the project, I sat down with Natsumi and we went through the plan, point by point.

"The basic background check — education, work history, criminal record, credit rating — is probably done by an outside contractor. All they're looking for is the facts, 'Did John Doe graduate from Colgate in 1983? Yes? Okay.' "

"Have you picked your John Doe?" she asked.

"Not yet, but I have a short list. The trickier bits are the reference checks."

"How so?"

I gave her the logic. Given today's labor laws, people giving references can easily get into trouble, so most refuse to do it. Those who do are highly circumspect. HR people are used to this. The trick for my fake reference-givers will be sounding credible while sidestepping things they know nothing about. Without sounding like they're hiding something.

"I'm ready," said Natsumi. "Not sure about Evelyn and Little Boy."

"They'll have to be. I don't have anyone else."

"Seems sketchy," she said. "You're just giving HR a name and a phone number?"

"HR prefers references over the phone. Much easier to get something close to an honest opinion. Reference givers are far more reserved in writing, so e-mail's out. The fact that I'm offering cell numbers encourages the idea that the reference-givers are letting HR into their personal space, and ergo, the opportunity for greater candor."

"You know a lot about this," she said.

"I spent years researching corporate HR. Unlike most of the wild stuff we've dealt with recently, I actually know this world pretty well."

"What if it blows up? How much trouble can Evelyn or Little Boy get into?"

"None. If HR gets even slightly suspicious, they'll just toss my résumé in a drawer and move on. The last thing they want is to talk to the cops."

"Why's that?"

"Most HR departments are overworked, underappreciated and marginalized, despite the importance of what they do. There's no percentage in bringing problems to upper management. Only solutions."

"You're already sounding corporate."

"Simply maximizing my potential as a proactive collaborator in achieving our mission of enhanced shareholder value."

After close study of my identity theft short list, I chose Martin Goldman, who, like me, had a graduate degree in mathematics from the University of Pennsylvania. I remembered Marty. He was quiet, calm, competent and even more disheveled than I was. He'd spent most of his career at a public policy think tank called Metreconica in Princeton, New Jersey. They were absorbed into another company ten years before, prompting Martin to move around a few times as a research analyst in the NGO social welfare arena before shipping out last year for Singapore.

There was no photo on his LinkedIn profile, but a Google image search threw up a few shots of him at his nephew's bar mitzvah five years earlier, when he was working in New York City. We would never be mistaken for identical twins, but it wouldn't take much for Natsumi and me to achieve a good family resemblance.

I called all his former employers and received confirmation on his dates of employment, with no further comment. The same with Penn and his undergraduate school, Trinity College in Hartford, Connecticut.

I put the finishing touches on Marty's résumé and before I could second-guess myself into indecision, sent it to the recruitment officer at The Société Commerciale Fontaine's offices in White Plains. Then, like millions of edgy, hopeful and slightly self-deluded job aspirants across America, I anxiously awaited a response.

CHAPTER 15

When the phone call came, it felt like a hallucination. Even though I was well prepared for the possibility the scam might work, the words coming though the earpiece seemed strangely detached from reality.

"Mr. Goldman?" the female voice asked.

"Yes. Yes it is," I said, in a near stammer.

"You're sure?" she said, amused.

"Yes. I'm absolutely positive."

"This is Jenny Richardson. I'm an internal recruiter for The Société Commerciale Fontaine. I was hoping we could talk about the position you applied for."

"That'd be really great," I said. "And thanks for using the whole company name. Now I know how to pronounce it."

"When did you get back from Singapore?"

"Actually, about a month ago. And I'm not yet officially gone, but I'd love to make a change if I can find the right position."

"Why's that?" she asked, with a forthright-

217

ness I both appreciated and felt a little unbalanced by.

"I'm in the process of breaking up with my girlfriend," I said. "She wants to stay over there. I definitely do not. But more importantly, I'm much more interested in the position you have open than continuing with my present responsibilities."

"Nice pivot. Could you come in for an interview? Just me for now, so nothing to worry about."

"I only worry about making a good impression. When would be good for you?"

She gave me a few dates and times and I picked the earliest, feeling that looking eager was better than chafing under further delay. She seemed pleased with the choice.

"Splendid. Business casual is fine."

Natsumi was nearly as taken aback as I was.

"I have to admit," she said, "I didn't think this would work."

"Hasn't worked yet, but it's a good start."

"We're certain Chuck won't recognize you."

"No. We're not certain about anything but ongoing ugly uncertainty."

"Okay."

The receptionist guarding Fontaine's human resources department had a professional's honed resistance to gratuitous charm. So after one frail attempt at conversation, I sat in my khaki slacks, open button-down collar shirt, V-neck sweater, blue blazer and tassel loafers, and proceeded to fill out the standard application form.

When I handed her the clipboard, she gave it a glance and whisked her hand in the general direction of the chair I'd just left. I sat back down, charmless but compliant.

When Jenny Richardson appeared, the mood in the waiting room took a dramatic turn for the better. She had the tidy, neatly proportioned shape of a former gymnast, complete with short, straight hair and an open, earnest cast to her face. She shook my hand and asked, "What's the weather like out there?"

"I can't remember," I said. "Sunny?"

"Good thing I'm not recruiting a meteorologist," she said, brightly. Then again, she said everything brightly.

"So you want your data analysts focused on the data instead of the weather?"

"I like that. Follow me."

We went through an unmarked door into a trackless room filled with cubicles as far as the eye could see. She led me along a circuitous route that I would never be able to retrace on my own. She held miniconversations with everyone we encountered, without actually slowing our pace. No one tried to make eye contact with me, not wanting to establish a relationship with a person they'd likely never see again. I smiled at them anyway.

We entered one of the rare semiprivate offices along an outside wall. The partition was glass, though you could close it off with a glass door. The space was large and equipped with both a desk set and a living room-like seating area. The solid walls were decorated with banal, corporate-issue artwork, and no sign that Jenny resided there as a regular thing. I sat on a rock-hard love seat. Jenny took a chair and spread a copy of my résumé out on her lap.

"How did you like Singapore?" she asked.

"They run a tight ship."

"I've never been there. Or anywhere but London, where my high school class took a two-week tour of famous landmarks. Do you think that makes me a lesser person?"

"No. Just less-well-traveled," I said. "You have time to make up for that."

"I do. I'm only twenty-nine years old, though I've worked in this office twice as many years as I spent in college, which makes me feel old. So why do you think you'd be great in this job?"

"I love data the way other people love puppies. Spreadsheets, compilations, bar charts, integers, vectors and algorithms make me feel safe and warm."

"Though you also love puppies," she said, helping me along.

"And kittens. Though it's not the data per se that's so compelling, it's what you do with it. That's where most people in the information industry fall down. They're far more comfortable telling you what *is* than what it all *means.*"

She took her hands away from the résumé and adjusted her skirt, pulling down the hem with a deft and barely noticeable maneuver.

"I'm so glad to hear you say that. I can barely do arithmetic, but I think I'm more sensible than my boyfriend, who works on Wall Street and thinks all truth lies within Generally Accepted Accounting Principles."

"Accepted by whom, I always want to ask."

"What can I tell you about our Economic and Cultural Development Department?"

"What do they most want the person in this position to achieve?"

"Excellent question. They're buried in

data that sloshes in continuously from all these public and private resources, from all over the world, in every imaginable format and level of sophistication, and they just don't know what the heck to do with it all. Those are my words, not what they tell me. But it looks like they most need what you most like to do — make sense out of a big old jumble of information."

"To what end?" I asked.

"To prove to management that the company's investment in this stuff actually helps our financial picture in addition to being a nice-to-have PR gimmick."

"What if I prove the investment is a colossal waste of money?"

"Then we'll have to fire you and get someone who knows how to prove what we want you to prove," she said, then quickly added, "Just kidding."

Though I wasn't too sure about that.

"Okay. Fair enough. Who do I need to convince I'm the right guy for the job?"

"Me. And Dr. Rajendra Gyawali, head of Corporate Research and Strategy. Chuck will go along with his recommendation."

"Charles Andalusky?" I asked.

"You are correct, sir. You've done your homework."

"Can you tell me anything about Dr.

Gyawali?"

"He's Nepali, like from Nepal, not Naples. They tell me he's a genius, and I've got no reason to argue with them. I've placed a half-dozen people into his office over the years, but I haven't the foggiest idea how he picks. I just know it helps if I like you."

I almost asked her if she did, then thought the test was avoiding putting her in an awkward position, even though she was the one who put herself there in the first place. So I kept silent, which I sensed from her manner was the right thing to do.

"So," she said, looking down at my résumé, "all your contact information is here?"

"The cell phone is the best. It never leaves my side."

"Splendid," she said, in an encouraging, yet inconclusive way.

Rajendra Gyawali worked in a completely different office, in another building across town that housed the corporation's technical support services. It made me wonder if the corporate structure was organized around social aptitude, which meant housing all the geeks and data wonks in the same building.

Where Jenny's habitat was fresh but sterile, Gyawali and his team of researchers lived under high ceilings, amongst military-style metal office furniture, lab benches, computer rooms and white boards spanning all four walls of messy conference rooms.

Gyawali himself, in contrast, was dressed for a gallery opening — all business, but hardly casual. A handsome man with a tall forehead that likely helped his reputation for genius, tightly packed hair, pale skin and Ricardo Montalbán features. He moved as gracefully as he dressed, and we spent the entire interview, more like a guided tour, strolling down the halls and through the building's cluttered, shopworn work areas.

He asked three highly technical questions related to probability theory, recursive functions and statistical analysis. He nodded when I answered, then spent the rest of the meeting sharing his frustration with an upper management that knew nothing about his department's inner workings, yet felt free to provide ongoing advice on how those workings might better perform.

"Thus my professional responsibilities are about 10 percent implementation and 90 percent justification."

"I can help you with that," I said.

"That's my fondest hope."

■ ■ ■ ■

Two weeks later I got the gig. My hopes had been on the rise ever since HR contacted Natsumi, who told me her recommendation was given with only the barest of reservations.

"Reservations?"

"It had to sound real. They were mostly about your girlfriend in Singapore, whom I made clear I didn't like. Jenny's not entirely comfortable with her own boyfriend, by the way. He might be a little too controlling."

Evelyn and Little Boy also left upbeat messages, the relief in Evelyn's voice palpable.

"I simply told the woman the truth," she said, "that I thought you were ideally suited for the job. I didn't tell her I've admired your analytical skills since you were three years old."

Little Boy thanked me for making him a doctor of arboriculture, for whom I'd ostensibly performed a study into the relationship between mental health and urban leaf biomass.

"I told her leaves make me happy. What can I say?"

That night, Natsumi cracked a bottle of

red wine and I went crazy over a single bottle of Sam Adams Winter Lager, still celebrating the occasion felt more than a little strange. Not just for me.

"Are we happy you got a job, under false pretenses, though a job you could legitimately win with your own credentials, or are we happy we found a way to sneak you into Andalusky's operation at Fontaine, or what?"

"We're happy the tree limbs are full of leaves. Leaves increase our happiness. I know this to be true. I did the study."

"You're right," said Natsumi. "A single beer does make you a little loopy."

A single beer chased with a carafe of fear, now that I'd actually figured out how to infiltrate the corporate lair of my enemy, with no idea what I was going to do once I got there.

With the exception of a few years working directly for a market research firm, I'd been a freelancer my whole career. This often involved long assignments, sometimes up to a year, so I had some sense of the rhythms of a steady job — getting up, showering, shaving, making coffee, driving into the parking garage, scanning my name tag at the turnstile, making more coffee, sitting at an assigned desk and tackling one or more defined projects, with or without the collaboration of fellow employees.

My inaugural duties at Fontaine focused on a water project in Jordan where their government, supported by a grant from the US State Department, was building a pilot desalinization plant. They needed to compare the cost of building and running the plant, meant to supply irrigation water for local, traditional agriculture, against a strategy of water conservation that would theoretically force farmers into higher value crops using more sophisticated technology.

After about a month of solitary, concentrated labor, I was able to show how an increase in the fresh water supply not only supported Jordanian exports, it dovetailed perfectly with the emotional and cultural needs of the farmers themselves. Presented properly, my report had the potential to represent a nice feather in the cap for Chuck Andalusky and his Economic and Cultural Development Department.

Rajendra Gyawali hadn't posed this initial project as a test, though we both knew it was. So I worked hard not only vetting the data underlying the report, but polishing the report itself into what I hoped was a gleaming demonstration of logic, insight and strategic acumen.

Gyawali left me alone to do this, a credit to his management style, asking only that I give him a date when I could go over my preliminary findings. I gave him the date, not telling him I planned to use the meeting to roll out a finished product.

There were other workers in neighboring cubicles with whom I was polite and friendly when they tried to engage, though with my face stuck all day in the computer screen, I hardly invited further conversation.

So I was somewhat surprised when I arrived at my meeting with Gyawali and found a conference room full of people, some of whom I saw every day at nearby workstations. Most of them displayed a jittery unease laced with arrogance that typified young techs. A few were my age and older, more jaded and wary. Two were women, one overweight blonde with short, thick fingers, too much makeup and masculine clothes, the other sylph-like and fragile, pretty in an unadorned way, as if placed by HR to balance out the group's female morphology.

"I might not have mentioned to you that we have a type of peer review system, not unlike what you remember from graduate school," said Gyawali, and I thought, no kidding you didn't mention it to me. "The only rule is no holds are barred. Everyone in the room has been given the same brief I gave you, with the same data streams and project parameters. While not asked to prepare a report, they've had plenty of time to review the materials, which I'm sure everyone has."

He looked around the room at expressions belying both embarrassment and coy triumph. I made a note to pitch my story at the triumphant.

"I'm sorry, but I went beyond the data provided to other sources," I said. "It's all there, just supplemented."

"That's fine, as long as it's documented," said Gyawali.

I used PowerPoint slides to present the highlights of the report and help glue together the chain of logic, though I delivered the meat of the matter orally, believing that mental pictures were always more potent and convincing than images thrown up on a screen. I had given probably hundreds of these presentations during my life as an independent researcher, without the benefit of administrative support, or the soothing protection of a large firm led by grey-haired Yodas and fueled by young, overeducated work dogs. So I had to be all things, naked before anxious clients, usually surrounded by jealous in-house staff waiting for any opportunity to unseat the interloper, to show their bosses the foolishness of seeking talent beyond what was readily at hand.

In some ways, the audience this time was a blessing, especially during the Q&A, when I could both reinforce my case and make instant allies by flattering the questioners and giving them room to hold forth in front of the boss.

Not every opinion, however, supported my position. In fact, several seized the opportunity to stage frontal assaults on both the logic of the presentation and the effrontery of the presenter.

"This all looks to me like yet another pandering to so-called native customs," said one roundish guy named Ansell Andersen, whose fleshy lower jaw, thrust forward, and narrow forehead, left only a small opening for his squinting eyes to peer through. "We're so hell bent on being culturally sensitive that we condemn these people to perpetual poverty."

He looked at everyone in the room but me when he spoke, but I answered him.

"While there is certainly poverty in Jordan, the farmers in question are anything but poor, except in affordable water resources," I said, referring back to statistics derived from the World Bank and the Gates Foundation.

"Compared to what?" Ansell asked. "I think the de-sal plant should go forward, but not to drown olive fields. The type of petrochemical industry that makes the most sense for the region needs water as much as it does crude oil, and it doesn't have to be potable."

"That's a reasonable proposition," I said, "though the data tell us that the agricultural benefits outlined in this report and industrial development can both easily be supported by the de-sal plant under consideration."

"Tells *you*, doesn't tell me. I assume you've done other studies on reverse osmosis and water utilization in arid climates. I didn't see that reflected in this presentation," he said, flipping through the papers in front of him as if just realizing they were there.

"You wouldn't because this is my first," I said.

"Oh," he said, as if grappling with the shock of it all, "then I guess it's fortunate Dr. Gyawali made our own extensive studies available for you to skim over."

Again, his eyes panned the room, yielding

a few smirks, and an equal number of averted eyes. Then he sat back and let his attention be diverted by scribbled-on sheets of chart paper left behind by a prior meeting.

Gyawali, whose face was blank as a statue throughout the presentation, and subsequent critiques, asked for other comments. After a pregnant pause, a guy with a Frank Zappa soul patch and a bald head gave a solid, positive review, pointedly avoiding eye contact with Ansell and his followers. Others followed suit, until the pleasant scent of approval cleared the room of negative vibes. When remarks from both sides appeared exhausted, Gyawali thanked everyone and sat patiently as they cleared the room.

"I hadn't asked for a final presentation," he said when the two of us were alone. "Just preliminary findings."

"It was hard to distinguish preliminary from conclusive as I did the research, so I just pushed on through to a logical end."

"You did."

"It's my first bit of work here," I said. "First impression and all that."

"You certainly made an impression."

"Your people all had good points," I said.

"Did they? You seemed reluctant to defend your work."

"It can defend itself. Or not." I slid the bound printout and a flash drive across the table. "If you want to share with anyone else."

He nodded, as if not quite hearing what I said.

"The PowerPoint was a little Hollywood for my taste," he said finally, "but the argument was sound and the conclusions hard to dispute, from my point of view, at least within the context of your operating premise and the data at hand."

"Thank you," I said.

"I'll need to vet your supplemental sources. They may not meet corporate standards. We're conservative. People in government stare at everything we do."

"They're as good or better than what you gave me. So I think we're okay there."

"You're not including the quote from Pink Floyd," he said, without humor. "The one on the first slide."

"That was for color, Dr. Gyawali."

"This is nearly ready to take to the big building. We'll need to do some tweaks. Edits, really. And no color," he said, his face darkening a little. "You'll need to trust me on this. I know the audience."

"Whatever you think," I said.

He nodded and told me we had to let go

of the room for the next meeting. Though he seemed to be lost in thought when I stood up. It wasn't hard to imagine a lot going on behind that towering forehead. I gathered up my papers and popped my presentation out of the AV computer and was heading for the door when he said, "Mr. Goldman."

I stood holding the doorknob.

"Dr. Gyawali."

"Rajendra. Where did you obtain that table you cited from the International Desalinization Bureau on the projected pace of membrane development?"

I tried to remember, having scooped up information from so many sources over such a short time period. Typical of my work style in those situations, I tended to capture, record, annotate and dash ahead, assuming I could reconstruct the pathway at some later date.

"Not sure, but it's in my notes. I can look it up."

He shook his head.

"Not necessary. It's just that I'm on the IDB steering committee on membrane technology and I wasn't aware we'd released that projection."

And then I remembered. I'd hacked their servers when I saw how it easy it was, and must have grabbed that chart as strong support for my hypothesis, forgetting in the flurry I was nosing around the bureau's confidential files, and completely unaware of Gyawali's involvement.

"The Internet sure makes it hard to keep stuff under wraps, doesn't it?" I said.

"Indeed. It's like the Wild West."

CHAPTER 16

"We know you don't do lunch, but we ordered pizza and won't be able to eat it all," said Manfred Getz, a native of Germany who sat a few cubicles away. He stood at my door with the slender, pale woman, who introduced herself as Imogene. Both had been at the peer review.

"Only if I can help split the cost," I said.

"We insist on it," said Imogene.

I followed them down the hall to a small conference room that also served as a staging area for IT, which meant there was barely room for the two pizza boxes, soda, stack of napkins and a large Styrofoam cup full of french fries.

"This is Manfred's idea," said Imogene, lifting the overflowing cup of fries. "As if there's inadequate trans fat and low-density lipoprotein content in the pizza."

"You always eat at least half."

She opened the two lids.

"One veggie and one carnivore. As if one is any better than the other."

"We curse the food before we consume it," said Manfred. "Helps the digestive process."

"All looks good to me," I said.

After we settled in and had pizza draped over our plates, Imogene said, "We liked what you did the other day. Your de-sal presentation."

"Thanks."

"Sorry about Ansell," said Manfred. "He's a bit of a provocateur."

"He's an asshole," said Imogene.

"That, too."

"There's nothing you could have presented that he wouldn't have challenged," she said. "It wasn't your argument, it was you."

"I've never spoken to the guy," I said.

"Gyawali hired you," said Imogene. "That's all Ansell needs to know. By definition, that makes you an enemy."

"Ansell was acting director of the department when they brought Rajendra in over him," said Manfred. "You can figure it out from there."

"I can't believe Martin hasn't had a single bite of pizza and we're already hanging out all our dirty laundry."

"That's okay," I said. "I'm used to that stuff. Gyawali should get points for having such an open environment. Tolerant guy."

"Unless you're crazy enough to use Power-Point."

They both smiled broadly.

"How so?" I asked.

"PowerPoint is forbidden."

"Really? I didn't know."

"Flip charts only. Not filled out ahead of time. Black markers, chisel point. Handouts eight and a half by eleven, twelve point type max for headings, eight point in the body of the text."

"He didn't tell me any of that," I said, talking around a slippery wad of pepperoni-soaked dough.

"It was supposed to be preliminary," Imogene said to Manfred. "He hadn't given you the presentation specs."

"Sometimes it pays to be ignorant," I said.

"That's yet to be decided," said Manfred.

"You've inspired me to add Kurt Cobain lyrics to my weekly summaries," Imogene said.

"But you like Gyawali," I said.

"He's brilliant," said Manfred.

"And repressed," said Imogene.

Manfred seemed distracted for a moment by an itch under his thick blond hair.

Imogene leaned back as he scratched as if to avoid flying debris.

"He was a muckety-muck in social anthropology at the University of Edinburgh," said Manfred, with a shake of his head. "I don't think he's reconciled yet the higher pay with the diminished prestige."

"He's an honorable man," said Imogene. "It isn't easy being Nepali."

"Is everyone here an anthropologist?" I asked, hoping to get off Gyawali as a subject.

Imogene chuckled. Though it sounded more like a clucking chicken.

"The worker bees are hardened geeks," she said. "Computer science one and all. Data crunchers. The analysts are from all over hell," she flicked her long finger at Manfred and herself. "I'm microbiology. We have an electrical engineer, a few chemists, a guy from an advertising agency, and I think at least one lion tamer. Ansell is a former undersecretary in the State Department. I don't know what his degree is in. Probably satanic studies. Manfred's a chess prodigy and professional fuckup, as far as I can determine."

"Fucking up is a highly underrated career path," he said, exaggerating his German accent.

"Why do you think they hired me?" I

asked, I hoped innocently, though who could be innocent about a question like that. Imogene took the ball without hesitation.

"Some people are frustrated with Rajendra. Most of the people here are go-go, rule-the-world, wham bam thank you ma'am. He's deliberate. Cautious. Meticulous."

"Fucking academic," said Manfred.

"Unlike Charles Andalusky," I said.

The room chilled off a few degrees.

"So you met Chuck," said Imogene.

I shook my head.

"No. Just tried to read up on him when I applied for the job."

Imogene's near white skin took on a faint pink flush.

"Chuck freaks her out," said Manfred, enjoying her discomfort.

"Manfred likes to say that, but I have nothing against the man," she said, moving a piece of pizza crust around on her paper plate.

"Without Chuck, none of us would be here," said Manfred. "He's the man with the money."

"He protects our funding," she said. "It's very admirable. And he likes Rajendra, despite pressure from the C suite for greater productivity."

"He likes you, too," said Manfred, folding his arms and leaning close to her.

She snapped off a piece of crust and tossed it at him.

"Cut it out. He likes Kallie better," she said, referring to the other woman on the analyst team.

"Right," said Manfred, looking me in the eye.

"Well, I think I'll get a chance to meet him," I said. "Gyawali wants me to give the presentation at the big building. I assume that means department management."

That brightened up the room again.

"That's great, Martin," said Imogene. "Well done. That's good for all of us."

Imogene dropped the rest of her leftover crust into his lap, and stood up, signaling the end of lunch. He took it well, and we wandered back to our workstations. I'd slid my chair back in front of the computer and was trying to locate where I'd left off when Imogene stuck her face around the corner.

"You wouldn't say anything to Rajendra about me and Chuck," she said. "What Manfred was saying, that I have a problem with him. I really don't. Rajendra might say something to the wrong person. He's so unaware of things."

"What things?"

She watched herself slide her fingers down the doorjamb, an odd gesture obviously meant to buy time. When she looked back at me, she appeared puzzled, as if responding to a rhetorical question.

"Good and evil," she said. "What else?"

That night, I checked in on the monitoring software I'd installed on Chuck's home computer. It was designed to capture information tied to certain keywords, like "mercenary," "British Virgin Islands" and "break-in." Only the last showed up. Apparently the effects of that trauma still lingered even after installing a security system. The contractor sent an order confirmation that specified the equipment and system configuration. Not a bad choice, I thought, though easily disabled at the site if you knew what you were doing. They also considered getting a dog, though Okayo's worries about allergies and the cost of daily dog walkers trumped Chuck's romantic vision of fishing with a loyal retriever at his side.

It made me think of our dog, Omni, with her head stuck over the side of the boat, snapping her jaws at flying fish. I wanted to tell the Andaluskys that another hazard of bringing a dog into your lives was the potential for long, painful separations.

Although Chuck occasionally conducted business through his personal e-mail, most of it was friendly, innocuous correspondence with associates and peers. Never with Rajendra Gyawali or anyone else I knew from our research office. The real meat of his operation was obviously conducted through his corporate e-mail, which I couldn't access from his home computer or smartphone.

And no sign of Alberta. I paid particular attention to any e-mail to or from women, but nothing remotely suggested knowledge of the events aboard the fishing boat off the BVI, no matter who Chuck was corresponding with. If I hadn't seen Chuck Andalusky face-to-face, I'd doubt we were dealing with the same person.

"I'm wondering how we could know so much about this guy without learning anything connected to our experience," I said to Natsumi, when she sat down next to me at the computer.

"How would you know it was connected?"

"I don't know. Something would jump out. It usually does."

"But if you don't know what you know, what good is all the information?" she asked.

"Now that we can capture more information than we know what to do with, the world is full of geniuses trying to figure out exactly that."

"They probably won't figure it out in time to help us."

"Another thing I don't know is how much better off we'd be if I had my old brain back," I said. "The computational part that got sprayed across my living room."

"You seem to be doing pretty well despite all that."

"Maybe now that I'm not so obsessed with the numbers, I might better see the big picture. Who knows."

She put her arms around my shoulders and gave me a squeeze.

"I know, Arthur. I have faith in you. Of that I am 100 percent certain."

Gyawali's mood on the drive over to the big building was almost ceremonial in its gravity and portentousness. He drove us in his Toyota Sienna minivan, both hands firmly gripping the wheel. I sat shotgun, Imogene and Manfred were in the rear seats.

They were there because I told Rajendra about their keen interest in the project and desire to see how it played out with management. It wasn't a hard sell; he seemed pleased to have them along.

I wore a tie and sport jacket, even though

I was told it was unnecessary, even counter-productive. But I couldn't help myself, as I tried to explain to Natsumi that morning.

"When you go before management, you wear a tie," I said. "It's all I can do to resist the grey suit."

"Is this the ghost of Arthur Cathcart past?"

"Yes."

"Is it strange for you, sort of being back in your old life, though not really?"

"Very disorienting. I find myself forgetting how I ended up at that desk at work, though it's helpful for sustaining the act. I really don't have to act. The work comes easily, though I forget I'm an employee and not a hired gun. That's more difficult. I used to fly over the sharks, now I'm swimming around in the same tank."

"You'd think it was enough to just do their jobs," she said.

"For a lot of corporate people, self-service is their job. Mostly at the expense of others. Their responsibilities toward the company's actual business is a sideline."

"Do you think your recent experience with professional killers and terrorists gives you a leg up with the corporate politics?"

I told her it might have been the other way around.

The big building was in the middle of a large tract of land, a mix of forest and open fields. It was built in the seventies when corporate planners thought marooning their employees on a so-called campus away from other commercial activity would produce a more docile, focused workforce. Since the vogue was now to tear down these isolated behemoths and move everyone back into the city, the planners must have gotten it wrong. Fontaine bought it for a song when they absorbed the American company Consolidated Global Energies, so they likely didn't care being out of step with architectural fashion.

The security people at the employee entrance were friendly with Gyawali, Manfred and Imogene, and mildly suspicious of me. They took a second look at my employee badge after letting me through the turnstile. The moment was also captured by a security camera up on the ceiling. I forced myself not to look at it directly.

A woman who worked in Andalusky's office met us inside. She was a spare, ageless person wearing a hair band and black sneakers. She did a quick head count, then turned and we followed her in silence down a series of hallways. I thought I heard Manfred whistling "We're Off To See The Wizard" under his breath.

The first stage of the journey ended at another reception room where our escort left us off with the words, "Wait here."

Manfred muttered something in Russian, which I didn't understand, though I made out "Colonel Klebb." Imogene gave him a gentle elbow in the ribs. Gyawali busied himself examining a piece of insipid art hanging beside an empty fish tank. I experienced a sudden craving for a cup of coffee. When the stern woman reappeared, she led us through another warren of offices, these a few clicks up in pay grade with solid walls and doors, and little kitchens with coffee machines thus far denied to our traveling band.

We came to a single elevator that the woman called to our floor with a key. We rode it up to the best address in the building, where the reception area was paneled in stainless steel and the receptionist an attractive young woman whose welcome involved the barest arch of her penciled-on eyebrows. Following a hushed exchange with our guide, she pushed a button on a console hidden behind her desk and spoke a few words into a nearly invisible black headset.

There were no chairs in the waiting room, so we stood. I was grateful no one tried to make small talk. I kept my eyes averted toward the floor, occupying myself admiring Gyawali's handmade, two-tone Oxford brogues, and wondering if Imogene knew how to polish the pointy-toed slip-ons that likely represented her finest footwear.

Another woman emerged from a door neatly blended into the room's gleaming walls. Our guide handed us off without a word and went over to the elevator, pushing the down button. Our new escort was very tall, angular and late middle-aged, with a hairdo so tightly held together I felt you could lift it like a helmet off her head. She introduced herself as Patricia Cheerborg and looked each of us closely in the eye when she shook our hands. She wore a thin sweater over her shoulders and her glasses hung around her neck on a beaded necklace.

"Mrs. Cheerborg handles communications for Chuck," said Gyawali. "She's the voice of Fontaine Cultural and Economic Development."

"Patricia, please," she said, though she allowed the grand characterization to stand.

Slightly stooped, she loped down a long

carpeted hallway and we followed, eventually arriving at a conference room anchored by a massive mahogany table. At each seating was a high-backed leather chair, a leather blotter, personal electrical and electronic connections that popped straight up from the table, and a black puck protected by a wire mesh I assumed was a microphone.

I gave her the flash drive with my presentation and she disappeared for a few minutes. She came back holding a remote, which she pointed at one end of the room. A screen descended out of the ceiling and the first page of my presentation appeared immediately after it stopped in place. She handed me the remote.

"Forward arrow makes it go forward, back arrow back," she said, helpfully.

Manfred nodded, as if pondering the wonder of it all.

Gyawali, after some indecision, assigned us our seats, which he had us claim by putting copies of our report on the leather blotters. In front of the opposite chairs we put our business cards, in neat vertical rows with his on top. Then we waited.

Andalusky didn't arrive so much as burst into the room. He wore an open-neck khaki shirt and olive drab Dockers, as if in vague mimicry of an army uniform. His grip was dry and solid and he used our first and last names as he shook our hands.

"Marty Goldman," he said to me, then paused before letting go of my hand. "Have we worked together before?"

"Not that I remember," I said.

"I meet a lot of people, but I'm good with faces, thank God, since I suck at names. I can barely remember my own."

"I'd remind you, but then you'd miss the chance to practice."

I could sense Gyawali stiffen as Andalusky chewed on what I said. Then he grinned.

"I get it. Pretty funny," he said, letting go of the handshake gradually, as if releasing me on my own recognizance.

"Imogene Nikolayevich," he said, taking her hand in both of his. "I always feel like bowing when I say that. So royal."

"Royalty in Russia usually meant getting shot in the head," she said. "After people bowed."

"That would be a terrible crime in your case."

"It's a terrible crime in every case," she said, gently pulling back her hand.

"You're right about that," he said, moving on to Manfred and Gyawali, then asking if we needed anything. Gyawali started to demur, but I said, "Coffee. Please. Black."

He looked over at Patricia, who got the hint and left the room after taking orders from the others, somewhat perturbed by Imogene's interest in organic tea.

"I'll see what they have in the little white cup things."

Andalusky sat on our side of the table and put his fists on the polished surface.

"Rajendra says you've got some interesting stuff on the Jordanian de-sal project. I tried to get more out of him, but his lips were sealed."

"I wanted you to see how the concept is laid out," said Gyawali. "It's better if Martin just takes us through it."

Andalusky spun around in his chair and looked up at the title page on the screen.

"I've already read a counterargument from Ansell Andersen," he said, looking back at me. "Made me even more curious."

Gyawali sat bolt upright in the chair he'd assigned himself.

"Ansell shared the report?" he asked Andalusky, in a hoarse voice.

"Just the high points as a way of telling me Marty was full of crap. Don't worry, Rajendra. You know I've got an open mind."

"I know you do, Chuck. I just wish Ansell would leave it to me to manage things."

"He does have a bug up his ass about something, that's for sure. But some people around here like him." He moved closer to Gyawali and put his hand on the other man's forearm. "I got your back, Rajendra. You're my guy in research, and that's the way it is. Okay?"

"Yes, Chuck. Thank you."

Patricia came back in the room nervously balancing a tray full of coffee, cream and sugar, and a tiny pot of tea, which she dropped without comment in front of Imogene.

"Okay, let's see this thing," said Andalusky. "We've got a lot of expensive talent burning up time in here."

I took him through a shorter, duller and less assertive version of what I showed in the peer review, but all the essentials were there. Andalusky concentrated keenly on each point, moving things along quickly by saying "okay," and "next slide," and making a clicking pantomime as if he held the remote. I skipped over some of the content I realized was more supportive than central to the case, and drove to the conclusion as rapidly as clarity would allow.

"Okay, got it," he said, when I finished. Then he asked several questions that betrayed how well he'd retained the material despite the brisk pace.

"Andersen thinks Jordanian agriculture could increase productivity dramatically with some fairly simple upgrades in technology and best practices," he said.

"Not without a capital infusion or consolidation of the type we experienced here in the States," I said. "Fewer family farms, more cultural disruption."

"But increased productivity will help the country overall," said Andalusky.

"Agreed. Which is why they need the desalinization plant," I said. "They don't need to revolutionize their farming techniques."

"Be a nice new market for American technology," he said.

"Does Fontaine sell agricultural machinery?" I asked.

He shook his head.

"Just chemical plants for making fertilizer. And we already have all the contracts in the region."

"Does our competition sell agricultural machinery?"

"Some do."

"Then why would we kill ourselves to enrich our competition while screwing up a segment of the population that just might not enjoy an American company screwing them up?" I asked. "When instead we can just irrigate the hell out of their fields, sit back and share the love with the Jordanian government, who I bet has more than one major capital project in the pipeline."

He pulled back from the table and crossed his legs, slumping slightly in his seat.

"That's what I'm thinking," he said to Gyawali. "All upside, no downside for Fontaine. Nice stuff."

"I'm pleased you agree," said Gyawali, though no hint of anything but cautious concern showed on his face.

"You two haven't said much," said Andalusky to Manfred and Imogene. "What do you think?"

"We agree, too," said Manfred, then went on for about fifteen minutes, ten minutes longer than Andalusky clearly wanted, reiterating points that had already been made. To his credit, Andalusky waited him out, then spun back around to Gyawali.

"It's good to have your people not only sell you on an idea, but tell you why you ought to be sold on it," he said.

He looked over at Patricia Cheerborg.

"You're not going to have a different opinion, are you?"

She took off her glasses and dropped them over her sunken chest.

"Heavens, no, Chuck. How ill-advised would that be at this point?"

"But you agree with Goldman."

"I didn't say I didn't."

"Isn't that a double negative? You're supposed to be our staff writer," he said.

"I'm your Director of Communications, Chuck. The staff writers work for me."

He looked around at all of us, grinning.

"Isn't she great?" he asked. "Don't know what we'd do without her."

"You'd hire another Director of Communications. She just wouldn't be as good as me. Now, can we let all this expensive talent go back to doing honest work?"

Andalusky had us take everything with us when we left.

"Otherwise, some pain in the ass will get hold of it and start whispering in the CEO's ear before I have a chance to give him the story."

"You have your own Ansell Andersens, perhaps?" asked Imogene.

Andalusky didn't comment, but at the door he stopped and thanked me for the report.

"And I'm going to remember where we worked together," he said, poking me gently

in the sternum. "I'm nothing if not persistent."

"Me, too, Chuck," I said.

CHAPTER 17

A week later, my sister called. Before I had a chance to feel bad about undercommunicating, she got to the point.

"Our mutual friend needs to hear from you," she said.

"Really. Do you know why?"

"I do. I'm afraid to say."

"How come?" I asked.

"He thinks they're watching me. In fact, this is the last time I'm calling on this phone."

"Okay. Anything else?"

"I don't think he's being paranoid," she said, and hung up.

I was in the kitchen leaning against the counter. Natsumi was putting two mugs of coffee on a tray with assorted muffins. It was Saturday, just after sunrise. Natsumi was in her sweat suit. She looked up when I put the phone back in my pocket.

"It was Evelyn," I said. "Shelly wants to

talk to us. She sounded spooked."

"More than usual?"

"Yeah."

"Do you know why?" she asked.

"No. She was in a hurry to get off the phone."

"Should we be worried?"

"Not until we talk to Shelly."

The family room, equipped with a large-screen TV we never watched, was our favorite room in the house. The attraction was a wall of windows and french doors that looked out over the woods. Squirrels and intrepid snowbirds were already up foraging. At other times, we'd seen fox, deer and coyotes. Having grown up in an apartment and living most of adulthood staring at books, paper reports and computer screens, the abundance of wildlife in a county adjacent to New York City was startling.

"They're just biding their time," Natsumi said. "Eventually we humans will screw everything up and they can have back all the real estate."

We sat on opposite couches, nursing our coffees.

"I set up Shelly with a secure phone number, online drop box and dedicated e-mail," I said. "Why would he send us a message through my sister?"

"None of those things are actually secure."

"That's part of the message," I said. "He's being monitored."

"So what do we do?"

"Fix his plumbing."

"Of course."

The next Wednesday morning, I called in sick. Gyawali was kind and sympathetic, as I expected him to be. He said nothing I was working on was so pressing that it couldn't wait a few days. Then he said he had some news for me, but thought it best to wait until I came in. I asked for a headline, but he insisted I forget about work and concentrate on feeling better. Since I couldn't tell him this made it impossible not to think about work, I thanked him and hung up.

Then I left Natsumi and drove up the Merritt Parkway into Connecticut to a diner in Stamford where I met up with Little Boy Boyanov and one of his men, a quietly vicious guy named Kresimir. Little Boy, a block of a man with a head the size of a medicine ball, greeted me with a bone-crushing handshake and an order of pancakes, sliced bananas and a side of ham.

"Need to keep your strength up for the caper," he said.

"Did you get everything?" I asked him.

He looked a little disappointed.

"Give me something hard to do, then you can ask if I got everything."

"Sorry. Of course you did."

"Nothing stolen," he said. "All borrowed from the brother of a friend of mine. Twenty-five hundred bucks will cover the whole day."

"That's not borrowed, that's rented."

"You're good for it, Mr. G., I know that." He handed me a baseball cap with the name of a plumbing contractor embroidered on the front. He and Kresimir put on caps of their own. "Tool belts and other plumbing shit is in the van. I'm wearing my tightest jeans so my ass hang out the back."

"Probably not necessary," I said.

"Describe possible threats," said Kresimir. "I want to be prepared."

It wasn't hard to imagine some of the supplies in the van were capable of firing off hundreds of rounds a minute.

"Should be zero," I said.

"Should be," said Kresimir.

"Shelly will be alone, but the place could be bugged. If other people show up, they could be federal agents. So don't shoot anybody."

"Unless our lives are threatened," said Little Boy.

"Unless your lives are threatened," I agreed.

"When aren't they?" Kresimir asked.

I followed the van, borrowed from an outfit called Brunoli Brothers Plumbing, which Little Boy explained was actually a pair of Bosniaks who'd borrowed the name for business purposes.

"You tell me how many people in the South End of Hartford will be calling Kovač Cousins Plumbing," he said. "Maybe next generation."

"Capice," I said.

We met up next in the parking lot of a restaurant just south of Rocky Hill owned by another friend of his. I left my car and climbed into the van. As promised he had a tool belt waiting for me, plus a clipboard and an iPad, which he handed me.

"If you're the boss, you gotta look like the boss," said Little Boy. "That's my daughter's. Don't drop it."

I watched as Kresimir slipped a Glock into a tool bag he planned to carry into the house. He had another gun taped to his right ankle. No doubt Little Boy was similarly armed. Since they'd no sooner go to a picnic any less prepared, I didn't bother to say anything.

"Don't worry, Mr. G," said Little Boy,

reading my thoughts, "we won't shoot you unless you get in the way."

It was a comfort that so far they hadn't shot me, even when I'd been technically in the way.

I hoped Shelly still tightly adhered to his daily schedule, which would mean he'd be just getting home from the gym when I drove the van down the street in front of his house. I wasn't disappointed, as we fell in behind his plain wrapper hybrid. I followed him up to his house and into the driveway. The garage door was going up, but he stopped and got out of his car.

"Hello there, sir," I said, as I left the van. "Looks like our timing is pretty good."

"Good for what?"

I looked down at my clipboard.

"There's some trouble with your kitchen sink?" I said, looking up again.

"Not me," he said.

I looked at the clipboard again, then showed it to him.

"Isn't this your address?" I asked.

He looked at where I was pointing.

"No, it's not," he said. "And that's not today's date."

He handed me back the clipboard, allowing his eyes to drift toward Little Boy and Kresimir, who were now out of the van and standing behind me.

"Fucking dispatcher," I said to my fellow plumbers.

"We got to get rid of that girl," said Little Boy. "Too bad she's such a hot babe," he added, an improvisation Kresimir seemed to enjoy.

"Though since you're here," said Shelly, looking toward his house, "I've got something you could take a look at."

Without waiting for an answer, he walked down his front walk. We followed. Inside the house, he showed the way down into the basement. We gathered around the water heater.

"Damn thing runs out of hot water when I'm halfway through a shower," he said. "Any ideas?"

"We don't have ideas," said Little Boy. "Only facts. Things work or they don't."

"Interesting philosophy," said Shelly. "For a plumber."

"Philosophers would do well to learn a little plumbing."

As Little Boy and Kresimir made what they thought were sounds of mechanics at work, Shelly pulled me over to a workbench. He took my clipboard and used a pencil from the bench to write, "They're connecting the dots."

"Who?" I wrote back.

"Don't know. Two heavies shoved their way into my house. Flashed bureau IDs too fast for me to verify. Showed me a dozen head shots. One of them was you."

"Which me?"

"Arthur," he wrote. "Circa 2005."

Before the shooting that killed Florencia.

"What did you tell them?"

He looked at me flatly.

"Nothing," he said, out loud.

"Did they tell you the reason for the interview?" I wrote.

He studied my face as he wrote the word.

"Cybercrime."

If he hoped for a look of recognition from me he was disappointed. Though he might have seen the fear cinch up around my heart. I gestured in a way that meant bafflement.

"You should leave the country," he wrote.

"What about Captain Perry?"

"I'm way too compromised. I'm afraid to connect. You could try."

"Risky?" I wrote.

"Very."

I asked him if there was anything else, and he shook his head. I went back over to where the Bozniaks were pretending to repair Shelly's water heater, happily chatting in their native language between metallic clanks and bangs. I wrote on the clipboard that we were done there and could leave any time.

Back upstairs on the way to the van, Shelly took my arm and handed me another note.

"Evelyn will go down with you," it said.

"Not going to happen," I wrote back, though we both knew that wasn't up to me.

Back at the restaurant parking lot, I gave Little Boy an envelope with thirty hundred dollar bills. It was more than he expected, though it would be hard to overpay the Bosnian gangster after all his past service, or overensure his help in the future. We parted after bear hugs and well wishes for our respective families.

I drove the rest of the way home in a fugue of muddled dread. There hadn't been a moment since I limped away from my sister's house, officially dead and driven by blind vengeance and grief, when I hadn't expected the ultimate reckoning. It helped to be utterly absorbed in the task at hand, in the hunting and being hunted by assorted antagonists on both sides of the legal divide, but that was getting harder to sustain.

Natsumi, ever perceptive, wouldn't let me speak when I first came in the door. She touched my lips with the tips of her fingers, took my hand and led me into the big living room with the wall of windows. The sun was getting near the horizon, drawing slender black shadows from the trees across the forest floor.

"You're frowning," she said. "What's wrong?"

I told her everything Shelly told me, describing the body language that accompanied his story. She listened impassively, at least by outward appearance.

"How much time do we have?" she asked.

"It's impossible to know. My image was only one of a couple dozen. It can't be a coincidence that I was included, but that doesn't tell us how close they are. Though no matter what, they're closer to Evelyn."

"You looked different in 2005," she said.

"Sixty pounds heavier, long dark hair, huge moustache. Nothing face-recognition software would have a problem with."

"What are your instincts telling you?"

"To cut and run."

"What does the rest of you want to do?"

"Stick it out at Fontaine. We've invested a lot in getting there. And risked a lot, but it's paying off. I'm getting closer to Andalusky by the day. Pulling this off again in the future is beyond unlikely. It's now or never."

266

"That's what I think," she said.

A squirrel hopped in front of a big picture window, stood up on its haunches and looked through the glass. Another squirrel ran into the scene and pounced, resulting in a squirming ball of grey fur. We watched silently until they took off again, one in pursuit of the other.

"Let's keep packed bags with cash and essentials in each of the vehicles," I said.

"Meanwhile," she said, "we stay here?"

"As good a place as any, now that we're dug in."

"Okayo is starting to speak to me. I'm the only one who can keep up with her workout. We talk about training and nutrition. I've never been in such good shape."

"Study up on microfinance," I said. "If e-mail is any indication, outside of her dermatology practice and working out, The People Project is all she does."

"And you'll be?"

"Working and worrying, like any red-blooded American corporate employee."

An urgent e-mail was waiting for me on my computer when I got back to the office the next day.

"M. Goldman:

Please see Ms. Jennifer Richardson in Human Resources at eleven A.M. today.

J. Richardson."

I wrote back to ask for specifics and if there was anything I should bring to the meeting. She didn't answer, so I left a message on her voice mail. Then I went to see Imogene, who was little help.

"I've never been asked to see HR," she said. "Is it like being sent to the vice principal? I never had that happen, either."

I went back to my workstation and pretended to focus on my current research assignment until quarter to eleven, when I started the long trek down the building's endless hallways to HR.

Jenny wore a skirt whose length I thought might not meet minimum HR standards, and black high heels with some sort of animal skin fabric across the toe. She had a loose, wide-neck knit sweater on top that exposed a lot of collarbone. She only needed a glass of wine and plate of mini egg rolls to complete the picture.

"My college reunion is tonight," she was quick to tell me. "I've been prepping for two weeks."

"With some success."

"You need to look young, trim, professionally successful, approachable, mature and a torment to the guy who never asked you out. Without stirring up enough jealousy with the women to make somebody slit your throat in your sleep."

"It might be easier to pretend you've had a sex change and just get yourself a nice business suit."

She guffawed loudly, drawing the eyes of her HR colleagues, with some lingering on her butt as we moved through the cubicles to the walled-off room. I sat in the interrogation chair, which she softened by pulling her own chair out from behind the desk and moving it so close our knees nearly touched. She held a big pad of paper in her lap.

"Are you liking it?" she asked "The job."

"I am."

"We have to ask you. It's just a formality."

"If I like the job?"

"No. What I'm about to ask you. About a transfer out of Gyawali's group."

"Oh. Not sure."

I just noticed she was holding a pen in time to see her stick it in the corner of her mouth. It made her look like she'd graduated from college the day before.

"It's a promotion, actually, as much as a transfer. You'll still be in Cultural and Economic Development, only working directly for Chuck Andalusky. More strategy stuff, less research. There might be some travel. You'll have to get your shots up to date. Still unsure?"

"What kind of shots?"

"Rabies? I don't know." She clicked her pen in and out a few times and held it poised over the clipboard. "Can I start the paperwork? You know we can't do anything around here without paperwork. We still have a division that builds paper mills. Makes you suspicious, doesn't it."

"Okay," I said, hoping whatever trepidation I felt would appear as appropriate as my excitement. "Let 'er rip."

"Oh, goody."

It took a week for the new job to be formalized, and after that, about ten minutes for the news to spread through the research division. Manfred and Imogene were the first to show up at my cubicle.

"So, they grab the new guy while he still doesn't know any better," said Manfred.

"Into the valley of the shadow of death," said Imogene.

"You *do* know what you're getting into," said Manfred.

"Obviously not," said Imogene.

"We both turned them down. Couldn't pay me enough."

"When do you start weapons training?"

"Don't worry about the Ebola vaccine. The side effects go away in a few weeks."

"Have they heard from the last guy who got the gig?"

"Do ransom notes count?"

"Gee, that sounds really encouraging," I said.

Imogene smiled with her lips clenched shut.

"We're kidding," she said. "It's what you do when you're jealous."

"Not me," said Manfred. "I just sulk and plan revenge."

"Speaking of revenge, I think Ansell's in his office sharpening knives," said Imogene.

I didn't see Ansell the rest of that day, but Gyawali asked me to stop in before I left for the night. He was in his stark, paperless office wearing an off-white shirt that looked like he'd ironed it a few minutes before. He swiveled away from his computer screen and offered his hand. The grip was soft and dry.

"I figured you for a short timer," he said. "So not a big surprise."

"It's only because you let me present at the big building."

He nodded.

"Chuck's been looking for somebody for a while. I thought you'd fill the bill."

"You wanted this to happen," I said.

271

"I planned it. The CEO wanted Ansell Andersen, but I convinced Chuck that even gratifying his boss wasn't worth the hazard of letting that snake into the garden. You're far more likely to support Chuck's agenda. The question is, will you support ours?"

"Whose?"

"Research. We're isolated over here in engineering. They look at us as technocrats, clueless number crunchers. We need someone in the inner circle to look after our interests. You haven't been here that long, but you can see our value. You can do that for us, I think."

He posed that last comment more as a question. I nodded.

"I think I can. I won't know how until I get over there."

"Good political answer," he said, without rancor. "You'll fit in well."

Then he swiveled back to his computer and I knew I was dismissed from that meeting, and likely forever more.

So it was past the end of normal working hours when I finally encountered Ansell Andersen in the mail room. He was pulling sheets of paper out of a printer as they shot into the tray. He managed to continue this chore while staring up at me.

"You must have pictures of Andalusky

having carnal relations with a spring ewe," he said, in a low monotone that still managed to sound aggressive.

"It's just a job," I said, cleaning out my mailbox.

"And a 1967 Ferrari 275 GTB Spyder is just a car."

"The Buddha would tell you wanting anything that badly is the surest way to never acquire it."

He fumbled the last few sheets from the printer, crinkling the edges. He swore and shoved them into a recycling bin.

"The Buddha can kiss my ass."

I turned to leave the room, but he grabbed me by the shoulder. The shock of the contact startled me, and I shook off his hand more violently than either of us expected, though it did little to calm his wrath.

"This isn't my fight," I said. "I'm just working here."

"You're right. It isn't you," he said. "You're just an asshole passing through. It's the fucking management of this place that should be jailed for criminal stupidity. But who's going to do that? The fucking board of directors, who're paid six figures to show up twice a year to cram their heads up the CEO's ass?"

"I'm walking out of here now," I said. "It's

probably a good idea not to put your hands on me again."

He just stood and glowered. I thought I saw a vein throbbing in his forehead. I thought, maybe I should just stand there and taunt him till he stroked out. But instead I backed out of the mail room and he made no move to stop me.

I made it out of there physically intact, with my meager office belongings and a letter to show security at the big building when I showed up the next day as their newest employee.

CHAPTER 18

The new job came with a serious upgrade in office accommodations. Four walls with a door and a window to the outside, a desk, computer station and credenza, and a bookcase prestocked with reference material left by the prior occupant.

I even had a theoretical percentage of an administrative assistant, though as the HR lady — the big building's equivalent of Jenny Richardson — introduced us, the slim middle-aged woman with a Turkish accent gave me a look that said, "Don't even think about it."

The most interesting part of the orientation came that afternoon when a guy named Brian showed up at my door carrying a laptop computer.

"The IT man cometh," he said. "Is now a good time?"

"For IT, any time's a good time," I said.

"That's the kind of attitude we like to

foster," he said, slapping the laptop in front of me on the desk and flipping open the lid. He explained that with my new job I was categorized as a power user, warranting a personal visit by tech support. I let him walk me through basic instructions, establishing myself as an amenable computer naïf, not entirely helpless, but unlikely to challenge or be much of a burden on the technology edifice.

When he got to the file servers, I was able to ask the question that had been on my mind since joining the company: "Just tell me where I'm allowed to go and where I'm not."

"I don't have to tell you," he said. "You don't go anywhere your password won't let you. But since you asked, anything with a little padlock icon, forget about it."

"I guess the security is sort of tight around here."

"Tighter than a gnat's rectum. Our cyber-security team is all ex-military. The rest of us aren't allowed to talk to them. Shit, we can't even look at 'em."

I held up my hands in abject surrender.

"They'll get no trouble from me," I said.

"You're right, they won't."

As soon as he left I took inventory of the files marked with the padlock icon. There weren't that many, which told me I couldn't see the really interesting stuff. I went into the list of corporate applications and wrote down the name and version of the Spam filter. Then I signed into the file folders I was allowed to see and did a little of the work they were paying me to do, which would all be recorded somewhere through an application buried deep inside the new laptop's operating system.

Before leaving for the day, I went back into the file servers and made a few alterations. I left the laptop where it was and went home, eager to tell Natsumi all about my first day on the new job.

The next day, as planned, I was blocked out of the file servers, so I called my new friend Brian.

"You're kidding," he said.

"I was just going through the various folders to see what I had access to and what I might need in the future, and some funny-looking windows popped open and I think I clicked some stuff I shouldn't have. I'm really sorry, I should know better."

"No worries, I'll be there in an hour."

He was true to his word, and without a lot of preamble, sat in front of my laptop and logged in.

"You somehow managed to delete all your

permissions," he said. "No big deal, I can do it from here. You're not a key tapper, are you?"

"A what?"

"People who get into trouble and just start hitting keys at random. You'd be amazed at the hole you can dig for yourself without even trying."

"I wouldn't be surprised. I've done it."

"That's obvious."

In less than ten minutes he had me back in business, with a minimum of condescension and tart warnings about staying in the cyber lanes.

"Got it, chief," I said to his back as he left my office.

I waited a prudent few minutes before opening up the application that had captured his log-in information — admin user name and password. Then I deleted all trace of the application on the laptop. It was possible that Fontaine's crack cybersecurity team's monitoring capabilities had spotted its presence within their network, if only for a few minutes. So it represented a risk, though one I had to take if I was going to keep moving.

Minutes later my desk phone rang and I almost leaped out of my chair. Amused and annoyed at myself, I picked up the receiver.

"Mr. Goldman," said a spritely female voice. I recognized it as Patricia Cheerborg's.

"Marty," I said.

"Marty, Chuck wants to buy you lunch. At noon. In the cafeteria."

"If I can find it."

"Just follow your nose. And I mean that in the nicest way. And by the way, welcome aboard. You'll be happy with your decision."

"I already am. No free lunch over there in research."

I did find the cafeteria with a minimum of effort. It was in a huge, glass-walled room, with shimmering chrome ceiling and aluminum tables and chairs. Chuck was waiting for me at the head of the food line, which featured preparations you'd find at a fine restaurant if any stooped low enough to offer a buffet. He shook my hand and gave me a small red ticket.

"Good for anything here," he said. "Backed by the full faith and credit of The Société Commerciale Fontaine."

"A pastrami sandwich should do it."

"You can take the boy out of Brooklyn," he said. "If I read your LinkedIn profile correctly."

"You did," I said, swallowing the bit of my heart that wanted to jump up into my throat. "Lost the accent, I'm afraid."

"If you say so. All you Easterners sound the same to me."

After securing our meals, we found a table well away from any possible eavesdropper.

"Well, I wanted to thank you for joining our little group," he said, awkwardly offering his hand for a second time. "I've wanted a staffer with some serious research skills for a while now. The good news these days is we're basically drowning in data. The bad news is we're drowning in data. Gyawali's team isn't up to it. They're fine for the big studies, but I need to know what's going on day-to-day. I can't be hauling those people over here every time some government agency, or NGO or God-knows what inter-office asshole dumps a pile of statistics in our laps. I need my own geek, no insult intended."

"None taken. Geeks are fashionable these days."

"You got that right," he said, grasping a fork in one hand and a knife in the other, as if prepared to either cut up his cordon bleu or attack his lunch guest. "From where I sit, you people are running the world. They say we're in a technology revolution; I say bullshit. The revolution's over and the techs have won. All that's left now is to complete the conquest."

"I guess I better get in line for my share of the spoils," I said.

"You got nothing to worry about. I knew that when you were presenting. I saw what you did there, fuckin' hacker."

I had another chance to calm my heart while he took a big bite of chicken, ham and cheese.

"Hacker?" I asked.

"You pulled data right out of Fontaine's archives in Zurich. It was from the early nineties before they were even over here. I know this because I used to work in that office. I recognized the branding on the Power-Point slide."

"Guilty as charged," I said, in a weak voice. "Though anyone in Fontaine has access to those files."

He shushed away the thought.

"I know. Just kidding about the hacker thing. Truth is, it's the kind of initiative I wish I could get out of Gyawali and his boys, but it just doesn't happen."

"His boys and girls. There're two of them."

"Don't go all feminist on me. I get enough of that crap from Patricia."

"Just noting."

"You probably noted Imogene. Freaky chick, if you ask me. Not to go running to

HR, but did she hit on you?"

I shook my head.

"Probably cause you're single. I think she goes for the married type. Whenever I talk to the girl, she invades my space. Gets too close for comfort. You know the type?"

"Not really," I said, honestly.

"I've got a five foot eleven Nubian princess at home. I don't need any of that career-killing shit, you know what I mean?"

"I understand what you're saying. I'm just a boring work dog. Politics of every kind, sexual or not, goes right over my head."

He nodded as he chewed through another wad of food, having shoveled about a pound more of his meal into his mouth. I remembered one of my research clients from years ago, an organizational psychologist, telling me to beware of people who ate like hungry lions. As with the big cats, it was a good idea to keep your distance.

"Don't get me wrong about Gyawali," he said, the feral look in his eyes deepening. "Smarter than shit. And Imogene, too, freak or no freak. They're all smart people, but they've got some kind of fucked-up notion about the politics around here."

That was for sure, I thought. But I said, "Research and analytics?"

"Yeah, but for who?" He took out a pen

and drew a few boxes connected by arrows on his napkin. "This is Gyawali's group. Nominally, they're supposed to support Economic and Cultural Development, which is me. But officially, they've only got a dotted-line responsibility. They support me, but don't actually *report* to me."

"Oh."

"Oh, yeah," said Andalusky. "The hard line goes right to the CEO. Even though most of their funding comes out of my budget. I mean, what the hell.

"To the CEO it's a black box. The son of a bitch got his chemical engineering degree in 1965, and hasn't cracked a technical manual since. Sales guy. Fucking Frenchman, could charm the pants off Angela Merkel. Rumor has it he actually did back in the day, proven by all the contracts we get from the Federal Republic. But he loves the damn numbers, the quantitative justification for whatever venal, greedy, exploitative shit the company wants to get into, and I mean that as a loyal Fontaine employee."

I wondered how the disloyal ones would have put it.

"Don't get me wrong," he said, a phrase he often used as a palliative to all the things he said that he didn't mean, or meant and didn't want you to think he did. "The contribution Fontaine makes to the well-being of millions of people around the world is incalculable. It's a multiplier, something like ten dollars returned to the local economy for every dollar invested in a Fontaine infrastructure project."

I wanted to say he just calculated the incalculable, but even my unpracticed political instincts knew that was a bad idea.

"What's the multiplier to Fontaine's income for every dollar invested in a local official's pet project?" I asked.

"That doesn't sound like the do-gooder I read about on your résumé," he said.

"Altruism feeds the soul, though it isn't too kind to the bank account. Especially when there's a negative balance big enough to choke a horse."

"Overextended are we?"

"Beer budget, champagne tastes. The usual dreary story. Since I'm not going to change my tastes, I better improve the budget."

"That's my attitude," said Chuck. "My wife struggles a bit with her good fortune, but most of her friends and family live in the worst kind of poverty in Haiti. It eats at her."

I couldn't tell him I already knew that

about Okayo, having read her personal e-mails over the last few weeks. While not necessarily driven by guilt, she clearly felt a strong responsibility toward those she left behind for her life as an affluent doctor in Westchester County, New York.

Andalusky sketched out my new responsibilities, which looked uncannily like my old responsibilities, with the added requirement of helping to present the department's quarterly status reports, bolstered, he assumed, by some of the same foundational research that lifted my Jordanian desalinization study.

I thought he'd covered everything when he mentioned one other thing.

"Now that you're attached to my office, it'd be very much in your interest to help me build a counterweight to Gyawali's data and policy recommendations," he said.

I told him I didn't quite understand. He handed me a piece of paper that listed the half-dozen areas of interest being researched by Gyawali's group, and the estimated dates of completion, along with check-in dates along the way.

"You probably worked on a lot of this," he said. "I want you to keep going, but go deeper, wider, use some of that data magic of yours. Find out where he's gone off the beam, or missed something important. Keep it close to the vest until we need it. If it all works out I'll introduce you to my discretionary bonus pool."

Then I understood.

"You want me to find ways to undermine his research, to gain us some leverage with the CEO."

He studied my face.

"It's sort of a crude way of putting it, but that's the gist. We break the cord between Gyawali and the CEO, or at least weaken it, allowing me to step in with a fresh alternative. Then maybe we get a better grip on Gyawali's operation, make him accountable to our divisional budget for a change. Can you kill three birds with one stone?"

He smirked as if charmed by the idea.

"And it could mean added compensation for me," I said, "if I deliver the goods."

"We all deserve a chance to get ahead."

I didn't know if I could duplicate his look of rapacious zeal, but I tried.

"Sounds like fun," I said.

I gave him my opinion on the Gyawali projects that offered the greatest opportunity, based on my assessment of certain shortcomings in Gyawali's methodology. I was able to paint a vivid picture of how we could encourage Gyawali to go down a

286

certain path, and then just as he commits to a given conclusion, spring the trap. It sounded a bit ambitious, I admitted, but if we were going to do it, better do it in a big way.

The more I talked, the more excited he became.

"That's the way to be transformative in this company," he said, tapping the table top with a tight fist. "You gotta go big."

Before we broke to go back to our offices, he put his hand on my shoulder. He brought his face close enough for me to smell the lunch on his breath.

"You know, Marty, if you happen to stumble on anything of a personal nature regarding Dr. Gyawali, or any of his top people, anything that they wouldn't want the world to know about, that wouldn't be such a bad thing. Could really ice the cake. You read me?"

His voice still danced with that good-natured, Midwestern bonhomie, but the set of his face had changed, to one I recognized, having last seen it on a beat-up fishing scow in the Caribbean.

"Read you loud and clear, Chuck," I said.

"I think it's going to be interesting having you around," he said, giving my shoulder a slight squeeze.

"I certainly intend it to be," I said.

I used about a week to familiarize myself with my new surroundings, the general rhythms of the building, the social climate and prevailing mood states. With a greater proportion of private offices, deep carpeting and sound insulation, a monastic quiet prevailed, with communications managed almost entirely through e-mail. Chuck's office was physically, and thus tellingly, directly outside the standard concentration of top management known as the C suite. The CEO, CIO, COO, etc., clustered defensively behind a locked glass wall, and sustained by a small cadre of administrative assistants. You rarely saw any of these people, despite the steady flow of upbeat, or instructive interoffice memos that drifted down into the rank and file.

Surveillance cameras were coyly concealed throughout the building, along hallways and within common areas and conference rooms. Having worked for a security equipment company, I knew what to look for, which meant never acting as if I did. Official staff in grey slacks and blue blazers moved regularly through the building, somehow being unobtrusive and obvious at the same time. Fit, composed and square-jawed, I didn't need the IT guy to tell me they were all ex-military.

Though I had virtually no contact with my fellow employees, I saw a fair amount of Chuck, the result of some of his pent-up demand for data analytics. The assignments came at me in a steady stream, though he was respectful of my time, allowing me to set my own reporting schedule. It wasn't difficult work if you had the right software, which Brian in IT was happy to provide.

Seeing a lot of Chuck also meant seeing a lot of Patricia Cheerborg. It was apparent she was his closest protégé and that they represented a duality through which ran the whole of the department's operations. He copied her on every e-mail he sent to me, so I made sure to consistently hit the "reply all" button. And on a few occasions, as I waited for an audience, I saw them move between each other's offices as if it were a common work space. This is what inspired a plan that would surely necessitate Natsumi's participation.

"You'll never fit in any of my things," she said, looking me up and down with a critical eye.

"I know. We need to go shopping."

"What's her size?" she asked.

"I don't know what that means. Sort of

tall, on the slim side, though big boned. A little stooped."

"That's a start."

I Googled her and found a few photographs from company events and her LinkedIn page. Even better, there was a video interview of her when acting as spokesperson for a Fontaine development project.

"You're lucky about the hair," she said. "We can buy it prepermed and ready to go."

As every male on his first attempt at going drag knows, even modestly high heels are very difficult to walk in. I tried them with a pair of panty hose, over shaved legs, and a knee-length light wool skirt in order to capture the whole experience.

"I wonder when I'll be able to look at you without at least a little smirk," said Natsumi.

"It'd be heartless to deny you that joy," I said, as I wobbled around the house.

"I bet your legs are better looking than Patricia's," she said.

"The kind of thing a guy waits his whole life to hear."

After we bought the wig, blouse, plastic-rimmed glasses and cardigan sweater, the greater challenge became more apparent. My shoulders.

"Maybe if I lost weight," I said.

"That won't make your skeleton any smaller."

"She stoops," I said, demonstrating as well as I could while still unsteady on my feet.

"How long can you sustain that?" she asked.

"Let's find out."

So I practiced for a few hours every night for over a week, until I mastered her long-legged loping walk and slope-shouldered posture, though after taping my performance with a camera similar to what security would install at Fontaine, it wasn't assuring.

"You're still too manly on top," said Natsumi. "You're not a good enough schlump."

After some thought, I resorted to one of the most versatile tools of the pragmatic and deceptive. Duct tape.

I assumed as slouched a posture as I could and Natsumi taped me into position, working around the stuffed bra. It was just shy of excruciating, but I had movement of my hands and could free myself of thinking about that unnatural shape.

"Too bad about the nose," said Natsumi, searching out the final flaw in the disguise.

"My mother used to say the same thing.

She blamed it on my father's side of the family."

"Just keep your head down."

I used this preparation time to do a little low-key network probing using Brian's admin password. I stayed in the outer rings of the file structure, mostly recording what was accessible without actually cracking into the folders. Though it was within this relatively safe realm I came across a valuable find — an appointment schedule one of the administrative assistants kept for Chuck, Patricia and a few other high-ranking people in the department. At that point in the process, there was no more precious asset.

Thus the opportunity arose about a week later when both Chuck and Patricia were scheduled to be at an evening presentation in the city. This was posted a few days before the event, giving me time to smuggle the women's clothes into the office along with a flash drive containing what I hoped was the key to the rest of Andalusky's electronic realm.

In the morning I asked Chuck for a brief chat at the end of the day. He said he could do it a few minutes before five. So I showed up when the two of them were getting ready to leave the building. As we chatted in the hallway, I sneaked another look at the camouflaged security cameras, assessing their likely angles and coverage.

Back in my office, I logged on to one of my approved servers, typing in the first section of a report I'd already composed at home. Installed on my computer was a program that picked up the report halfway through and continued with a recording of the keystrokes, creating the appearance I was diligently working away at my desk while I adopted my Patricia Cheerborg identity.

Around seven o'clock I left my office and headed down a nearby stairwell connected with the parking garage. I was wearing a long raincoat, underneath which I wore the Patricia outfit down to my calves, which were covered in cut-off pant legs taped to my knees. I got in my car, and after climbing into the passenger seat, completed the conversion. One of the greatest points of exposure came next, when I left the car and followed a different route back to the stairwell. My hope was that unless my movements were being directly monitored, which in the garage would have to be from some distance, it was unlikely anyone would notice Marty Goldman get in his car and Patricia Cheerborg emerge from the passenger side moments later.

I climbed back up the stairwell, passing my floor on the way to the next, the top floor where they housed company top management.

When I reached the hallway, I adopted my best Patricia Cheerborg walk and headed for her office. I'd made another guess, that security would be unaware of her meeting in the city, assuming that keeping tabs on executive meetings would be too burdensome. Seeing her appear at her office after hours, on the other hand, would be commonplace, and unworthy of extra attention.

Head down, I walked with Patricia's purposeful stride directly into her office, which was unlocked, answering yet another worrisome possibility. I sat at her desk, swiveled around to face the credenza and took a deep breath. Though presumably hidden from view by people or cameras, I pretended to go through some papers on the credenza while I waited for the storm troopers to appear. Or not.

When it felt like I was in the clear, with my heart rate down to a steady trip hammer, I took a bunch of Kleenex tissues out of my skirt pocket, gathered up a few file folders and left the office, making a show of sneezing and snuffling into the Kleenex. Again, with clear purpose, I made the quick turn into Andalusky's office, also blessedly unlocked, and shut the door.

This time, I didn't hesitate, but went right for his desktop computer. I put the flash drive into the USB port and switched it on. When the user name and password request popped up, I used Brian's admin credentials, and hit enter. As the machine booted up, an invisible little app slithered out of the flash drive and attached itself to Chuck's computer at the operating system level, expressing itself as a legitimate slice of communications code and thus undetectable by known security software.

"Known" being the operative word. In the arms race between spyware hackers and the people committed to their defeat, the balance of power shifted nearly by the minute. Though I'd acquired the latest version of my app from a reliable source, no one could know if it weren't already tagged and targeted by the righteous opposition. There was no way to know.

The advantage I had, warranting the mighty risk I was taking, was being able to inject the agent directly into the computer at the start-up phase, bypassing any network presence where automated sentries guarded the gates.

It was tempting to cruise around Andalusky's e-mail and file folders, but as soon as the app was safely tucked away, I logged off and shut down the computer. This part of the mission presumably accomplished, my entire nervous system decided it was time to jump up and run like hell.

Luckily, running of any kind in Patricia's modest heels was out of the question. Instead I went back into her office to let another reasonable length of time pass before making the last run through the building.

I sat at her desk and attempted to breathe normally, steady breaths despite the pull of the duct tape, and compose myself for whatever would come next.

Which turned out to be a knock on the door.

CHAPTER 19

I actually opened the window the allowable few inches, proving the impossibility of fitting through. Even if I could, the four-story fall would surely kill me, and then there'd be no way to explain the skirt, heels and frothy wig.

So I sat down at Patricia's small, round conference table and looked at the closed door, disappointed to hear another knock.

"*Perdoname ¿hay alguien en la sala?* Eez anybody here?" came the female voice from the other side of the door.

I got up and opened the door, again holding a wad of tissues to my face.

"Oh, sorry, I come back," said the tiny woman in a grey uniform armed with an industrial-strength vacuum cleaner.

"*No, no es una molestia. Voy a salir pronto,*" I said, automatically, using my best version of a female voice, sounding more like a comic imitation of Julia Child than Patricia

Cheerborg.

"Señora, no sabía que hablaba español."
Madame, I didn't know you spoke Spanish,
she'd said, clearly taken aback.

I kept the tissues firmly planted to my face
and shook my head, not daring to risk
another word. I pulled on my coat with one
hand, grabbed a few files and fled the scene.

Rattled, I started to run down the stairwell
to the garage, then forced myself into a
more acceptable pace. The click of my heels
on the cement stairs sounded like little
muffled gunshots.

I made it to the car without encountering
anyone. Before starting the engine, I ripped
off the wig, took off the heels and tucked
the coat around me. There was nothing to
be done right then about the makeup,
though I made a few feeble attempts with
some napkins from the glove compartment,
only achieving a few ugly smears across my
forehead from the eyeliner and an unwel-
come mouthful of lipstick.

You had to go through a gate on the way
into the parking lot, but luckily, not on the
way out, which I always found curious, but
in this case highly convenient. I kept to a
reasonable speed as I drove out of the
complex, though once hitting the public
road, I let myself give it a little extra gas on

the way to the highway, and after that, the quick trip up to the blessed woods of Pound Ridge.

The next day, when Andalusky turned on his computer, the first thing it asked him for was his user name and password. When he typed these in, it unlocked his computer, giving him entrée to most of the corporation's file servers and his e-mail account, which lived on the Internet up in the cloud. The user name and password were also transmitted through a mini network within his office group, and thus well inside the corporate firewall, to a common administrative file that had lain dormant since the system had been installed. A split second after this file received the information, the communications link disappeared and the app slid back into the cyber shadows.

Seconds after that, I opened the administrative file from my office desktop using Brian's system administrator permissions. I copied the information, then deleted the file and purged all sign of its existence from the directories.

Using Andalusky's e-mail address and password, I went to the e-mail provider in the cloud and created a duplicate of his account with its own login instructions. This I could access from anywhere at any time.

Although this contrivance was theoretically invisible to the company's security measures, I thought it better to wait until I got home to start exploring.

So all that was left to do that day was to wait impatiently for it to end.

Back at my table full of computers in the house in Pound Ridge, I poured what I thought would be the final cup of coffee of the day and brought up Chuck's e-mail. The first thing I did was type the name Alberta into the search box, though before I could type past "Alb" about a thousand e-mails appeared on the screen, the name Albalita highlighted in brilliant yellow.

Albalita Suarez, Executive Director, The People Project. The institution into which Okayo poured her zeal and devotion, where she sat on the board of directors.

I went to their website and in a few moments had a portrait of Albalita, in starkly professional suit and expression to match the gravity of her mission — to bring health and social well-being to the world's poor through the opportunity to be financially independent and secure. To us, she was Alberta, the woman on the fishing boat in the Caribbean, whose mission was to abuse, terrify, interrogate and then condemn Natsumi and me to death.

I couldn't help but note the apparent disconnect.

I managed to read a few hundred of the e-mails between Chuck and Albalita, starting from the earliest dates and working forward in time, before falling asleep on the keyboard. The story they told was of the wealthiest power on Earth, the US Federal Government, in a complex dance with the planet's poorest individuals.

That the notion of winning hearts and minds has become easily lampoonable doesn't mean it isn't essential if any large-scale military power hopes to succeed in a conflict with a weaker, yet culturally cohesive local population. So the central planners in huge, air-conditioned concrete buildings in Washington, eager to find a supplement to the tanks, drones and infantrymen to hurl into foreign communities, saw a lot of merit in The People Project's approach to hurling money at their constituencies.

Not hurling so much as scattering, as one does when hand-seeding a garden. As a concept, microfinancing is relatively simple. Rather than lending large amounts to big institutions which are then charged with providing services to the general population, you lend tiny amounts to thousands of individuals directly so they can put the money to work in the most effective and efficient way possible. At the same time, you foster personal responsibility and a sense of self-reliance on the part of the borrowers, teaching them the particulars of good money management while bringing them into the larger financial universe.

Those in the federal government who thought this was a good idea also knew executing such a program was well beyond the logistical capability of the State Department or the Pentagon, or any other government agency, even the United Nations. In an unusual moment of thoughtfulness and clarity, someone decided this was a job for specialists, people who understood the staggering administrative challenges to qualifying applicants, then lending to and collecting from people who often lived on dirt floors and whose greatest financial asset might be a single goat.

So even the selection of the right subcontractor in this case fell to another organization that had proven its talent for sourcing anything and everything, worldwide.

The Société Commerciale Fontaine.

As it turned out, the man in charge of dispensing these contracts had only to travel the width of the marital bed to find the perfect enterprise. To circumvent conflict-of-interest charges, he put the assignment out to bid. Okayo publicly recused herself from the decision making and The People Project mounted a robust and ultimately successful campaign to win the contract, led by their executive director, Albalita Suarez.

Thus began a fruitful relationship between the dispensers of US foreign aid, their fiduciary — contractor Fontaine — and The People Project as the NGO specialist in the field. In the process, a billion and a half dollars found its way into the hands of millions of impoverished people throughout the world striving to build more financially secure, self-sustaining lives.

Out of this success came a strong mutual regard between Chuck and Albalita. It grew more intense and demonstrative with every milestone achieved, every triumph celebrated. As I concentrated on the messages there was nothing that would reconcile the reality expressed in these e-mails and what had happened to Natsumi and me.

No wonder I succumbed to exhaustion.

■ ■ ■ ■

I drove into work the next day, resisting the urge to go deeper into Andalusky's e-mail. I was fairly bludgeoned by lack of sleep, my late night in front of the computer made worse by waking up early to brief Natsumi. She took it all in, made coffee and entreated me to be careful.

"I know you always are," she said. "It just makes me feel better saying it."

Everything else about the morning was routine. I pulled into my usual parking spot, used my ID badge to get through the employee entrance turnstile and said hello to the guard, carrying my briefcase and coffee mug freshened at a deli along the way. Everything routine but for the security guy standing outside my office and the other one suddenly walking behind me.

"Good morning, Mr. Goldman," said the guy at the door. "Could you come with us please?"

He moved away from the door and I felt a gentle herding vibe from the other man, so I followed along compliantly, feeling a brief urge to dive down a passing stairwell, though I knew I'd be pinned to the floor before I had a chance to take half a step.

As we walked I took out my smartphone and speed-dialed Natsumi's panic phone. I let it ring three times, then hung up and put the phone away before the security people decided they should stop me.

We went through an unmarked door into an area that housed the security detail. Faces looked up from desks as we walked through to a conference room, where Ansell Andersen sat with a laptop computer facing away from him, as if prepared to give a presentation. Which he was.

They stood behind me while I sat in front of the computer. Ansell looked either jubilant or argumentative, which for him was likely one and the same.

"Hello, Ansell," I said to him. "What's up?"

"The jig, if you can call it that," he said.

He stood up and tapped on the computer's space bar, typed in the code to unlock it, and up popped a video of Martin Goldman, my old classmate, being interviewed by an Asian woman on what looked like a television newscast. I noticed Marty looked pretty good, and not much like me despite my effort at disguise. I didn't follow the content of the interview very well, distracted as I was by a nearly overwhelming surge of fight/flight.

"It seems there's more than one Martin Goldman with Martin Goldman's résumé," said Ansell. "Only, unfortunately for you, this one appears to be the real Magilla."

"Appears to be?" I said.

With some flourish, Ansell took out his smartphone, tapped a few buttons, then put it on the table.

"For the record, I'm absolutely me and I'm here in Singapore," said Marty. "I'm about to go out to dinner with some friends who can also vouch for me, and if I'm not me, we're all in for a big surprise. Hope this is what you need, and tell that other guy I'm flattered. Not every day you get impersonated."

I looked up at the security guy on my left.

"Where's Jenny?" I asked him.

"Who?"

"Jenny Richardson. From HR. You can't talk to me without HR in the room. If you continue, I can sue all three of your asses and it won't matter if I'm Santa Claus, I'll win."

Ansell's face fell a little, but the security people seemed unperturbed. Nonetheless, one of them walked over to a phone and called Jenny.

"I don't know what she's going to do for

you," said Ansell. "You're fucked no matter what."

"Who else have you notified?" I asked one of the security people.

"Mr. Andalusky was away from his desk. We left a message."

The guy checked his watch as if it would tell him when Chuck would be picking up his messages.

"I don't know how you thought you'd get away with it," said Ansell. "You think we're stupid?"

"Who's head of security?" I asked the guys.

"That'd be me," said the one who'd called Jenny.

"So you know you can't restrain me," I said, "as long as I'm not behaving in a way that endangers anyone's safety."

"Let's just wait for Ms. Richardson," he said.

"What a bunch of bullshit," said Ansell. "Why aren't you calling the cops?"

"Maybe because they're doing their job, which is to look after the best interests of the corporation," I said to him.

Jenny came into the room with a look of surprise and wonder on her face. The two security guys moved a few steps away from me, as if deferring to the diminutive woman.

Ansell muttered under his breath.

"Can someone please tell me what this is about?" she asked.

"The guy's a phony," said Ansell. "I always thought so. But to please people like you, I got some proof. The real Martin Goldman's still in Singapore."

He reached for his computer, but I stopped him by saying, "Not necessary. I'll stipulate that it's true. I'm not Martin Goldman."

She bent over me and actually put her hand on my shoulder. The wonder on her face turned to concern.

"Why?" she asked me.

"I needed a job," I said quietly, staring deeply into her eyes. "I was desperate. No one gets hired when they're unemployed more than six months. I've been out for a year. You can't imagine how hard it can be. The kids love their school. We were going to lose the house and we'd have to move, God knows where."

"Jesus Christ, the guy's a fucking con man," said Ansell.

"I'll leave quietly," I said, a slight whine creeping into my voice. "There's no reason to bother Mr. Andalusky. This is embarrassing enough."

"What are you talking about?" Ansell

nearly shouted. "This is a gross violation of the law. You can't go around pretending to be other people and taking money and acting like you know what the fuck you're doing, bullshitting your way into a job you have absolutely no business being anywhere *near.*"

He would have gone on, but I put my hand in front of his face, interrupting him. I looked straight at Jenny and spoke so softly she had to lean farther in.

"As of now, with the exception of Mr. Andalusky, who has a message on his phone, the only people who know about me are in this room. While I'm sure your management will be unhappy to hear how easy it was to get though the human resource hiring process, perform well enough in the job to be promoted into a position within walking distance of the C-suite, I guarantee they'll be much happier if it isn't broadcast to the entire world. All you have to do is let me walk out of here and that'll be the end of it. It's in no one's interest, certainly not mine, to let any of this be known."

Jenny nodded, thinking about it. She looked up at the head of security.

"What do you say, Carl. Can we just escort him out of the building?"

"No," said Ansell. "No, no, no."

He stood up and tried to grab me by the shoulder. As I reared back, Carl got between us and used both oversized hands to move Ansell out of the way.

"None of that, sir," said Carl.

"I can't fucking believe this," said Ansell. "Are you people out of your fucking minds?"

Jenny drew to her full height, even gaining an inch by lifting up on her toes. She pointed a finger at Ansell.

"Listen. You do not get to make decisions for this corporation. And if you even think about violating confidentiality in this matter or any other relating to human resources, your sorry ass will be out of a job before you can say 'spit.' "

I thought this was a good time to stand up myself, clutching my briefcase to my chest with pathetic defensiveness.

"I need to get home to break the news to my family," I said.

Jenny's eyes shot another set of knives at Ansell before guiding me out of the conference room. I led the way to the employee entrance followed by Jenny with Carl bringing up the rear. When we got to the turnstile I handed Carl my ID badge and let him look through my briefcase. He thanked me and took everything but an empty pad of paper.

"Good luck," said Jenny, shaking my hand.

I forced myself to walk to the Jeep like a dejected sad sack and not the adrenaline-addled lunatic I actually was. I was out of the garage and partway down the long, curvy driveway when a security car came racing up behind me with its blue light flashing. I pulled over and watched two uniformed guards in my rear view mirror get out of the car. When he reached my door I gunned the accelerator. In the time it took him to scramble back to his car I was nearly to the guard shack. I could see the driveway blocked by the barrier with two men standing there waiting for me.

To my right was a field of tall grass. I shoved the Jeep into four-wheel drive and flew into the field. It was a lot lumpier than it looked from the road, which was fine for me as long as the Jeep and I could take the punishment. The same didn't seem possible for the car driven by security, though they gave it a try.

I could barely hold the steering wheel as I flopped around in the Jeep's passenger compartment, with only the seat belt preventing me from smashing into the dashboard or up into the ceiling. The options before me weren't promising. Another few hundred yards of grassland, a ditch, and a cyclone fence. Beyond that was a public road. Cyclone fences are little impediment for Hollywood, which generally has the stunt driver ripping through the chain-link as if it were cheesecloth, which it isn't. I took a counterintuitive approach, aiming instead for one of the poles, hoping it would snap off or crimp at the base. But first, I had to clear the ditch.

There wasn't much more speed I could get out of the Jeep, even with the accelerator on the floor. The lumpy terrain just wouldn't allow it. All I could do was hold the wheel in a death grip and try to keep the Jeep perpendicular to the ditch, and subsequently, the fence.

I guess I was moving better than I thought, because the Jeep actually became airborne at the bank of the ditch, clearing the distance to the fence, which I hit like a ballistic missile.

The airbags finally had enough, which was a good thing. Cushioned in their rough embrace, I survived the crash with consciousness and all four limbs intact. The Jeep as well, even after whipping around to the right and nearly launching into a roll.

The bigger problem was regaining freedom of movement from the deflating airbags surrounding me. With one hand on the wheel, I used the other to push the slippery synthetic material out of the way. I still had a stretch of grassy ground to cover, but it was much smoother and the Jeep's steering and suspension system felt fully operational.

The hood was crimped toward the front, but a look at the instrument panel showed I still had oil and coolant. Seconds later I was at the roadside, waiting for a few cars to pass before calmly entering the flow of traffic.

My thinking now moved to the strategic. I couldn't know why security suddenly reversed their decision to let me go, but my money was on Andalusky picking up their voice message. Security probably decided that, facing demands by a big shot like Andalusky, they were in their legal authority to restrain me while still on corporate property. After that was another matter. I tried to imagine the reaction of a police dispatcher being asked by some corporate hack to please chase down one of their ex-employees for lying on his résumé.

I turned onto a side street and stopped to look at the GPS on my smartphone. I mapped out a route away from White Plains that avoided most of the main roads and set off. Then I called Natsumi.

"Have you heard from your mother lately?" I asked.

"Yes, she's well, thank you," said Natsumi, completing the prearranged signal that all was clear.

"I'm blown at Fontaine," I said. "Some asshole in Gyawali's group tracked down the real Marty Goldman. Don't know if there's more damage beyond that. They let me go, but then changed their minds and I had to bust my way out of there."

I told her my theory of Andalusky picking up his messages and likely grasping implications well beyond the simple fraud.

"I grabbed our ID supply and your external hard drives, but left everything else at the house," she said.

"I gave HR a PO Box connected to a phony address, so Fontaine doesn't know where we live. As long as I'm not followed, and I'll make sure of that, there's no reason to think we've lost the house."

"Think about that," she said.

I knew what she meant. I needed to run through all the possible scenarios, hitches, possible holes in the argument, threats imminent and improbable. Our lives depended on it.

I told her I'd call her back in an hour or

314

two. I drove a desultory route around the Westchester and Fairfield County area until nightfall, fitting in a couple of errands as I went, since I needed to ditch the Jeep. The security people didn't need to record my license plate in the midst of a car chase, they just had to go to my employee file and look it up. No matter what, that made the vehicle a big liability.

So I bought a bottle of cleaner and a roll of paper towels. Then I drove to a parking lot of a big shopping mall, wiped down the interior, locked the doors and left it, smashed-in grill and all.

I caught a bus that took me to a car rental outlet where I picked up another SUV, this one a Ford Explorer. I'd long ago stripped off the Marty Goldman wig, but I also stopped at a clothing store so I could dump the business casual in favor of a baseball cap, flannel shirt and jeans. Aside from being smart tradecraft, I felt renewed by the look and feel of the clothes, a protective layer against encircling threats.

"I still think the house is good," I told Natsumi, when I called her back, adding that I'd switched out my ride and ensemble. "We're all done with drab corporate drone. The new look is lumberjack."

"I'll work on a hearty meal."

I took another long and winding route up to the house in Pound Ridge, watchful as a timid herbivore for any hint of threat, while continuing my endless brooding deliberations and calculations, and plotting alternate futures, searching for paths out of the chaos that was closing in on me.

CHAPTER 20

"I'm not going to draw the blinds and cower in a corner," said Natsumi. "That might be the best survival tactic, but I just can't."

We were in the big basement of the rental, which had a set of comfy, well-used sofas clustered around its own fireplace. It also had my bank of computers and storehouse of munitions and protective gear. When I got home, she met me there, a place with only two small windows high up on the wall and a door leading directly to the garage on the same lower level. Noticing the fortress feel, Natsumi had clearly felt a surge of rebellion.

"Me neither," I said. "Why don't you go get some coffee?"

"Up there? What're you crazy?"

She left anyway and came back later with coffee and lunch. I had a Google search of Albalita Suarez up on the computer from which I was downloading text, photo and video information and storing it on one of my bottomless external hard drives. Natsumi put down the tray and sat next to me.

"That's definitely her," she said.

Born Albalita Drechsler. Daughter of an Argentine mother and a German immigrant father, also Argentine.

"Probably a Nazi," said Natsumi.

Married to an American, Pedro Suarez, subsequently divorced. BA in sociology from the University of Wisconsin-Madison. Started at UNICEF, moved through different NGOs till landing the executive director spot at The People Project, headquartered in Zurich. The usual awards, accolades, published articles and honorary degrees. Photos of her drinking tea on the floor of a yurt, loading relief supplies onto flatbed trucks, holding skinny African babies, stalking through a Middle East refugee camp in a calf-length skirt and hiking shoes, standing at a podium pointing her finger at someone out in the audience likely being flattened by a withering retort.

I switched over to Andalusky's company e-mail account, but saw nothing current relating to Albalita. Then I looked at the software monitoring his smartphone and saw a call not long after I fled the big building to a number in Zurich, Switzerland. I pulled it up and hit the audio button.

"Albalita, it's Chuck."

"Odd time to call, Chuck."

"We had a security breach this morning at White Plains. I'm not happy about it."

"Why're you telling me?"

"I think I fucked up."

There was silence on the line for a moment. I could imagine Albalita sitting up a little straighter in her chair.

"How so?" she asked.

"We hired a guy into my department who slipped in under false pretenses. Thing is, he knew his shit. Really well. But there was something familiar about him. Something I didn't like. But I couldn't put my finger on it. You're going to think I'm nuts, but I think it was him."

"Who are you talking about?" she asked, clearly exasperated.

"Him. The hacker with the Asian woman."

There was a longer silence this time.

"That's impossible," she finally said.

"The hell it is. Those fucking mercs double-crossed us. I never trusted those bastards."

"They were your idea," she said, in a tone that nearly froze the phone line.

"You didn't have anything better," he shot back, the stress building in his voice.

"Tell me more about this imposter," she said evenly, pulling back from the impending argument.

"He was a researcher Gyawali picked up. I needed someone to run analytics out of this office. So I got this smart son-of-a-bitch, though kind of a loose cannon. He's the right age, but had this big head of hair and thick glasses. 'Course you have wigs."

"Chuck," she said to him, the way you'd address a defiant teenager, "don't you remember what our Basque friend said about this guy? He's a world-class hacker, and he's been inside your building, on your servers."

It was his turn to pause in silence.

"Shit," he said. "The phone."

"Dammit," she said, and hung up.

That was the last call he made. I tried to switch over to his company e-mail account, but it was gone. Not locked up, or defended by a new password. Gone, like it never existed. I switched again, this time to Andalusky's home computer. Also gone.

I tried to slip into Fontaine's servers with Brian's administrative log-ins, with no luck. I checked the GPS monitors stuck to Chuck and Okayo's cars, and they were gone. As were the video monitors I'd set up outside their house, though I knew that already, having checked on my circuitous route back home.

It was as if everything I'd done in the last few weeks was a hallucination. As if I'd been living inside a massive delusion.

Prompted by such thoughts, I checked in on our finances. The investment accounts were all there, but another two bank accounts had disappeared. About thirty-eight thousand dollars had evaporated.

"Fuck," I yelled, slamming the top of the table with my open palm.

Natsumi, who'd drifted away as I worked at the computer, ran back down the stairs to the basement.

"What."

I gave her the news.

"Have you heard from Strider?" she asked, reminding me I'd asked the young hacker to look into the original vanishing account.

"No. Now I'm afraid to contact her again."

"What's happening?" Natsumi asked, her voice nearly a register below normal.

"It's coming apart."

"What?"

"They're breaching the outer perimeter. Eventually, they'll get to the core."

"Who are they?" she asked.

"I don't know. And now I've lost Andalusky. Fontaine's security is sweeping up after him. Very effectively. We're cut off. Weeks of work gone poof."

"But we're smarter," she said.

She was right. We'd identified Alberta as Albalita, confirmed her connection with Andalusky and acquired convincing evidence that they'd conspired to capture and do us great harm.

So we knew a lot more, but it was cold comfort, as our security seemed to erode faster than our awareness could increase.

"We can't go backward," I said. "It's too late to stop."

"I'll start packing," said Natsumi, leaving me again with exhilaration, terror and paranoia competing for purchase on my weary heart.

We made one stop at a big international bank where I'd consolidated all our remaining liquid funds, and then subsequently withdrew in fat stacks of traveler's checks. It took awhile to complete the task, though no one at the bank seemed to think it out of the ordinary, testament to the type of clientele served at that level.

A few hours later we were at JFK airport, inching our way along a serpentine queue that terminated at a podium behind which a humorless TSA agent scrutinized passport photos and the matching human face there before her.

Passing the visual test was of little concern. It was all the other stuff — name, address, date of birth, place of birth, passport number, fraudulent all. The source of the passports came with impeccable credentials, though for all we knew he'd been turned by the authorities and was now in the business of setting snares for his unsuspecting customers.

I hoped we'd perfected a look of bored indifference laced with impatience, which pretty well captured the manner of most international travelers. There was a time when such attitudes mattered little, before the TSA ran software that could spot a possible terrorist by the mood state captured on a security camera.

So I was disappointed when the TSA agency at the podium looked at my passport, then at me, and then asked me to step out of the line. She asked the same of Natsumi.

I held firm to my insouciance and walked with my rolling bag over to where another TSA agent, this one looking very comfortable in a body about twice the size of the woman's at the podium. While we stood there a third agent brought the large man our passports. He opened them, one in each hand, moving his head back and forth as he absorbed the information.

"You two travelin' together?" he asked.

"We are."

"Hm," he said, nodding. "Married?"

I felt Natsumi stiffen. Our adopted personas by necessity had to be single. The degree of difficulty in obtaining a married pair was nearly insurmountable.

"No," she said, with an edge of annoyance.

"Jes' askin'," he said, his eyes still fixed on the passports. "Stamp says you been to Martinique. Like it there?"

I never had, so I probably stiffened myself.

"On business," I said.

"My people are from down that way. La Trinité."

"Never left the resort," I said. "Wish it weren't so."

Natsumi said something in Japanese. I replied with "Don't worry," in the same language, two of a handful of words I knew. She nodded, then bowed her head.

"Don't speak English?" the agent said.

"Of course she does," I said. "She's just nervous we'll miss our plane."

He smiled.

"I was stationed four years in Okinawa,"

he said. "I know the lingo for 'airplane.' "

"So, is there a problem?" I asked.

"Prob'ly not," he said, then looked directly at Natsumi, and said, "Dealer's holdin' a king and a five. Player's got an ace showin'. Who folds?"

Natsumi cocked her head, her face a torment of unease.

"I'm sorry," she said. "I do not understand. What is a king of a five?"

His laugh was more of a grunt. He handed us our passports.

"Have a nice flight," he said. "And keep this kid out of the casinos, if they got 'em over there in Switzerland."

"I have no idea," I said, fussing with my passport and luggage and fawning over my timid Japanese girlfriend, who, once we were clear of the security, said, "Fucking asshole."

I shook my head, warning her into silence, broken only when we were on the plane as it rumbled down the runway.

"What just happened?" Natsumi asked.

"They're looking for a Caucasian male traveling with a female Japanese blackjack dealer," I said.

"Why not just hold us till they're sure?"

"We're not the only mixed-race couple traveling today. They'd have to hold dozens for hours. The media would have a field day. He had to make a quick call. He'll duly note the stop in his regular report. They'll have video images. It'll all be processed through a central database. We still have a seven-hour flight and have to get through Swiss customs. Plenty of time for things to go awry."

So it was a less-than-relaxing trip over the Atlantic. Natsumi took full advantage of the beverage service in business class while I built and discarded scenarios. The prevailing stereotype of researchers is of coldly dispassionate, computer-like people bolted irrevocably to the available facts. That's part of the story. But it doesn't account for hypotheses. What-ifs and if-thens. This requires the ability to imagine, to extract, often out of pure ether, possibilities and potentials. Einstein famously claimed he began with an answer, a version of nature that to others would appear in utter conflict with observed reality. Then he'd backfill the math, the proof that his mad vision was in fact the true state of being.

And Einstein's visions were nearly common sense when compared to the prophesies of the quantum physicists. Among their many incomprehensible theories was that every action, no matter how small, had an infinite number of possible outcomes. Even that each of these was actually realized in an infinite number of universes. Fine, I thought, mulling this. We don't need infinite answers to the anguishing questions before us. Just one will do. The right one.

Chapter 21

After the aggressive brio of the New York TSA, the dignified Swiss almost made the airport gauntlet refreshing. I wasted mental energy studying the customs agents' faces as they studied our passports, and then let us through without hesitation. It wasn't until we were in the cab on the way into the city that I felt the grip on my nerves ease up a little.

"Hypervigilance," said Natsumi, when I shared my feelings. "With physical exercise, repetitive stress on your body makes you stronger. Constant stress on your nervous system has the opposite effect. It's why virtually no soldier will last more than a few months of steady combat without succumbing to some sort of psychological degradation, PTSD or what have you."

"That doesn't make me happy."

"Shelly was right. You think the rules don't apply to you. But no one can live as we've been living and stay the same. As your resilience decays, your sensory sensitivity is sharpened and your environmental aware- ness becomes far more acute than neces- sary. I'm seeing it happen to you, and feel it happening to me. But there's no shame in it. We're human after all."

"I can't have it fog up my brain."

"I certainly haven't seen that. Maybe the rules don't apply to you."

When we got to the hotel, I abandoned a long-held jet lag strategy by lying flat on my back and passing out. When consciousness eventually returned, it was slow going, weighed down by lingering fatigue and clut- tered with the fractured remnants of frantic dreams. It took longer than usual to place where I was, but it all came back abruptly when I saw Natsumi come out of the bath- room wearing only a towel on her head.

She told me she'd sat in a chair and watched me until night fell, then she passed out, and both of us were gone to the world until the following day.

"You're kidding," I said.

"You slept about eighteen hours. How do you feel?"

"Less vigilant."

She joined me on the bed and helped complete the waking-up process. I knew I was merely freshened and hardly cured of my nervous exhaustion, but I took it as a gift and a warning that I probably wouldn't get another one until the state of our lives was resolved, one way or another.

It only took a few minutes to restore full computer operations using my laptop and a solid state, terabyte external hard drive. I didn't bother trying to check on Chuck Andalusky's home and office e-mail accounts, or his telephone conversations, knowing they were now securely locked up with new passwords, and fearing the possibility Fontaine's security people had a way to detect and trace infiltrators.

I was about to check my own e-mail when a little window popped up, alerting me that a message had hit the mailbox I'd set up to communicate with Shelly Gross. With a mixture of pleasant anticipation and dread, I clicked on the window.

"Let's meet on the *Quaibrücke*. Half hour from the time you respond."

It was signed Captain Perry.

"Ah!" I yelled.

"What?" asked Natsumi, alarmed.

I felt heat spread across my chest and a bell literally ring in my ears. So much for a respite from hypervigilance.

"Fuck," I said.

"Fuck what?" she asked, looking over my shoulder. "Oh fuck."

According to the GPS on my smartphone, *Quaibrücke* was a bridge in the city that crossed the head of the Limmat River where it poured out of Lake Zurich.

"What does this mean?" Natsumi asked.

"It's very good or very bad."

"What are you going to do?"

I looked around at her.

"Einstein said imagination was more important than knowledge," I told her. "I could analyze the facts at hand for the rest of my life and not make a better decision than you'll make in the next ten seconds by simply getting in touch with your feelings."

"I'm feeling sick," she said.

"What do we do?"

"Write him back and tell him to expect a bald Caucasian and stylish Japanese woman. But in an hour. Style like mine doesn't come quickly." I started to object, but she shut me up with the obvious. "You don't let me decide then second-guess the decision."

And that's how we were walking along the River Limmat, arm in arm. The morning air was cool, even though spring had nearly surrendered to summer and there were flowers aplenty in the parks, planters and window boxes around the city. I was in a light fleece and Natsumi had fulfilled on her promise by wearing a skirt, scarf and suede jacket. I watched men of all ages watch her as she passed by.

We actually managed to be a little early, so we detoured up into the Old Town to use up the extra time.

"What are you thinking?" Natsumi asked as we wove our way through the narrow, ancient streets.

"Nothing. I'm done with all that."

"Intuition only from now on?"

"You got it."

"Maybe you should see how this next bit turns out before you decide," she said.

"If that's what your intuition is telling you."

We walked the last block along the river and turned off onto the busy *Quaibrücke*. Captain Perry hadn't specified which of the two broad sidewalks to meet on, so Natsumi picked the south side, facing the lake.

A few minutes later, her impulse was validated when a tall man who'd been leaning on the railing, looking out over the lake, turned around just as we were approaching. His ball of steel-wool hair might have been a little shorter, and his face a little less tan, but it was unmistakably Jersey Mitchell, former FBI agent, late of the good ship *That's a Moray.*

He stuck out his hand and Natsumi took it.

"Captain," she said.

"I almost bought the Jonathan Cornwall routine," he said to her. "But you never seemed like a Natalie. Ian says hello," he said to me as we also shook hands. "Or maybe it was 'Go fuck yourself.' Can't remember which."

"He brought you in," I said.

"He did. After a fifth of whisky and a serious bout of conscience."

"Over Angela?"

"Over selling out his former employer. He damn near ate a gun over that one."

"I'm sorry," I said.

"He's in rehab and finally free of that harpy of a wife, so maybe you saved his life."

"I thought you were retired," said Natsumi.

He smiled.

"Are you accusing me of deception? Come on, let's walk and talk," he said, moving down the sidewalk.

Without going into detail, Jersey told us he was only semiretired, staying in the game by being eyes and ears for the FBI in the Caribbean. That's why, when Ian contacted him, he was able to pull agents from the Boston field office to pay us a call. No one expected us to dodge the interview.

"A less impressive evasion would have aroused less interest," he said.

The report from Boston made its way to Washington, which resulted in Jersey being ordered on a plane north. Again, without revealing the FBI's inner workings, he let us know a very important person wanted Jersey to brief him and only him.

"He's the real Captain Perry. I just got to borrow the name to get your attention."

"So you're not here to arrest us and bring us back to the States," said Natsumi.

I didn't like it that he took his time answering.

"That depends," he said, eventually.

"On what?" I asked.

"How the rest of this conversation goes. Who's in the mood for coffee and a snack?"

By that time we were well west of the river in an area that was new to me. Jersey seemed to know his way around, however, and we were soon in a booth inside a dark little joint run by a husband and wife. Jersey ordered in German.

"They claim not to speak a lick of English, but everybody in Switzerland speaks a *leetle,*" he said, using the standard Swiss

334

pronunciation.

"You'll forgive us if we aren't into small talk," said Natsumi, "since our lives depend on the quality of the conversation."

"Not afraid of the quality," said Jersey. "It's more about the content."

"This feels like a game," she said. "Only we don't know the rules."

"The only rule is honesty," he said.

"Now that we have a table," said Natsumi, "it would help if we got all the cards out."

"Spoken like a blackjack dealer," said Jersey.

"What did Shelly tell you?" I asked.

"Shelly Gross isn't part of this conversation," he said. "I'm here as Captain Perry's proxy. He's keenly interested in an organization that seems to interest you. There may be a way to work something out that could help you, while helping us, which is why we're sitting here today."

"The Société Commerciale Fontaine," I said.

He nodded, and said, "In particular, Charles Andalusky."

"He's dirty," said Natsumi.

"Is that a question or a statement?" asked Jersey.

"Why the interest in Andalusky?" I asked.

"That's one of our questions for you."

Natsumi told him how we'd been woken up on our boat, trussed up and shipped blindfolded to the old fishing scow. How we'd been held in grim metal rooms, then interrogated by Andalusky, drugged, and handed over to mercenaries who ignored his order to kill us. She told a reasonably complete story, while leaving out a lot, including our encounters with the Cuban mercenaries, my brief tenure as a research analyst with Fontaine, Albalita Suarez and Joselito Gorrotxategi, the financial IT wizard I'd helped the FBI ship off to penitentiary oblivion, and thus far the only connection between our past lives and the whole inexplicable swirl that had come since.

"And you have no idea why Andalusky, a man of serious international prestige, would behave in such a way?" he asked.

"We're hoping you could ask him," said Natsumi.

The set of Jersey's shoulders seemed to relax slightly and he sat back in his seat. He took a long sip of his coffee, then said, "That'd be difficult."

"The FBI's afraid to talk to some corporate poo-bah?" she asked.

"It's not that," he said. "Nobody's talking to him, now or ever again."

Which is when I realized the true reason we were having this chat with Jersey Mitchell in the dim little coffee shop in Zurich, Switzerland, and not in a brightly lit, windowless room in some nameless location, or on an official plane on its way back to Washington, DC.

It's when I saw, among a nearly infinite number of possibilities, one likelihood emerge, one sure outcome coalesce out of the fog of uncertainty. Although I hadn't thought out all the details. In fact, I hadn't thought at all. I'd merely felt.

"He's dead," I said.

Jersey nodded.

"Shot through the head, sitting in his car in the garage. Not a suicide, unless he figured out how to make the weapon, bullet and shell casing miraculously disappear."

Natsumi broke the resulting silence during which Jersey's usually friendly, jovial face seemed to assume a harder set.

"And you know who did this?" she asked.

"Sure," he said. "The guy sitting next to you. Arthur Cathcart."

CHAPTER 22

Sometimes an event can alter a person's life so dramatically that the versions of himself, before and after, are best described as two people. For me, it wasn't just the bullet in the brain, with all the attendant physical and psychological consequences, it was why it happened, and how. The horror and the violence of it all.

I forgive everyone who calls me lucky. They aren't wrong, in that I lived, and the aftereffects, while devastating, could have been much worse. Most head trauma of that severity leaves partial amnesia, especially about the trauma itself. Another bit of luck, good or bad, depending on your point of view, is I remembered everything that happened.

I also remembered what I was like in my old life. I knew that person well, and I will never stop envying the extraordinarily blessed life he lived. Blessed most certainly in his innocence, which more than anything was obliterated by the assassin's bullet.

It would be inconceivable that the blissfully innocent Arthur Cathcart could kill another human being. Not true of Arthur Cathcart's successors. I'd proven that more than once.

"But you're not bringing us back to the States," said Natsumi.

"No," he said. "Not yet anyway. Captain Perry wants to have a conversation before all that stuff becomes necessary."

As I listened to Jersey, I wondered how difficult it would be to injure him badly enough to escape the coffee shop and make a run for it. He was at least ten years older than me, but far bigger, and as a career FBI field agent, not an easy opponent, even if I got in the first shot.

And with what, my fists? I hadn't successfully hit anyone since high school, and then I had the element of surprise. No one back then thought a nerd like me would ever throw a punch. I needed more of an advantage, so I ordered a draft beer, which I'd seen served to a nearby table in a heavy glass mug. Without missing a beat, Natsumi ordered herself a glass of red wine.

Jersey looked at his watch.

"A little early, isn't it?" he asked.

"We might be a bit nervous," said Natsumi.

"Fair enough."

"Captain Mitchell," said Natsumi, "I understand the value of both holding and showing your cards. As you pointed out, I'm a professional blackjack dealer. But it's very hard for the opposite player to know what to do when so many of your cards are face down. In this game, you have the greater advantage. We've turned over quite a bit. In good faith. It's your turn."

He liked that.

"I wouldn't need your file to know you're a psychologist," he said.

He took a moment to gather his thoughts.

"In order to lighten the mountain of shit that was falling on him, our friend Joselito was more than eager to sell out anybody and everybody he might have helped in their illegal enterprise," he said. "It was quite a treasure trove of material, and the FBI and the Justice Department are still happily working their way through some very promising opportunities. The stickler, however, was Joselito fingering Chuck Andalusky, which was a little like saying the Sisters of Mercy have been selling orphans to McDonald's to make into cheeseburgers."

"They haven't?" said Natsumi.

"By one estimate, The Société Commerciale Fontaine has managed, or been the fiduciary for, about thirty billion dollars in taxpayer money," said Jersey. "A big piece of this has flowed through Chuck Andalusky's office in White Plains. Do you think maybe some people in Washington might be just a *leetle* bit concerned to hear that Mr. Andalusky might have been engaged in even a *leetle* hanky-panky?"

"And what are we supposed to know about this?" Natsumi asked.

"He hasn't told you?" Jersey asked, looking over at me. "You two should talk more often."

Natsumi kept her eyes on Jersey.

"I don't know what you mean," she said.

"Where did Arthur go after they chased him out of Fontaine?" he asked her.

"He came home."

"Directly?" he asked. She sat silent. "My guess is no. Andalusky was gunned down less than an hour after those bozos in security let Arthur drive away. I'm betting an hour after that Arthur shows up in a new ride. We have the Jeep, by the way. Nice job cleaning up, though you left behind a partial and enough DNA to make a match with the guy we've decided is you. What's really interesting is that Andalusky's next-door neighbor saw the same Jeep parked outside their house that same morning. Arthur doesn't happen to own an automatic pistol, does he Natsumi? Fitted with a suppressor?"

I finished off the last of my beer, looking down into the mug the way I'd seen people do who needed a beer far more often than me. Gripping the handle, I tested the balance and calculated the weight, and ballistic potential.

"If you really believe what you're saying, why aren't we in custody?" Natsumi asked.

"You're the psychologist," he said to her. "Do you really know who you've been living with?"

"Please, Mr. Mitchell," said Natsumi. "Don't insult me with the oldest trick in the book."

"Arthur's a smart guy, but I've spent my whole life with guys like him. He cons everyone he knows. Why would you be different? Because you're sleeping with him? Since when does that matter? Sorry, but it never does. Sure, he's probably pretty good to you, if you ignore making you an accessory to enough shit to put you away for the rest of your life. I like you, Natsumi, but frankly, I don't care what you think. You're going to find out soon enough, as soon as the stakes get so high that even you move into the liability column. Right Arthur?"

She didn't let him move her gaze on to me. Instead, she said to him, "I think the stakes are already as high as they can get."

"Really?" said Jersey. "Why do you think Andalusky grabbed you off your boat in the Caribbean?"

This time I tried to make eye contact with Natsumi, but she stayed fixed on Jersey.

"They wanted something from us," she said.

"What."

"Information."

"About what."

"Money," she said.

"Ah, money," said Jersey. "It always gets back to money, doesn't it Arthur?"

"Not always," I said.

"It does when you're talking about a really, really big pile of money. Big enough that the gravitational pull starts to warp and bend and everything in its path, including the hearts and minds of otherwise decent, honorable people."

"Ostensibly decent and honorable," I said.

Jersey nodded, as if conceding the point.

"Fair enough," he said, "but let me ask you, Natsumi, how much money are we talking about here? Did Arthur tell you?"

I'd never mentioned to Natsumi that Albalita, then Alberta, had told me the only thing she wanted to discuss with me was a billion, with a B.

"A considerable amount," said Natsumi. "I'd rather not share the exact number."

Jersey gave the top of the table a light smack.

"God, I miss talking to liars," he said. "The good ones, I mean. With all due respect."

Natsumi maintained her stillness and poise.

"Maybe you should share your version of the truth," I said to Jersey.

He liked that, too.

"There's only one that matters, Arthur. The FBI's. And our truth is that about a billion dollars of taxpayer money has been stolen and we want it back. The only thing left to decide is whether you correct the situation or disappear into some anonymous hole in the wall somewhere where you might as well be dead, this time for real."

"And how do you think we could possibly help, as you say, correct the situation?" Natsumi asked.

"Another question for Arthur," he said. "Geez, I feel like a marriage counselor. Maybe I should go into that. When I'm all the way retired."

Natsumi finally broke eye contact with Jersey and looked at me, though revealing nothing in her gaze. I made it easy for her.

"He thinks I know where it is," I said.

"Why does he think that?" she asked, this time not rhetorically.

"Because he took it," said Jersey, as he reached across the table and gently took the heavy beer mug out of my hand.

It took a few hours involving multiple cab rides, back-door exits and even a quick trip to an outlying town, but eventually we made it back to our hotel. I didn't know if we'd managed to evade the tails, if there were any, but just going through the motions felt like a meaningful thing to do.

The room had a tight little seating area, a reasonably comfortable place for us to sit and try to plan out the remainder of our lives.

Jersey had left us with a phone number and a deadline. Two weeks to hand over whatever would allow retrieval of the money — account numbers, routing codes, stock certificates, Krugerrands, treasure map — he didn't care as long as it happened. After that, the government would decide what to do with us. So there was no clear quid pro quo. We returned the money or else, and even when we did, further consequences were impending.

"Why did he let us go?" asked Natsumi.

"They think we can get the money more easily if we're free to move around."

"I don't see how, but even so, it shows they're confident they can capture us again if they want to. When they want to."

"It does."

"Do you think that confidence is warranted?" she asked.

"Probably. They know too much and we know too little about what they know. Though I think we can take him at his word about the two weeks. That's our window."

"To do what?"

"Get the money."

She closed her eyes and let her head fall slightly forward.

"And you know where it is?" she asked.

"Yes."

She opened her eyes again.

"Maybe this is something you could share with me."

"I don't know exactly, but I know where to look."

"That's an important distinction," she said.

"We need a car, ski masks, leather gloves

and duct tape."

"Roger that."

If you drive south from Zurich along the lake shore you come to an area called the Gold Coast, ostensibly because sunsets turn the hills amber, though the real reason is the same as the Gold Coast of Connecticut — bucolic suburbs in close proximity to an international financial center.

This was where Albalita Suarez lived alone in a house behind a high white wall with a locked gate, with the second floor likely affording a good view of the lake, as suggested by the 360-degree street view on Google Maps.

Employing basic precautions as we worked through the preparations and secured supplies, we were ready in the little grey Audi hatchback driving down Route 17 toward the Gold Coast village of Küsnacht. It was two o'clock in the morning, a time when even dynamic cities like Zurich were tucked in for the night, yet with plenty of darkness left to carry out the mission.

We had a simple plan, one familiar to anyone who'd seen any run-of-the-mill television drama. Beginning with our outfits, all in black.

"You really look like a ninja warrior," I

347

told her. "It's kind of hot."

"Stereotyping won't get you anywhere with me."

She didn't argue when I said I looked more like a ninja accountant.

Before reaching the village, we exited the highway and drove up into the hills, following the GPS instructions until we reached the red dot pinned to Albalita's villa. Even in the darkness, partially relieved by a single streetlight, the property was easily matched to the street-view image captured on my iPad. We drove by and turned off onto a side street.

We took our black knapsacks and carrier vests out of the back of the Audi and put on the ski masks. Underneath were headpieces linked together via mobile phone connections, another simple expedient.

"Okay," I said, in a whisper over the phone, "let's do it."

We walked back to the house and turned down the neighbor's driveway, which paralleled the white wall on the south side. Halfway down, we stopped and I hoisted Natsumi up to the top of the wall. She jumped down on the other side and secured a rope to the base of a big ornamental bush. I pulled myself up with the rope, an approach that's far more difficult than it looks on TV. Natsumi did her best to help drag me over the top and we both landed more noisily than hoped for on another clutch of shrubbery.

We moved on to clear ground where we lay on our stomachs and listened for unwanted sounds, like a barking dog or burglar alarm. It stayed quiet long enough to encourage us to move toward the house. I looked through a pair of night vision goggles pulled from my pack, scanning for security cameras, but saw nothing, not even outdoor flood lighting. It didn't surprise me, Switzerland being such a safe country, Albalita's white wall more a matter of privacy than defense.

On the other hand, a lot of people in Switzerland owned guns.

At the side of the house, we stood to either side of a set of tall casement windows. I looked through the uncovered, single-pane glass and over a kitchen counter. I used the night vision goggles to scan the ceiling and saw that both corners within view were free of motion detectors.

I took a pair of suction cups and a diamond-tipped glass cutter out of my pack. I cut a hole large enough for me to fit through and used the suction cups to pull the cutout free of the window. The smell of cooking and cigarette smoke spilled out into the clear night air.

In a brief moment of indignity for Natsumi, I stepped on her back and wormed my way through the hole in the window. She fed our backpacks through, then followed. It was a tricky enough maneuver under any circumstances, though performing it soundlessly consumed most of the physical effort. Frequently pausing to listen for sounds inside the house, it took a painfully long time for both of us to be crouched up against the kitchen cabinets.

From there, we moved off into the house, praying for the kind of sturdy, squeak-free floor construction you'd expect from the Swiss.

The staircase was in the sitting room near the front door. I led the way up to the second floor. When we were in the hallway at the top of the stairs a cat stepped out of a bedroom door and let off a guttural meow that sounded as if it were amplified through a PA system. We both froze.

"Bernicia! *Tranquilo, calma!*" came a muffled woman's voice from inside the bedroom.

Bernicia moved toward us, her tail waving whip-like above arched haunches. She yowled again.

"Bernicia!" Albalita yelled, this time more clearly.

I moved past the cat, who swatted at my pant leg, and walked into the bedroom. Albalita was in a bed directly across the room, lying on her back. I took two long steps to cover the distance and jumped on top of her.

She didn't scream so much as make a wet animal sound not unlike her cat's. I sat hard on her stomach, my knees pinning her arms to the bed, and grabbed her by the throat, squeezing until her skinny but sinewy body stopped thrashing about.

I let the pressure off her throat. Natsumi came up and turned on the lamp on the bedside table. I took off the night goggles and looked down at the blurry image of Albalita as she also struggled to adjust to the incandescent light. Though not for long.

"You," she said, her panicked eyes fixed on mine.

"Hello, Albalita," I said. "You remember Natsumi?"

"Hello," said Natsumi.

"You can't be doing this," said Albalita.

"We need to have a candid conversation," I said. "I don't want to waste a lot of time debating. And I'm sure there're things you'd rather be doing. Like going back to sleep."

"What do you want?" she asked.

"To know why you tried to kill us. Why not just let us go?"

"I don't know what you're talking about."

"Because we saw your faces? That's what I think. We could identify you. You knew we could, and would. Pretty cold."

"You'll go to prison for this," she said.

"Did you know Chuck Andalusky was shot through the head?"

She stiffened underneath me.

"Ridiculous."

"Don't you wonder why? Unless you're the one who ordered the hit."

"That's nonsense."

"You thought you'd murdered us," I said. "What's another dead body?"

"Get off of me."

Instead I took my hands from her throat and gripped her head, with my thumbs pressed into her cheeks.

"Why did you capture us in the first place?"

"That was all Chuck's idea."

"Don't forget we were there," said Natsumi. "You were a willing participant."

She wiggled some more under my weight, to little avail. I tightened my grip on her head.

"Why," I repeated.

"You took something from us."

"How could I do that?" I asked. "I don't even know you."

Her eyes darted over to Natsumi.

"Is that what he told you?" she asked her.

"You haven't answered the question," said Natsumi.

"*Tu sabes la respuesta,* El Timador."

You know the answer, she said, calling me by the alias I'd used back when I was confronting the Basque terrorists. I moved my thumbs up from her cheeks to her eyes, which she involuntarily flicked closed. I put the pads of my thumbs on her eyelids.

"Say it," I told her, applying slight pressure to her eyes. With surprising strength, she tried to wrench her head to the side, but I held her firm. "After your eyeballs burst like a pair of ripe grapes, I will keep pushing until my thumbs penetrate the most human part of your brain." I pushed a little harder. "And from there, I'll just see how far I can get."

Her body writhed in fury as she absurdly tried to bite my hands. Gurgling noises came out of her throat, the precursor of an anguished scream. I put a little more pressure on her eyes.

"*Bastante! Por el amor de Dios!*" Enough, for the love of God.

I let up some of the pressure.

"Tell me."

"You took it from Joselito. You betrayed him," she said. "Why are you making me say this?"

I took my thumbs off her eyelids and her eyes snapped open, wide enough to show circles of white.

"How much did he take?" Natsumi asked.

I still had Albalita's head in my grasp, but her eyes looked over at Natsumi.

"I don't know for sure," she said. "We think about a billion."

"Where is Joselito?" I asked her.

Her panicked confusion deepened.

"In prison somewhere, of course. You put him there."

"When did you last have contact?" I asked.

"When your FBI arrested him. He sent me an e-mail through a friend on the outside. He told me the whole story, said to go to the accounts and look for myself. He wrote not to expect any more communication, that he was a dead man walking. He was afraid, I could tell."

"I still don't see what this has to do with El Timador," said Natsumi.

"Would you have let him poke out my eyes?" Albalita asked.

"Would you have forced him to watch me

354

be tortured?"

Albalita put her eyes back on me.

"Joselito worked for me. He showed me how to take the money. I was going to use it for good, just not the good your government had in mind." She shifted her eyes again toward Natsumi. I eased the grip on her head to make it easier. "Chuck was with me. We shared a vision. No one would ever have to know. And then you penetrated Joselito's computer and discovered everything. What were we to do? We faced ruin, personal and professional. And all those wonderful things we could have done slipped away like ghosts in the night. You don't know this?" she asked Natsumi, who stood silently.

"Then I pity you," said Albalita.

"How did you find us in the Caribbean?" I asked, regaining Albalita's attention.

"I don't know," she said. "That was all Chuck. Is he really dead?"

"Yes," said Natsumi.

"That's awful. He could be a brash man, but a good one."

"We're prepared to argue that," said Natsumi.

"Of course," said Albalita. "How would you know."

Bernicia chose that moment to jump on the bed and walk across Albalita's face. Albalita turned her head side to side to mitigate the effect.

"Bajar, tu gata loca!" Get off, you crazy cat.

I scooped Bernicia off the bed and handed her to Natsumi.

"I want a copy of that e-mail from Joselito," I said.

"You can't. I destroyed it," said Albalita.

"What computer did it come in on?"

"The one in my office. I deleted it."

I eased up off the supine form, though she made no effort to move. Bernicia popped back up on the bed, her little cat face filled with accusation. Albalita reached out and scratched under her chin.

I got all the way off the bed and Albalita quickly pulled herself up against the backboard, her bedclothes clutched to her chest. She shook as if recently dragged from a freezer. Bernicia made a grey ball of herself in the middle of the woman's lap and looked at us with wary malevolence.

"What was the good you were going to do," I asked Albalita, "with all that money."

She shook her head, pulling a sheet all the way to her mouth.

"Oh, no. That's not for you to know. Torture me if you want. I'll never tell El Timador, the ruiner of dreams."

We found her mobile phone and the junction box for the landlines, which I pulled off the wall. Before we left, I wrapped her wrists and ankles with duct tape. She took it with nearly listless resignation, the comparison with her treatment of us on the fishing boat floating around in the air, unsaid.

Halfway to Zurich, I sent a text to the cops in Küsnacht, telling them about the woman tied up in her house and asking for an immediate acknowledgment of the call. The second I got the message — demanding that I identify myself, describe my location, and wait in place for the authorities — I tossed the phone in Lake Zurich and drove north into the city.

Light was seeping up from the horizon as we pulled into the parking garage and replaced our black outfits with baseball caps, T-shirts, running shorts and shoes. The hotel's security cameras would record a couple back from a predawn run, their faces obscured by the hats, their gait slightly diminished by recent exertion.

I slept well for the next few hours, on top of the covers and still dressed in the workout gear. Natsumi wasn't as lucky, and as she reported, spent the time in a stuffed chair drinking wine and watching my chest calmly rise and fall.

CHAPTER 23

"How do you hide a billion dollars?" asked Natsumi, still sitting in the stuffed chair when I woke to the grey light settled over Zurich.

"With some difficulty," I said, as I swam up into full consciousness. "Create a series of shell businesses, buy off corrupt government officials in some equally corrupt country — no shortage of those. Break it up among a lot of different banks, mostly in places like the Cayman Islands, Liechtenstein, Bermuda, and Switzerland of course, though the rules governing tax havens are getting tighter all the time. It helps to be a criminal organization or kleptocracy with no aspirations of legitimacy."

"But how does a person do it, a single regular person?"

"How regular?"

"I don't know. As regular as me," she said.

"You don't. It's too big a number. You

hear the word 'billion' so much in the news you get inured to what it really means. To be a billionaire, you have to be a millionaire a thousand times over. That's way too much money to bury in the backyard."

She seemed to ponder that while sipping a cup of coffee that had taken the place of her wine of the night before.

"What about as regular as you," she said.

"I think we're getting rhetorical."

"Because you're not regular," she said.

"If modesty permits, no. I can do things most regular people wouldn't know how to do. On the other hand, even I can't hide a billion dollars."

"I wouldn't say that," she said, lightly. "I'm constantly astonished by what you can do. What you're capable of."

"In a good way?"

"Usually."

I got off the bed and went into the bathroom, where I threw cold water on my face and over my bald head, and brushed my teeth. As always, whenever I was in front of a mirror, I focused on the dent in my upper forehead left by the assassin's bullet. In addition to a general obsession with the old wound, I found it easier than looking myself in the eye.

When I came back to the bedroom, Natsumi was still in her chair, nursing her coffee.

"We have to split up," she said.

"Haven't we had this conversation before?"

"You're a fine analytical thinker, Arthur, except when you're so smart you miss the obvious."

There was something in her tone, more than her words, that stirred a twinge of panic somewhere deep in my nether regions.

"I don't think I'm going to like what you're about to say."

"Because you know it's true," she said. "We're finished. We're only here talking to each other because they want something from us. We can do things they can't. Like we did last night. Our freedom's an illusion. We're actually tagged animals they can scoop up anytime they want."

"I'm not so sure about that."

"I am. Jersey was fine leaving us on our own. He knows our true status. We're not dead anymore, we're official living breathing fugitives, prominent data points in a global database of bad actors. Worse, we don't know what they know. We don't know which of our aliases and stolen identities are compromised. So we can't trust anything digital — e-mail accounts, IP addresses, mobile phones, none of it. To say nothing of passports and driver's licenses."

"We still have clean identities in reserve."

"Okay, but what are we going to live on? Our working assets are starting to disappear. It's only a matter of time before they uncover the rest of our assets. You don't know if they haven't already, with the Feds just waiting around to snatch us up when it's convenient."

By training and temperament, I'd devoted my life to separating truth from fiction, to following the facts wherever they led, no matter where. So I had little experience with denial and avoidance, which was a pity, since at that moment I truly wished I could run from the words coming out of Natsumi's mouth.

Instead, I said, "I'm not giving up."

"We can't go on as a male Caucasian and female Asian. Way too easy to spot and track."

"What are you proposing?" I asked.

"It's no coincidence that TSA guy in New York asked me about blackjack. I'm a big, fat target. So I'm going to use the same passport to fly somewhere, and then do my best to shake the tail and disappear. You're going to use one of your reserve identities to hopefully disappear as well, and then figure out what to do next. I don't want to know what that is, because I can't reveal what I don't know."

"I don't want to lose you."

"When you really want something, you find a way," she said.

I told her I'd think about it, and went to take a shower. I had the door nearly closed when she called out to me.

"I have another question."

I leaned out the door, supporting myself on the doorknob.

"Okay."

"How does a person bring himself to shoot another person through the head?"

I wanted to give her an honest answer, so it took a moment.

"Self-preservation?" I asked.

Reading Natsumi's Asian countenance was never an easy thing, but she seemed satisfied with that answer. I went ahead and took my shower.

When I came back out of the bathroom, she was gone. The note on the dresser said, "My mother will know what to do."

I sat on the bed, naked, with the towel in my lap, and stared at the door. I'm not sure for how long. I used the time to think, or more accurately, to not think in the calculating, analytical way I knew best. My mind would never go entirely blank, but I got close, until I knew it was time to start thinking again.

I used that day to buy makeup and prosthetics from a theatrical supply house and change the shape of my face. The nose was the easiest part to bulk up a little, though I also added some extra flesh around my eyes. I bleached all the color out of my eyebrows and configured a convincing thatch of thinning white hair over my bald head.

The next morning, after downloading a few indispensable files onto a flash drive, I packed my day-to-day laptop and big external hard drive in a shipping box and crammed it into the black backpack. I stuffed a complete change of clothes, including sneakers, in the remaining space.

I took the service elevators to the ground floor and exited via the loading dock. I found a DHL office and shipped off the computer and external hard drive to one of their self-storage units.

I took a long hike to an aging industrial area, found a narrow brick alleyway that led to a concealed space where I burned all the potentially corrupted IDs. Then I took a train to Paris, and after a few days changing hotels, and ducking in and out of stores and restaurants, caught a ride through the

Chunnel with a chatty Brit I met in a café, who during the long trip to London exhausted my capacity for wholesale invention.

At Heathrow I used my remaining, as yet untested, passport and flew to JFK. Outside the terminal, behind a dumpster, I stripped off the white hair and cleaned the prosthetics off my face. I changed into worn jeans, sneakers and an old chambray shirt, and tossed my stylish traveling clothes into the dumpster.

From there, I used public transportation to get to New Haven, where I slept in the train station, then various outdoor spots around the city until my physical aspect took on the character of my apparent circumstances. In dire need of a shower, I tried to check into the YMCA. It was full, but I learned of an opening at "Second Chance University," a shelter for homeless, mostly drug-addicted and mentally ill men operating out of a rambling Victorian house a few blocks north of Yale.

In the attic was a big open room that served as a transient dorm for about twenty guys at a time. It wasn't directly supervised, but you had to go through a metal detector at the base of the stairs and be in for the night by nine o'clock.

To take possession of the free bed I had to pass muster with the staff psychologist. For this I drew on another research project, this one focused on finding employment for people with long-term intellectual disabilities. I chose bipolar disorder, since the manic phase most closely matched my normal disposition.

"You seem a little agitated," said the young man with a fine-haired beard and caring eyes. "Are you okay to talk?"

The office where we sat in the old house had ultrahigh ceilings, overpainted woodwork and the smell of decades without a deep cleaning. The psychologist sat in an ancient, wooden swivel chair and I was nearly swallowed up by an exhausted leather couch.

"Sure, talking's entirely cool with me," I said, tapping out a loose rhythm on the top of my knee.

"They tell me you have no identification."

"They tell you right. I got rolled sleepin' under a bridge in Wilmington, Delaware. Took my wallet, my pen knife, my meds and my lucky airplane."

"Airplane?"

"Little plastic airplane on a key ring. Had it since I was a kid."

"I'm sorry. What sort of meds?"

"I had the lithium and the aripiprazole. *Olé!*" I added, waving an invisible red cape.

"Who is your physician?"

"Now, that'd be hard to say since I was in a loony bin outside Phoenix, and the truth is, I stole about a six months supply of those pills out of an unlocked closet, for which they'd be more'n happy to throw my sorry ass in jail, so I'd rather not tell you anymore'n that. And I'm not particularly concerned with them meds so much as havin' a place to sleep where I'm not gonna get my ass kicked just for breathin' some other asshole's air."

"So you're feeling pretty good?" he asked me.

"Good? I'm feeling fan-fucking-tastic," I said. "Would feel even better if I got some sleep as it's goin' on three days of being scared to shut my eyes. TV would be nice, too. I used to steal TVs out of the dorm rooms at Michigan State, the big console ones, not as a living exactly, just 'cause it was so easy to do that in those days. Those TVs can pile up, though, big as they are. Too old to do that now. Can't handle the weight, though that's not as big a problem with the new flat screens. Just harder to get off the wall. You think Yale has a lot of flat screens?"

"I imagine they do, but I wouldn't advise stealing any of them," said the psychologist.

"Why not? Jail's one way to get three hots and a cot. Man, am I a poet or what?"

I got the cot anyway, and three hot meals, with no more questions asked. I felt reasonably safe, given the metal detector and brawny staff only one story away, but as a further precaution I bought a cheap plastic toothbrush and used my Swiss Army knife to whittle a sharp point out of the handle. I kept it in the back pocket of my jeans and kept my jeans on when I slept. The Swiss Army knife had to stay with the guys running the metal detector.

They also gave me a cocktail of psychotropic drugs, and fortunately didn't insist on watching me wash them down every day with my morning coffee. I told them I'd worked as a systems administrator back when I could still hold down a regular job, so I was able to be useful upgrading their software and troubleshooting hardware and network issues. In return I was left alone to wander about the little city and poke around Yale until I found what I wanted most. Secure broadband access.

It was in the basement of a satellite library supporting the anthropology department. A postdoc working on a paper took to me in a bookstore cum coffee shop across from the campus after I'd told her the story of my fall from social grace into mad vagrancy. I apparently fit into her thesis, which she tried to explain, though it made no more sense to me than it would have to an authentic street person.

Most importantly, she slipped me the password to the computer the university had given her to use over the course of her research, which provided me at least one tidy level of security.

The study room was little bigger than a closet — windowless, all white, with a black office chair and a silver Mac. A kind of academic tomb. Perfect for my state of mind.

I invested my first two online hours tracking down Strider.

"Long time, no hear," she wrote, once we snuck into a private chat room. "I have things for you."

"Good. I need things."

"Has to be a sit-down," she wrote, in other words, the web wasn't safe enough. "Shouldn't be hard for you, Spankman. It's, like, reality. The Final Frontier."

Then she signed off.

"Great," I told the stark, white room.

■ ■ ■ ■

Second Chance University didn't mind listing me as John Doe on their resident register. I wasn't the only one there with that name. They allowed us a week's anonymous stay under a type of rescue status. But if I wanted longer than that, I needed to fork over a name, some type of history, and financial capability.

I had taped to my torso enough money to buy their building, but it was more useful to appear broke. So I offered the psychologist, whose name was Cary McNichol, a form of community service.

"Here's the deal," I said, after pulling him into a private room. "If I volunteer my time to one of the do-gooder operations you got around this town, can I stick here for like another month or so? If things go well, I'll get a credential I can use to get a regular job. Then I'm out of your hair."

"You're not in our hair," said Cary, with a kind smile. "Not yet, anyway. I suppose it's worth a try. How're you feeling?"

He meant, are you in control of your mania.

"Right as rain. Seriously." I held up my hand to show how steady it was. "Totally in control."

"Okay, have any organization in mind?"

"Yeah, in fact I have. The People Project. You just gotta tell 'em I'm a resident in good standing and a great man to have around a computer. Everybody's got computer issues. Look at yourselves."

He didn't argue that.

"I know the director, Sylvan," he said. "It's only a satellite office focused on fundraising. Their headquarters are in Switzerland. Why them?"

"Fund-raisers have big databases, which means data-crunching applications that I guarantee are in need of scrubbing and polishing. That's me all over. Mr. Cleanup."

He took my elbow and gently moved me back into the hall and toward his office.

"I can make the introduction, but no guarantees. Sylvan's a really good guy, but he doesn't have the bandwidth for micromanagement."

Another tacit warning not to act like a crazy person.

"Read you loud and clear, Cary. You won't get any blowback over me."

"You just owe me one more thing," he said.

"What's that?"

"A name."

"Stan Lee?"

"Inventor of super powers?"

"Something like that."

He let me sit in his office while he had a friendly call with Sylvan van Leeuwan, clearly a brother in New Haven's fraternity of social welfare professionals. He pitched my concept like a seasoned sales pro, and partway through gave me a thumbs-up. Cary McNichol was an easy man to like.

He made it even easier by walking me south to The People Project offices, which were above a corner restaurant on Chapel Street across from the New Haven Green. A big woman with a colossal head of unkempt frizzy hair jumped up from her desk and threw her arms around Cary, who took it as well as you could expect. Neither her cranberry-colored sweater or matching polyester pants were big enough to conceal her lumpy bulk. She looked me fiercely in the eye when she shook my hand and introduced herself as Finnegan.

"Geek, huh?" she said to me. "Where's your pocket protector?"

"The geek police made us turn 'em in. They're upgrading our image."

Her laugh was mostly a snort.

"We don't want any police trouble around here," she said.

"Won't get any from me," I said, looking around her at her computer screen. "What're you running for your back-end database?"

"C-View Plus. I think the plus part means extra aggravation."

"Stayin' current on updates?" I asked.

"That's the problem. Every time I update it gets worse."

An older, slightly heavier version of Cary came out of his office. The men hugged and traded laughs in the opaque way insiders usually do.

"Cary has good things to say about your computer skills," he said, as if just realizing I was standing there. He had the accent of a Dutch person who'd likely spoken English his whole life.

"I know C-View well enough," I said, telling him I'd trained on the original open source application that C-View was derived from. The speed with which his eyes began to glaze over was encouraging. There would be plenty of systems work there at The People Project satellite office.

"What do you know about vacuum cleaners?" said Finnegan. "Havin' trouble with one of them, too. Kidding," she added, looking over at Sylvan.

They told me to come back the next

morning so they had a chance to set up my own workstation and decide how to get me started. I thanked them with more gratitude than appropriate, though actually heartfelt.

Cary walked me back to the big Victorian house.

"When was the last time you had a regular job?" he asked, as we walked.

"Depends how you define regular," I said. "I've actually learned a lot more since things have been a little irregular. Necessity bein' the best of all mothers of invention."

"Can I ask you a personal question?"

"You're a fuckin' shrink, man. You can ask me anything you want."

"I know, but I respect your privacy."

"So ask," I said.

"Did you leave anybody behind? When you left, wherever you left from."

"Whoa, Nelly. I didn't mean you could ask me *that* kinda shit."

"I thought so."

We walked in silence for a while, both of us with our hands stuffed in the pockets of our jackets. Bulling along over the tattered but irrepressible New Haven sidewalks.

"How'd you know?" I asked, eventually giving in.

"How do you know how to fix computers?"

That was the last we spoke of it. I left him and went upstairs, through the metal detector and into the big open room where a few of the guys, like me, were in early, taking advantage of the daylight to organize their paltry belongings, sleep off a hit of meds or simply lie on their beds and either ignore or bathe in their respective sorrows and regret.

CHAPTER 24

Things come to people in the middle of the night. I'm no different. That night two things came to me simultaneously. In a half dream, I knew how to find Strider, and as I rose up into a much more wakeful state, realized I was being robbed.

I was lying on my side in such a way that I could see the pale movements of a man with his hand inside the front pocket of my backpack. I stayed still and watched through partially closed eyes, getting my bearings and gaining full consciousness.

It was the guy who'd just taken possession of the bunk next to me. I'd barely noticed him since the men came and went with such regularity it rarely made sense to get sociable. Though I did recall he had long hair, more haphazard than entirely unkempt. A younger man than me, but not by much. Clearly stronger, judging by the shape of his forearm.

Hoping he was too focused on the backpack to see me slide the tips of my fingers into the back pocket of my jeans until I felt the bristle end of my modified toothbrush. I slipped my hand deeper into the pocket until I established a firm grip. Then I waited to see what the man would do next.

I was disappointed to see him move from the front pocket that only held a small notebook, to the zipper that opened the pack's principal compartment. However, the greater angle forced him into a more awkward position, so that much of his upper torso had slid off his bunk.

In more or less a single motion, I rolled over far enough to free my left hand, which I used to grab a handful of his stringy hair, and used my right to bring the business end of the toothbrush up under his chin.

He froze. I growled.

"Not cool, dude," I said.

"Easy, brother," said the guy, in a near whisper. "Don't mean to offend."

"I'm extremely offended. You think you can steal from me?" I asked.

"I did, yes. Apparently I was wrong."

"No shit. So I shouldn't shove this shiv up into your brain?"

"You could," he said. "Though the prosecution will consider manslaughter a disproportionate response to attempted petty theft. The point of that thing is actually beginning to puncture my skin. What do you say?"

I pulled back on the shiv and he rolled back onto his bed.

"At least you've succeeded in stealing my sleep," I said. "What little I get of it."

"I can see how that would be. Sorry."

"I'm gonna get your ass tossed out of here."

"You won't have to. I'll go voluntarily."

"What did you do it for?"

"Meds. I like to experiment."

"I would've given you some if you'd asked," I said.

"How am I supposed to know that?"

"By asking. I just said that."

"Want to guess what's wrong with me?" he asked.

"I'm not into 'What's My Disease.' "

"Schizoaffective disorder. How 'bout you?"

"I don't want a friend. Especially one who steals my shit."

"That's simply your assumption. *Cogitationis poenam nemo patitur.*"

"Bullshit. *Animus nocendi,*" I answered, despite myself.

"Lawyer?"

377

"Polyglot."

"I had my own law firm specializing in intellectual property, and then I lost my mind. Uh? You don't think that's funny? They tossed me out of the bar when I got sick. Clearly discriminatory, don't you agree?"

"You should get yourself a lawyer."

I lay on my side facing him. I took my pack off the floor and clutched it to my chest.

"My name is Davis," the guy said. "My first name, not my last. I have to explain this every time. I think it might be the origin of my trouble."

"I'm going to sleep now. Please keep your hands off my stuff."

"The threat of death is a decent deterrent, no matter what they say." He rolled over with his back to me. "You could tell me your name. I told you mine."

"Stan."

"*Compos mentis* to all, and to all a good night."

The next day was Saturday. I took the train down to New York and made the quick walk from Grand Central Station to the giant hotel where the Star Trek convention was in its first big day. I had a simple strategy —

expose myself, as myself, to as many convention-goers as possible. I might have spotted Strider in the guise of Uhura, Deanna Troi or Captain Janeway, but un-likely. That I also might be spotted by an FBI agent or a known threat like Ian MacPhail was a distinct possibility, but I had no other way to proceed.

There were thousands of people at the conference. I moved from room to room, standing at doorways when large audiences flowed out of ballrooms, mingled at recep-tions and coffee stations, hung in the bar and gently avoided attempts to engage me in conversation. It was a long day of study-ing faces and negotiating crowds of aliens and Starfleet personnel.

I'd booked a room a few blocks away, and was making one last pass through the bar area before retreating to my hotel room when a small hand took me by the sleeve.

It was T'Pol, the Vulcan liaison officer. Actually, Strider's nicely rendered imper-sonation.

"You continue to impress, Spanky," she said.

The magnitude of my pleasure at seeing her there in the flesh, albeit in modified form, surprised me. I told her as much.

"I'm happy to see you, too," she said. "I'm

worried about you."

"I'm worried about me, too."

"Let's find a dark corner."

I let her buy me one of her hurricanes, further proof that I'd become slightly unhinged by the bizarre nature of the day. We clinked.

"You actually look a lot like T'Pol," I told her.

"The one thing these boobs are good for."

"Did you just spot me?"

"This morning. I've been stalking you all day. Making sure you're alone."

"Why wouldn't I be?"

"If you were already busted. You're not, are you?" she asked.

"I don't think so. I'm off the net. Actually, pretty much off the grid."

"That's why I got worried," she said. "You disappeared."

"Except for the connection I made with you. I had to chance that."

"A rare exposure for such a sneaky guy," she said. "El Timador."

"So you know the name."

"Whoever hacked your bank account is chasing the handle El Timador. I put two and two together."

"So who's the hacker?" I asked.

"No hard ID, but I know a few things.

Operates outside of the usual crowd. Stays out of discussions except to ask about El Timador. Otherwise, just lurks. No luck so far chasing down his IP. Very good at covering his tracks."

"You don't think it's a team."

"No. He works alone. In fact, a total loner."

"So not the government?"

"No, not at all. Unless they hired him freelance. That could be. Those people are getting smarter by the day. Makes me feel like we're all doomed."

She held her hurricane with two hands and drew a large portion down through the straw. Her fingernails were still chewed up, though much cleaner, as if recently scrubbed.

"I don't like the sound of that," I said.

She smiled at me over the top of her drink.

"You are such a romantic," she said. "Look, the next war will absolutely be fought in cyberspace. That means governments are putting the best brains they can buy into hacking each other's networks, public and private. Talk about an arms race. Or a Cold War. The fun times, when banks and universities and all these other dumb institutions were like naive little lambs any of us could lead to slaughter, that's ending

381

fast. That's how I know you got a lone wolf on your ass. If it were a government attack team, you'd already be splatter."

I sat back in my seat and tried to process what she was saying. She noticed.

"I can't believe you don't know this," she said. "You really are off the grid."

"I'm a little lost," I said, surprising myself yet again.

"I wish I knew your story," she said. "I can't help it. You interest me."

It might have been the effects of social isolation, Internet withdrawal, or the hotel's hurricane recipe, but without hesitation, I launched into a description of my past and the path that had led me to that moment. Her face was uncharacteristically filled with wonder.

"Holy crap."

"I have no right to ask for your help," I said, "but I need it."

"Just don't say it's a mission. Everyone in this hotel is on a mission."

"Okay, a project. Specifically The People Project. Get in there as deep as you can get."

"What am I looking for?" she asked.

"Hidden money. A lot of it."

She flagged down the waiter and ordered another hurricane. I demurred.

"Okay," she said. "And I assume you'll be

doing the same?"

"I will. We'll probably meet somewhere deep in the bowels of their global database."

"Thanks for that visual."

We talked for another hour, exchanging signals and signs and other ways to identify each other and communicate within The People Project infrastructure and cyberspace at large. We also managed to exchange a few laughs, which made me feel bathed in comfort and understanding.

By then the hour had grown late and the crowd in the bar had thinned to the usual noisy few. I felt exhausted and overexposed. Strider read my mind.

"Time to go," she said.

"It is."

"I'm not inviting you to my room, but that doesn't mean I don't like you," she said.

"I wouldn't accept the invitation, but that doesn't mean I don't like you as well."

"Good answer."

We parted and I made it to my much smaller and cheaper hotel with no incident or occasion to feel any less hopeful or invigorated. It was profoundly odd to enter a room without a computer, tablet or smartphone to obsessively check in on. No e-mails, texts or voice messages demanding an instant response. All I had was a bed crammed into a tiny room, lots of street noise outside and a stream of frantic and unwanted mental images to subdue before I could fall into a deep, yet restless sleep.

Back at The People Project New Haven, I gained a better grasp on their standing within the hierarchy of the organization. Tenuous.

Their stated purpose was to raise funds from the abundant wealth and charitable impulses within the high-net-worth community along the Connecticut shoreline. The reality was more nuanced. There was indeed a lot of money slopping around the coasts of Long Island Sound, but competition for those dollars was fierce. And the expectations of The People Project home office in Zurich, driven by highly optimistic statistical models, guaranteed that nothing New Haven ever did was good enough. The stress showed.

Sylvan van Leeuwan was always in the office when I arrived in the morning, and there when I left at night. His pale face had a sheen as if overwork had degraded his basic hygiene. But he was friendly to me, and it wasn't hard to engage him in conversation and ask him important questions, such as his heart's desire for his New Haven operation.

"I want a couple of millionaires who have us in their will to drop dead," he said.

"I might be able to help you with that."

"Debugging software would be fine for now."

It took a few days to untangle the mess Finnegan had made of the database and fund-raising application that served as the front end. It was satisfying work, but most importantly, I was able to poke around the interface with The People Project's home network under her administrative password. Eventually, I found a wormhole through the e-mail system. Strider was surely right about the tightening noose of cybersecurity, but the latest precautions had yet to reach the IT department at The People Project.

I looked over the top of my monitor at Finnegan working just a few feet away. I could see her screen, but she couldn't see mine. I sent her an e-mail with a list of things she'd need to do as part of the database cleanup.

"Thanks a lot," she said over her shoulder. "Do I have to do it now?"

"It would help."

As she bent to the task, I slipped into the servers in Zurich and made a survey of the file structures. I wrote everything out on a pad of paper, tearing off the pages and stuffing them into my back pocket before Finnegan emerged from her labors with a triumphant, "Got it. Done!"

At the next opportunity, I went directly to Albalita's e-mail in search of correspondence with Andalusky or Joselito, but whatever might have been there, it wasn't there anymore. Not just deleted, which I knew how to recover. Gone, like it never existed.

But I pressed on. Over the next week, I not only gained mastery over The People Project's global network, I made contact with Strider and set up communications within a folder buried deep inside an administrative backwater. As hoped, she already had burrowed her way through the accounting department, and had deposited a copy of "Audited Financials, Current and Year Prior" into our secret file. I thanked her and loaded the documents onto a flash drive, which I took to an office supply place around the corner and had printed out and secured inside a ring binder.

On lunch hours I sat on the New Haven Green and lost myself inside columns of numbers and arid financial commentary. Luckily, everything was in English, as required by the people for whom the audit was most importantly undertaken. The Société Commerciale Fontaine, fiduciaries for the US State Department.

While I could find my way around reasonably well, accounting and finance weren't strengths of mine. Luckily, they were Strider's, who revealed to me she had her CPA and a master's in economics.

"Why else do you think I'd want to hack banks?" she'd written when I was back on the computer in the Yale study room. "It takes a crook to know a bunch of crooks."

So I felt confident in where our joint inquiry eventually netted out. The books were clean as a whistle, and so was The People Project. Over the course of five years, a billion and a half dollars had flowed from the US Treasury through Fontaine to The People Project, which distributed the money in the form of microloans to thousands of tiny businesses throughout the world.

"Every penny's accounted for," Strider wrote.

"If you believe the audit."

"We have to. The auditors are a giant accounting firm who'd be ruined if they screwed up anything attached to federal money."

"Albalita said she and Joselito took a billion dollars. Which I then somehow stole out of the accounts."

"Not a chance. You can't just swipe a billion dollars."

"That's what I keep saying."

"I need to get behind the numbers the auditing firm was using. It'll take some pretty serious forensics. And time."

"I understand."

We confirmed our communications protocols and I watched her blink away, while ignoring, almost successfully, a faint pang of renewed loneliness. Which is probably why I leapt without hesitation into a role I'd played before, and had hoped to never repeat.

Bait.

It was absurdly easy. I merely had to go to websites run by Black Hats and White Hats, hackers and those in the service of defeating hacking, and post this simple message:

"Yo bank robber. Catch me if you can. El Timador."

Then I logged into a site run by market researchers, to kill time, and consume what amounted to intellectual comfort food, before jumping back into the world of cybersecurity.

The message was in Spanish: "El Timador. You're a dead man."

I wrote back: "I've heard that before."

"This time it's true. You ruin my life, I ruin yours."

"Joselito?"

The man who'd served Spanish death squads, whom I helped put away in a federal prison so deep he'd likely never be heard from again. A man who was supposed to be banished from the Internet for the rest of his life.

"Si, El Timador. I'm coming."

Having had a bullet smash through my skull, I was sensitive to the psychologist's claim that the brain could be smarter than the mind. That there were thoughts going on in the background that your consciousness wasn't privy to, but were nevertheless far more brilliant and perceptive. I don't know about that, but I do know at the moment I read those lines from Joselito, I knew what had happened, and what I had to do about it.

"I'll be waiting," I wrote.

I forwarded the e-mail chain to Strider, then logged off the site and the computer, picked up my backpack and walked slowly back to my dorm bed at the Second Chance University.

CHAPTER 25

There were two packages wrapped like birthday presents on my bunk when I got to the open dorm. My next-door neighbor, Davis, the guy who tried to steal my meds, was sitting on his own bunk, waiting for me.

"They're from me," he said. "I bought them for you."

"New strategy? More blessed to give than receive? By stealing?"

"If you insist on putting it that way, which happened a long time ago, by the way."

"It did. Sorry."

"Go ahead. Open them up, but don't take anything out." He looked around the room. I got the message. "Start with the one on the right."

Inside the package was a slim knife handle, yellow, etched with the name "Stan."

"It's a switchblade. Ceramic. Almost weightless. I made it on the 3D printer. Open the other one."

Inside that box was a tiny automatic pistol, bright red, with my name on the grip.

"Also ceramic," Davis whispered. "It takes real .32-caliber rounds. Not a lot of range or accuracy, but close in, it'll do the job. Kind of a chick gun, but fun, right?"

"How did you get this stuff in here?"

He laughed and slapped me on the shoulder.

"They're ceramic. Go through any metal detector. But you knew that already. You'll have to buy the bullets on the outside."

"Okay," I said. "Why?"

He laughed again, though more of a whinny.

"I wanted to prove a point. If I'd meant to kill you, you'd be dead by now. But I didn't. I just wanted to steal your meds."

"You're still worryin' about that?"

"Not worrying, obsessing. I'm a moral animal. I'm not a thief. It troubles me deeply that you'd think so."

"I forgot about it long ago," I said.

"I didn't. So there you go. Now you can kill me if you want to."

"When did you do this?"

"My clients have a prototyping business here in New Haven. I just had to hack into the CAD-CAM and download designs I pulled off the web. Ran it remotely over the

391

weekend and broke through a window Sunday night to retrieve the goods. Easy peasy."

I put the lids back on the boxes and put them in my backpack.

"Have you noticed our world has become exceedingly strange?" I asked him.

"Are you kidding me? I'm legally insane. Who knows better?"

I slept that night with both the ceramic gun and switchblade under my pillow. Though not so soundly.

I spent a good part of the next day in the tougher parts of New Haven scoring a handful of .32-caliber bullets, which I loaded in the ceramic gun and test-fired in a state park about an hour by bus north of the city. My hand and the gun came through intact, and true to Davis's word, it wasn't a straight shooter, but would put a hole in anything less than four feet away.

Easy peasy.

Since I could think of no reason not to, I had both the knife and gun in my pocket the next time I went to the study room at Yale to work on the computer. Traffic through the building was always light, so it wasn't that big an accomplishment to notice two sturdy-looking white guys with short hair in khakis and polo shirts hanging around the front door engaged in a nearly theatrically phony semblance of a conversation.

As I approached, one of them opened the door and welcomed me in Spanish. I acted befuddled and said, "Yes, of course. Whatever you say."

I headed through the building and down the stairs to the study room, daring a few looks over my shoulder, but saw no one following. I went into the sterile study room and shut the door. I noticed for the first time there was no lock. I thought about that for a moment, and after examining the tiny window up near the ceiling, I left the room, just in time to hear the sound of footsteps descending the stairway at the end of the echoing basement corridor. I moved quickly in the opposite direction.

I'd never been in that part of the building, a lapse I mentally kicked myself for making. It was quite a warren of study rooms and comfortable seating areas, kitchenettes and open areas often filled with folding chairs set in a circle. But no exits, as far as I could see.

The footfalls I'd heard on the stairs started coming down the hall. I picked up the pace, though shy of a full run. The hallway was filled with angles, seemingly endless and utterly devoid of escape routes. I kept moving and looking.

The footsteps grew loud enough for me to steal another glance behind, but it was clear. I started to run in earnest, though that made it harder to try for unlocked doors, so I went back to a fast walk.

I found a stairwell and bounded up to the next floor. When I pushed open the door leading to the hallway I nearly bowled over a young woman who had her face stuck in a book as she walked. She pulled back, alarmed, and I apologized as I rushed by. Other students were moving down the hallway, through which I moved quickly until I came to a lounge where at least a half dozen of them were nestled into comfortable sofas and chairs, plugged into earphones, smartphones, laptops and tablets. I sat on a sofa, put my hands in my lap and waited.

The two men I'd seen in front of the building stopped at the door, looked in the room, then moved on. The girl sitting next to me pulled her white earphones from her ears and looked at me curiously. As a bald man in his forties with no devices, I'm sure I presented a profound oddity. I smiled at her and left the room. More students were filling the hall. I went back outside and looked up and down the street, but my pursuers were nowhere in sight.

I headed back toward Second Chance. Before I got there, I saw a young man speaking on a smartphone. I stood there until he ended his call and offered him two hundred dollars if he let me use it.

"I'll only be a couple minutes. You can stand there and watch me."

"You're shittin' me, right?"

I handed him the two hundred dollar bills and he shrugged and gave me his phone. I used the browser to go into a website where I left a message for Strider:

"Keep looking. It's there for sure."

I found Cary McNichol in his office. He seemed happy to see me.

"Stan the Man. Have a seat."

I held my backpack in my lap when I sat down.

"Can you tell if a person's insane, even if they don't know themselves?" I asked.

"Sometimes," he said. "It depends."

"I had a serious traumatic brain injury."

"I know. From the scars, I'm guessing a bullet. I did my residency at Yale New Haven in psychiatric emergency. We had a lot of that kind of thing."

"Went straight through," I said. "Skimmed the frontal and took out a piece of the parietal and somatosensory cortex."

"You've retained considerable function."

"Some of it rewiring. Most of it, I think. I've had a lot to keep my brain busy."

"You're to be commended," he said.

"Not so sure. Is there a guy named Davis in the bunk next to me?"

He cocked his head and looked at me more closely.

"Davis Anderson. The man with two last names. Why do you ask?"

"I'm wondering about delusions."

"You're not bipolar, are you."

"No," I said. "But I did have a bad brain injury. I'm wondering how things might evolve after general recovery. That is, after you think you're okay, can things start to go wrong?"

"Without diagnostic equipment and a rigorous workup, I'd be guessing, too."

"That's okay," I said. "I won't hold you to anything."

"Then I guess scar tissue," he said.

"What do you mean?"

"Not the brain itself, but the skull and related material. It can harden and push down on the grey matter. Shows up over time. It can cause a cascade of mental abnormalities, though nobody exactly knows the process. It's too rare to get much research attention, but back in the psych ER we saw it enough."

"The symptoms come on gradually, as the pressure builds," I suggested.

"Something like that. That scar in front looks very close to important executive functions. That's where I'd start to look."

"Personality?" I asked.

"That's part of it."

"Paranoid delusion?"

"Sometimes, sure."

I thanked him and gave him two thousand dollars that I'd extracted from the money belt around my waist when I was in the bathroom a few moments before.

"Wow. Nice surprise," he said.

"It's to help out around here. Just don't give any to The People Project," I told him. "They're fine."

"You should know."

"I should."

I walked to the New Haven train station and caught Metro North into Grand Central. From there, I found another shelter specializing in homeless, anonymous men and crawled into another bunk with clean, white, stiff sheets and fell into a paranoia-free sleep for the next twelve hours.

I got hold of Strider from a computer in the cathedral that is the New York Public Library. I was in a room with soaring, coffered ceilings, walls lined with real books and desks lit by brass lamps. There were a lot of people surrounding me, but the voices rarely rose above a murmur, even from the tourists passing through, their faces behind clicking smartphones.

"I found it," she wrote.

"In plain sight," I wrote back.

"Pretty much. You knew?"

"I had a theory."

"You could have shared."

"I needed you to get there on your own," I wrote. "Did you document?"

"Of course."

"Can you bar access?"

"Already done. I just had to change a single string of code. Incredibly elegant, but ultimately a little sloppy, if you ask me."

"Any luck on the IP address of that e-mail string I sent you?"

"Haven't really been concentrating on that."

"Could you?"

"Come back in a half hour."

I logged off and used the time to walk

398

around the stacks and read book spines. I opened a few and enjoyed the typeset pages and aroma of aging paper. I recalled little of the subject matter, probably because I wasn't really reading, just wandering aimlessly, the working part of my mind preoccupied with other things.

I gave Strider another forty-five minutes before logging back on.

"Didn't you say you're from Connecticut?" she wrote.

"I am. Stamford."

"Greenwich is next door, right?"

"Yup."

"That's where the IP is. The e-mail came from somewhere in Downtown Greenwich."

She gave me a physical address. It was a law firm — Calle, Cowles and Espinoza.

"What's he doing there?" I asked.

"That's where the e-mail came from. Don't know if it's a him, a her, or an it. To get any closer I'd have to hack their firewall, which is doable, but probably won't give you a name."

"That's okay. Close enough. And nice work."

"It wasn't easy," she wrote. "I'm half dead from lack of sleep and Red Bull overdose. And I had to call in a lot of favors. Exposed myself."

"Secure the data, pack everything up and take a seriously off-line vacation. On me."

"You're scary," she wrote.

"I'm grateful," I said.

"Is there an end to this?"

"Wait for my signal," I wrote and signed off.

America isn't a kind place to a person without a car. Luckily, with an abundance of public transportation, not always the cleanest or easiest to navigate, the New York metro area was the least unkind. A string of cabs, trains and shuttle buses got me to La Guardia in Queens. From there, it was a simple matter of finding the sort of limousine service airport security stridently cautioned you to avoid.

Even as a law-abiding market researcher, it was a technique I often used: lurk around where the drivers dropped off their fares and look for the face of a bored, defiant or simply greedy individual. There was no lack of these at La Guardia.

It helped if the driver worked for himself and had a car with impenetrable windows. I profiled a guy with a gross belly, loosened tie and cigarette sticking out of an unkempt face. He told me to go fuck myself. So I tried another guy, slim and elegantly put together, who looked skeptical, but perked up at the roll of cash I flicked in front of him.

"Not here," he said. "Go to the next terminal and wait at the crosswalk."

I thought the odds were fifty-fifty, but he showed up and I jumped in.

"What'll it take for the whole day?" I asked. "Up to Connecticut and back."

He told me and I said okay, let's do it.

It was so comfortable in the backseat of the impeccably preserved Crown Vic I almost slid into sleep. The driver, with whom I never exchanged names, felt no need for casual conversation. More likely, chose reserve as the safer choice. He just nodded and punched the address I gave him into his dash-mounted GPS and we swept up through the urban majesty of New York and onto Connecticut's narrow greenways.

When we got to Rocky Hill, I asked him to park at the diner a few buildings down from the Jason P. Fellingham Academy of the Military Arts. I gave him half the fee we'd agreed upon and expressed hope that he'd wait for me to earn the other half.

"For an hour. Tops," he said.

"More than I need."

The massive woman was at her station at the front entrance. She greeted me as if she'd never seen me before. I bought a ticket, but didn't bother to ask for Colonel Gross. I knew where to find him.

The door to Archives was open, but Shelly wasn't at the worktable. I stood and listened, and finally heard shuffling noises coming from inside the towering shelves. I cleared my throat and out he came, holding a stack of accordion folders with both hands.

"Like a bad penny," he said.

"Nice to see you, too."

He sat at the worktable and called security, telling them he had a rude, but approved visitor. He assured them he'd hit the alert should any concern arise.

"Will concerns arise?" he asked me, as he hung up the phone.

"That depends."

"Where's Miss Fitzgerald?"

"I don't know. We split up."

"Sorry about that."

"It was after we got a visit from Jersey Mitchell. In Zurich. It was the only way to shake the tail. At least I hope we shook the tail."

"I wouldn't know," he said, patting his stack of folders, as if assuring them they'd have his attention back in a moment. "Nobody tells me anything."

"Then how did you know Joselito Gorrotxategi was in an undisclosed maximum security prison?"

"Because they used to tell me things."

"What if they're lying?" I said.

"Not a chance. And it's not a they, it's a him. Cleanest possible source."

"Captain Perry?"

"Yes," he said, without hesitation. "Not that I owe you an explanation."

"Joselito isn't in custody. At least the most important part of him isn't. He's online, free to roam the web at will."

"Impossible."

"You could say that with a bit more conviction."

"Why's that?" he asked.

"Because you knew."

Shelly never looked his age to me, despite the white hair and age spots on his hands. Looking at him then, I wasn't so sure.

"That's quite an accusation," he said.

"Captain Perry's been your go-to guy all along. He's your dear friend at the bureau. You've been feeding him information about us in return for getting back on the inside. You sold us out for a bagful of ego."

"The young man on the other end of this phone can crack you in half with one hand," he said.

"You knew about Joselito all along. But

no warning. How come?"

"I'm not in the position to discuss national security with you, of all people."

"You knew what Joselito planned to do to me. And to Natsumi. That doesn't bother you?"

"My personal feelings have nothing to do with this. And don't be so quick to condemn. I could have had you collared whenever I wanted to."

"But you didn't. Though not out of the goodness of your heart. We were supposed to operate freely. Why?"

"Your sister is safe," he said. "I made sure of that." He picked up the phone and redialed the security guy. "My visitor needs to be escorted from the building."

I stood back from the door with my arms held parallel to the ground. Moments later the dark-skinned man with the light blue eyes was a few feet away from me in a semi-crouched stance.

"Stay cool, sergeant," I said to him. "Just leaving."

He followed me through the museum, past the big woman who held a hand to her heart as she watched us go through the front door. The young military man stood there until I was through the gate and on my way to my reticent, but honorable limo driver.

CHAPTER 26

Instead of going all the way to the city, I asked the driver to drop me off in Stamford. It felt good to be back on home turf. Good, though a bit strange.

There was little danger anyone would recognize me, since I didn't look much like the guy who disappeared off the face of the earth several years before. Never a very social person, the few people I chatted with around the neighborhood were out toward the suburbs, and thus several socioeconomic light years from the tired city street where the limo driver dropped me off.

But it was where the home advantage mattered. In the midst of the AIDS epidemic, I'd done some pro bono work for a non-profit which was trying to distribute clean needles to a community the group tactfully described as highly disorganized. After a few weeks of face-to-face interviews, I'd learned how well organized their daily commerce actually was.

It taught me a lot about secure communications, transportation and housing. The last in the form of a motel that took cash for time increments beginning by the hour. No one stayed there long enough to determine limits at the other end.

I paid a week in advance and wrote the name of a famous baseball player in the register.

"Good luck with the season," said the old lady behind the counter.

I asked her where I could buy a ride, cheap. She directed me to a gentleman named Mo, who operated out of a muffler shop a few blocks over. Mo was about the same vintage, his hair mostly white and his skin reminiscent of weathered Naugahyde.

"I don't want to have to change the plates," I told him, when he asked for my specifications.

"Then you're talkin' a rental. I don't do rentals."

"Not exactly. I'll buy it, drive it, then give it back to you when I'm done."

"Hm," he said, pondering the opportunity. "That sounds like a pretty good deal for me, till the po-lice are here wonderin' what my car's doin' somewhere it ain't supposed to be."

"How about a combo? You rent it to me, then I steal it. Like a week from now."

"Innovative," he said.

"You'll probably still get it back. Either way, you're ahead."

He bought the logic and I bought a '95 Toyota Corolla, probably the closest thing to a generic car ever produced. It was clean and in good repair, despite the odometer reading that approached 200,000.

"Is that the actual mileage?" I asked the guy, as he handed me the keys.

"Probably not, actually. Do you care?"

"No."

I used the car to drive to a menswear shop specializing in business suits about as eye-catching as the Toyota. A few doors down, I bought an attaché case to match. The third purchase was more difficult, since the number of places you could buy a fake moustache in Stamford wasn't unlimited. The result was a mighty walrus affair that went with a Civil War uniform on sale at a costume shop.

The young girls in the shop convinced me their giggling shouldn't be misinterpreted, that in fact the moustache made me look quite distinguished. We used a high quality adhesive, which helped me to bring the thing under control after just a few minutes in front of a mirror with a pair of sharp scissors.

I drove to Greenwich and located the offices of Calle, Cowles and Espinoza.

They were just outside the denser part of town in a low, free-standing building. Across the street was the landscaped corner of another office complex, this one much larger. There was no easy place to park or lurk, though you could watch the entrance to the firm's building from an enclosed bus stop about fifty yards down the street.

Not good enough.

So I parked in the parking lot and found their office, which only occupied about a quarter of the second floor, though they'd dedicated a fair amount of floor space to the enclosed reception area. A man with a large head covered in a mat of buzz-cut white hair sat at the raised desk, on the front of which the name of the firm was elegantly etched in frosted glass.

"Can I help you?" he asked, as if that was the last thing he wanted to do.

"I'm here to talk about your documents."

"Do you have an appointment?"

"There's someone in this office who wakes up every night at three A.M. worrying about document security."

"That could be," he said, "but you won't

be putting them back to sleep without an appointment."

"In an office this size, that person is probably the managing partner. And I bet you're his direct report."

"Hers. If you leave me your card, I'll get it to her."

I imagined a wastebasket under his desk filled to overflowing with business cards.

"We're supposed to give it to the person directly," I said.

He looked at me as if deciding between a polite refusal and a swift kick. Then a door well hidden in the wall opened and a roundish young woman with pale troubled skin walked into the room.

"Ah, perfect timing," I said, "You must be the managing partner."

"That'll be the day," she said.

"Oh," I said, disappointed. "We were about to give her a call."

"Wait a minute," said the guy.

"Do you mind bringing me back?" I asked. "I just need to give her some documents. I'm not allowed to leave them at the desk. Chain of custody."

"Whoa," said the guy. "Hold the phone."

The woman looked at him with ill-disguised annoyance.

"I can handle this," she said. "Ms. Franklin is in her office, but she's probably busy."

I held up my briefcase.

"Two seconds. I hand her the documents and walk right out the door. On tippy-toes."

"Hey," said the guy.

The woman smiled at me in a way clearly meant for him.

"Not necessary. Follow me."

We went through the secret door into an open area with more reception seating surrounded by private offices.

"I'm assuming Ms. Franklin handles electronic discovery for your office. But maybe I'm wrong," I said.

"That'd be Miguel Ángel. He's our man in security."

"Hah. Can we bother him instead?"

She stopped and turned toward me.

"That'd be a lot easier," she said. "Even I outrank Miguel."

"Then lead on."

She took me to a door marked "Server Room." I could hear the whir of cooling fans and air conditioners. Inside the windowless room were metal racks filled with blinking electronic equipment and a flabby-looking dark-haired man staring into a monitor. Pulling his eyes away from the screen, his face went from curious annoyance to something entirely different, though

410

likely unnoticed by my escort.

She introduced us and he reflexively reached around the monitor and took my hand. The grip was as soft as a jellyfish.

"I have some pretty interesting stuff on document security I'd love to share with you," I said, "if you could just give me a few minutes."

"That's up to you," she said to the man. "You busy?"

"I'm willing to bet that nobody in the world is more interested in what I have to say than Miguel," I said.

He nodded.

"We can talk in here," he said, in a low voice, gently graced with Spanish inflection.

"Suit yourself," she said, pulling up a chair for me and leaving us alone. When I heard the click of the door, I said, "Hola, Joselito."

"El Timador."

The only time I'd seen him was in the midst of extreme circumstances, but I'd never forget his face. What I saw sitting in the server room was a much more pallid and deflated version of the grandiose cyber desperado I thought I'd flushed down the drain.

"Federal maximum security is even cushier than I thought."

"You won't get away with it," he said.

"What?"

"Hurting me."

"Any hurt to you will be entirely self-inflicted. I just want to know how you did it. Not the money. I know all about that. I'm more curious about why you aren't in the deep dark hole you're supposed to be in."

"I'm not telling you anything," his voice hardening, as hate reemerged from alarm.

"I know that. Just had to ask. By the way, your access has been cut off."

A pink haze started to relieve his pasty complexion.

"I don't know what you're talking about."

"The code that gave you access to the funds. It's been changed. You're locked out."

His fingers flew over the keyboard for a few minutes, his eyes narrowing at the screen as he worked. I watched impassively, ignoring the little twist of fear that perhaps Strider had been too optimistic, or maybe too tired, to have actually slammed the door. Or doors.

The fear lifted when Joselito banged his fist on the keyboard and looked up in a blaze of panic and fury.

"*Estúpido,* do you know what you've done?"

"You convinced them I took the money.

The only reason you're free is you promised to track me down and get it back. But you still had it, neatly tucked away. In a digital sense," I said.

The implications, the cascade of eventualities, and likely a surge of faith that his shrewdness and determination would yet prevail, flew across his face. Or maybe it was the face of a cornered rat, if the rat had plenty of experience finding trapdoors.

"You won't survive this," he said. "You can't."

"I've noticed something about constant reminders of one's mortality," I said. "After a while, you stop caring."

I didn't see much point in going back to my room in Stamford, since everything of importance was in my backpack, so I just drove on from Greenwich through New York City and down the Jersey Turnpike, and eventually to Washington, DC, where I found another flophouse willing to take cash and waive the nuisance of identification.

But then I needed some computer time — there was no way around it. It was an obvious necessity, and anyway, the withdrawal from a laptop with wireless broadband Internet access had become unbearable.

I bought the equipment I needed with cash, so no credit card exposure. All I needed after that was a coffee shop with free wireless and a screen angled away from prying eyes.

Thus established, I eased into familiar applications with a joy akin to what a soldier might feel returning to the bosom of his loving family.

I loved everything about my old job as a researcher, but nothing compared to the sheer delight of tracking people down. It combined a lot of appealing elements — primary and secondary research, detective work online and in the field, even a bit of psychoanalysis as I divined the person's location based on past behavior and known peccadillos. And it was, by definition, personal. The end of the search wasn't just a hunk of data or executive summary, it was a flesh-and-blood human being.

Working in the coffee shop, I felt the familiar pull of the process, though I was still in the throes of hypervigilance. Little bolts of fear, like I'd felt with Joselito, struck at my nervous system. But they got easier to ignore as I reminded myself that if the next project failed, none of the exposure would matter.

There'd be nothing left to save.

■ ■ ■ ■

There are places within commuting distance of Washington, DC, that remind you how southerly the capital's location really is. It was meant as a compromise by the original colonies, an approximate midpoint to ease the burdens of travel to all, and the possibility of dominance by either region. In fact, the indigenous culture of the surrounding countryside was far more reminiscent of antebellum Kentucky than the industrial North.

I reflected on this as I drove past endless rows of white fencing enclosing thoroughbreds and established privilege, consumed as I was by upcoming timing and logistics. The usual mental movie reel of scenarios, what-ifs and possible outcomes.

In the midst of the analysis, however, I decided to just act without a lot of thought and see what happened. Given all that had come before, it seemed most appropriate for a last act.

The house was at the end of a long driveway shaded by big oaks to either side. A giant willow was in the front yard, its long feathery fronds swept haphazardly by the breeze. A silver Lexus was parked out front.

I felt the hood as I walked past. It was warm.

I'd put on my business suit and carried the attaché, but left off the moustache, believing a pair of dark sunglasses was the better disguise and least likely to disturb the occupant of the house.

I put the attaché, open at the top, under my left arm and rang the doorbell. This way, when the door opened I was able to reach in and remove the ceramic pistol in a fairly fluid motion, sticking the end of the blunt barrel into the forehead of the tall man standing there in a dress shirt and loosened tie.

"Captain Perry, I presume?"

He slowly stepped backward into the house, prompted by the pressure of the gun at his head. His face was stern, but cautious, in keeping with a man who'd seen his share of perilous situations.

I maneuvered him into the living room and pushed him down into the sofa. I sat across from him in a stiff wooden chair, an antique reproduction that fit in perfectly with his sumptuous Colonial décor.

"Did you hire a decorator or do all this yourself?" I asked him.

"What do you want?" he asked.

"My life back."

"Do you know who I am?"

"You're Stephen Holt, the FBI's Assistant Director for International Operations. Though to me you'll always be Captain Perry."

"Then you know how serious it is to threaten me."

"What makes you think this is a threat?"

He looked to be in his fifties, but clearly the type who shamed much younger men around the gym. He had all his hair, longer than you'd think for a federal man, and his face, while handsome, looked like it could take a punch.

"I have a wife and children."

"I had a wife once. Yours works in New York, home on the weekends, am I right?"

He saw no advantage in answering, so he didn't.

"What were you going to do with all of it?" I asked.

"I don't know what you're talking about."

"The money. A billion dollars. How would you even spend it all?"

"If anything happens to me, they'll know who did it. You'll never get away."

I wanted to smile at that, but I'm not sure I did.

"That's what's so great about this," I said. "Nobody knows but you. This is your own private project. Joselito is probably halfway to Argentina by now, Andalusky is dead and Albalita is cowering in Zurich, waiting for a loud knock on the door. This gun is completely untraceable. I'm still officially a dead man. You might have pulled a few strings around the bureau to chase us around, and convinced Shelly Gross and Jersey Mitchell that you were working a legitimate case, but that won't matter when they find out what you've been up to. Will they really want to get your killer? Why kick up a bunch of unwanted publicity when I've essentially solved their problem?"

He remained tense, but poised, calculating the odds.

"If you make the slightest move in my direction," I said, "I will shoot you in the midsection. You won't die right away, but it'll be messy."

He seemed to settle back a bit in the couch.

"You talk a lot about killing me, as if there's no other way to work this out."

"What, with the billion bucks? You'll be interested to know Joselito had it all along. He pinned it on me as a bargaining chip to keep his ass out of enemy combatant no-man's-land. But that's been fixed. Now I've actually got it, well out of Joselito's grasp.

And all the bargaining chips are off the table. Any other ideas?"

He didn't react as poorly as Joselito, but a trace of desperation managed to break free of his professional reserve.

"You said you wanted your life back."

If a person's life exists within his mind, I wondered if such a thing could still be possible for me, given what I'd become. As I weighed the possibilities, indulging for a moment a return to analysis and calculation, I couldn't help observing myself taking more careful aim at Captain Perry's head, focusing the bright red gun on a spot just above his right eye.

CHAPTER 27

I asked the cabbie if he could turn off the air conditioning and let me open the window. I'd barely left the canned air of the plane in from JFK, and keenly desired the embrace of hot, dense Caribbean air.

"Fine for me," he said. "I was born breathin' it."

The cabbie, François-Marie, had also driven a cab in Manhattan for ten years before returning to his hometown of Port-au-Prince, so he represented a welcomed point of continuity. The cab was a model car I didn't recognize, and he explained its provenance, beginning in France and arriving in Haiti after traveling through Trinidad and Guadeloupe, where it was turned into commercial transport.

Traffic was tight, but moving steadily. Lanes were less than precisely honored, though the greatest distractions were the hand-painted phantasmagoria that covered many of the vehicles, including impromptu buses. I was reminded of Ken Kesey by way of Vincent van Gogh.

Foot traffic was denser still, though it lessened as we rose and fell over the hills and through narrow streets lined with high concrete walls, many of which bore commentary in a French that resisted translation.

"Not all French," said François-Marie, when I asked him what the writing meant. "Creole and warnings by NGOs after the earthquake of dangerous buildings. Not that anyone pays any attention."

The Caribbean penchant for brilliant color was also on display at a market we passed, where the blast of the sun was blocked by umbrellas in every vivid hue. The fruits and vegetables in overflowing bins did their part as well, as did the shoppers and vendors' T-shirts and occasional poster ad or giant billboard looming over the scene.

The color dimmed as we moved into the outer parts of the city, and the walls of laid-up cement block were less artistically festooned. The sidewalks, alleys and curbsides were still amply filled with people on their daily missions of survival. Behind the walls I began to see an occasional cluster of private villas, or a hillside covered in crisp-looking homes of identical composition, painted into a sun-bleached rainbow. Though not long after, we'd passed a residential warren formed from scavenged debris, corrugated metal and blue tarps.

Everywhere the rubble of the big earthquake lay strewn across open areas and in piles of masonry and twisted rebar. François-Marie, assuming I was too diplomatic to note it myself, said, "You don't want to think what's under there."

We followed a pickup carrying several men in the bed and clinging to the tailgate through the last of the urban jumble and into the countryside. The land rolled to either side, covered in grey-green Caribbean scrub interrupted occasionally by a clump of masonry buildings fully intact, or in various stages of collapse, giving witness to the capricious nature of earthquake destruction.

François-Marie reached back for my smartphone GPS, as he had several times during the trip.

"Tell me again where you going?" he said.

"Don't know how to pronounce it. I just have the latitude and longitude."

These were written on a tattered piece of

paper handed to me by an elderly Japanese woman who forked it over after I answered a series of questions that only a person deeply intimate with her daughter, Natsumi, could answer.

We were in a small garden temple down a narrow alley off a major thoroughfare in Kyoto, shielded by the koi pool and miniature foliage from the off-world neon lunacy just a half block away.

"Glad you know what it means," the old woman told me. "Just a bunch of gibberish to me."

"It's a waypoint," I said. "A dot on the globe."

"Don't lose it," she said. "It's the only copy I have. She sent it to me inside a Chinese puzzle box. She loved those things. When I got it in the mail, I figured it was some weird thing from her. Took a hell of a long time to get it open."

I thanked her and tried to make polite small talk, but she waved me off.

"Look, when you see her, tell her to give me a call. We do have phones over here in Japan. I take it she's been keeping busy," she added.

I said she'd been thoroughly occupied, though I wasn't up to date.

"We have some catching up to do," I said.

"Well, me too. The last I heard she'd met some geek with a limp and a bald head. That must be you. Try to look after her, will you? I love her, but she's a pig-headed one."

"I'll do my best."

François-Marie handed back the GPS, which I'd set on a chart-plotter program that placed the position of our vehicle and the waypoint on the same map. According to the red and blue dots, we were closing in fast.

It was at the end of a long unpaved drive. The dust kicked up by the cab followed us to where we stopped at a sign that read in French, English and Japanese: "Free Health and Well-Being Center. Japanese-Haitian Earthquake Relief and Goodwill Foundation. All Welcome."

Farther on, we came to a plain, white-washed building with the same words in larger, friendlier type painted above the big double front doors. Several cars and small panel trucks were parked to either side and people in various states of health and well-being sat at park benches and under the building's wide eaves.

I asked François-Marie to wait and I went inside. There was a wide hallway lined with benches and blocked off by a table covered with white cotton at which sat two bright-eyed young men, one Japanese and one Haitian. I said hello in their respective languages, and held up a photo of Natsumi on my smartphone.

"She's with her afternoon group," said the Japanese guy, calling her by an unfamiliar name in barely inflected English. "You can wait here. Will only be about ten minutes."

I waited and watched them field a steady stream of other inquiries, performing the waiting room triage with calm and dignity. Eventually, the Japanese guy checked the time on his own phone, and left. He came back a few minutes later with Natsumi, wearing her Caribbean tan and native floral garb. Her face sparkled and she skipped up to me and jumped into my arms.

"What did you think of my mother?" she asked.

"Nonstandard."

"She's a nut."

"Interesting place," I said, looking around the foyer.

"It's full of French-speaking Japanese mental health professionals. Feels good to finally blend in. Those conversations at the gym with Okayo actually got to me. Most of the time I'm so involved with these people I forget everything. Except for missing you.

Horribly."

"I missed you, too. When do you get off?"

She gave me a time she could meet me at her house about a mile away. She gave me the key and told me what to pick up on the way over. While we talked she reset the smartphone GPS, placing the red dot in the middle of her neighborhood.

So I just had to hand the phone to François-Marie again, and he got me there via the local outdoor market. We shook hands, I overtipped and we wished each other great future success.

"Text me when you're ready to go back to the airport," he said, handing me his business card. "Unless you're moving in. In which case, invite me over to dinner. We can talk about the Yankees."

Natsumi arrived when promised in a Toyota crossover SUV. I had the food and drinks she prescribed waiting on a tray in her small walled garden behind the house. It was green and well tended, with tiny stone replicas of Shinto temples and seating mats on raked gravel. All it needed was a koi pond.

"No reliably clean water," she explained.

She told me how she left the room in Zurich and attached herself to a group of Japanese tourists, all of whom were too polite to object, even though it was a major social offense. She stayed with them until they entered the underground shopping mall, which had a convenient entrance to the train station. From there she hopped from Northern Italy, through Croatia, then by boat to Malta, where she joined another group of Japanese travelers, these college kids who enjoyed having the older, English-speaking countrywoman along for the ride.

"I am now conversant in current Asian pop music trends and preferences," she said.

She hung with them all the way to Marseille, where she risked passport exposure to fly to DeGaulle, then Port-au-Prince.

"As I told you, Okayo moved me with stories about the Japanese-Haitian Relief Fund," she said. "It was how I finally got to her, invoking her greatest passion. Not surprisingly, the Japanese know a thing or two about earthquakes. When we had our own big one, Haiti lost a lot of the relief workers that were here. There were plenty of spots open, even for psychologists to treat PTSD."

"Hypervigilance," I said.

"I had been reading up on the subject."

Another lucky happenstance came a few months after settling in, when an unexpected gush of fresh funding hit the

Japanese-Haitian Relief Fund ledgers.

"We manage the country's People Project microfinancing program. Suddenly each of our clients got a one-time grant for twice what they'd originally borrowed. We get a cut on every loan that goes through, same with the grants. We all got a special bonus."

"Remarkable," I said, smiling.

"I should have known it was you."

"Not directly."

"You're going to explain."

"After I make another pot of tea."

"You know the old joke about the guy who asked a woman if she'd sleep with a man for a million dollars," I said, when we were comfortably back on the seating mats. "The woman thinks about it for a moment, then says she would. So the guy asks if she'd sleep with him for a dollar. The woman, offended, says, 'What do you think I am, a whore?' And the guy says, 'We've already established that. Now we're merely haggling over the price.' "

"So every man has his price?" she asked.

"Not every man. Though some do. And some women."

"Like a billion dollars?"

"The Congress, and subsequently the State Department, earmarked the money that flowed through Fontaine into The People Project for their microfinancing program. Say what you will about the federal government, if your contract calls for you to buy popsicles, you can buy them for ten dollars a pop, but you better not spend a dime on ice cream cones."

"Albalita thought there were better places to spend some of that money."

"Chuck Andalusky convinced her that was true. Haiti, for example, his darling wife's all-consuming obsession."

"They felt the ends justified the means?" she asked.

"Sure. Even if the ends included a major enhancement of their personal bank accounts. Regular people get desensitized to big numbers hearing about them in the media. What if it's flowing by, right under your nose, day in and day out. You know that somewhere downstream, waste and corruption are busy diverting much of what you've been stewarding with the utmost care and responsibility. You might think, 'Why can't I have some, too? Don't I deserve it more, for all I've done for humanity?' "

"You've got motive, what about means?"

"That's where Joselito comes in. Knowing the evil little weasel like I do, I'm sure he brought the idea to Albalita in the first place. He made it look easy, and it was, sort of. If you were expert enough in financial manipulation, accounting hijinks and digital security. And thought you were way too smart to ever get caught."

"But he did."

"Sure, by me, for aiding and abetting international terrorism. Not the massive embezzlement scheme."

"So when Joselito got busted he had a little leverage to use with the FBI," said Natsumi.

"Oh, yeah. He'd always been deep into their international division, as an informer, consultant, general fixer and Latin lover to one of their embassy liaisons, who worked directly for Stephen Holt. It takes a rat to know a rat. Joselito tells him the whole story and shows him the proof. Holt confronts Andalusky and Albalita, but instead of dragging them down the perp walk, he says, 'It's time to play *Let's Make a Deal.*' "

"But there was one little catch."

"The money suddenly goes missing," I said. "According to Joselito, stolen by the same crafty bastard who nailed him in the first place. A shadowy figure, and the only man in the world capable of outwitting the master money manipulator. His nemesis."

"El Timador. The Trickster. Aka, too many

names to list."

"But Joselito convinces the other conspirators that only he had the chops to get it back," I said. "He just needed a safe haven, a cover story and a computer. And a little help from Holt's ties within the FBI."

"But El Timador didn't make it easy for them," she said.

"No he didn't. Joselito looked a little strained when I saw him in Greenwich. I think he was running out of time."

"Because you hadn't actually stolen the money, right darling?"

"Would you rather I had?" I asked.

"Not really."

"It would have been hard, since I knew nothing about it. But I was the perfect fall guy for Joselito. He truly hated me, and wanted revenge, but better yet, I fit the profile as a decent hacker and fulltime outlaw. When asked by Holt, our friend Shelly Gross validated that, and essentially gave up our entire story."

"Was he in on the plot?"

"Shelly thought it was a legitimate operation. Holt was the only one he talked to. Shelly can be an asshole, but he's an honest asshole."

Natsumi looked like she wanted to debate

that a little, but instead asked, "What about Jersey?"

"When Holt learned we'd extorted Andalusky's name out of Ian MacPhail, alarms went off. He had to bring Jersey into the game, but still keep a lid on his ulterior motives. But like Shelly, Jersey's a company man, so he bought the story."

"You're sure about that," she said.

"You can ask him yourself. We're meeting him for dinner on *Detour* back in Saint Thomas as soon as you can get away."

"I can get away whenever I want."

I took out François-Marie's card and gave him a call.

They arrived by pontoon boat, a big red affair about the size of the one the mercenaries used to carry us away. Jersey worked the engines while Desiree stumbled from stem to stern tossing us lines to secure the boat raft-style to *Detour.*

They both looked as brown, rangy and disheveled as they had when we first met on Saint John's. Natsumi took drink orders while I convinced Omni to stop barking.

It wasn't till everyone was settled in the cockpit that Natsumi asked Jersey the obvious.

"So you're not arresting us?"

Jersey beamed at her.

"No ma'am. Nobody's arresting you. You're both free and clear."

Except for a little wetness in the eyes, she took it calmly.

"That's nice to know," she said, then looked at me. "This is the news you were referring to?"

"It was only confirmed a few hours ago," said Jersey, saving me. "Arthur didn't know for sure."

I told her about visiting Stephen Holt in his Maryland home. How I'd taken him at gunpoint to a hotel room where Jersey had agreed to meet after I'd laid out the whole embezzlement story and all the players involved, supported by evidence that Strider had neatly arranged into a step-by-step narrative, complete with charts, graphs and screenshots of accounting ledgers.

Jersey was a bit startled to see his boss sitting on the hotel bed, but he let me play the recording I'd made of our conversation in the car on the way over, where Holt told me he'd make sure I'd live in exile, unmolested and fabulously wealthy, for the rest of my life.

Not good enough, I'd told him.

It wasn't an easy process, but eventually the internal investigators at the FBI were convinced by Strider's overwhelming evidence to charge Holt with a long list of offenses and issue a warrant for Albalita, who disappeared before they had a chance to pluck her out of Switzerland.

"We also lost track of Joselito," said Jersey. "Holt accused him of killing Andalusky, pretty convincingly, since Holt's alibi on that one is airtight. We assume he's in Latin America somewhere."

Desiree, who'd mostly been an attentive audience till then, suddenly had a question.

"What happened to the billion dollars?"

Jersey insisted on giving the answer.

"Before bringing me Holt, Arthur made a deal with the bureau to exchange the money stolen from The People Project for blanket immunity. Implicit in all this was the threat of wicked bad publicity, which everyone from the State Department on down was very eager to avoid."

"How big a blanket?" Natsumi asked.

"As big as we need," I said. "Shelly brokered the deal."

"So you got to him after all," Natsumi asked.

"No. Evelyn did."

At that point, Natsumi and Desiree broke free and went down to the galley to make dinner. Jersey and I played with Omni and talked about sailboats and the relative merits of sloops over cutters when sailing into the wind. We ate as darkness shrank the surrounding sea and opened up the sky above to the infinite stars. Jersey and Desiree agreed to stay onboard for the night, so we were all there when Jersey said there was a little more of the story left to tell. Natsumi looked concerned until he laughed and patted her knee.

"Don't worry, Arthur's got his deal," he said, "and the bureau's got its renegade Holt. But then somebody realized it was time for the State Department to get its money. And son of a bitch, wouldn't you know, it disappeared again. Poof."

"Arthur?" said Natsumi.

Jersey started to explain, but then turned it back over to me.

"Go ahead, Arthur. You know this better than I do."

I reminded them of some of the background before embarking on new territory.

"The concept behind The People Project's microfinancing program was to take a big hunk of money and distribute it in small amounts to thousands of people all over the world. When Albalita brought Joselito in as a consultant, he immediately saw an opportunity. The reason there isn't a lot more

435

thievery of government funds in programs like this are the auditors. Even if everyone's crooked, including the fiduciary — which in this case he was — you still have the auditors checking over the books in meticulous detail."

Omni chose that moment to bring me the gnarled remains of a stuffed dinosaur.

"She wants you to throw it to the bow," said Natsumi. "It's taken me weeks to keep those things out of the water."

The trick was repeated about a dozen times before she had enough, stopping amidships to chew on the slobbered fabric. I continued the story.

"Standard practice in any audit is checking with the recipients at the end of a disbursal to make sure they got the money they were supposed to get. It's impractical to check with everybody, so they pick a sample of recipients, say 10 percent, at random, and survey them. But what if your recipients are impoverished people in remote areas with shaky communications and minimum financial sophistication? And what if there are thousands of them? Not really a problem if all the recipients you manage to reach report receiving every penny of the money promised, standard audit procedure confirms that all the money's been disbursed."

"But it hasn't," said Natsumi.

"No. Because two-thirds of the people on the list of recipients don't exist. The proper information was there, in rigorous detail, but none of it was real. Joselito wrote a software program that generated thousands of these phony approved loans, each with their own account number. These accounts were labeled with their own special code, so when the time came, Joselito could punch in a few commands and transfer the orphaned money however and wherever he wanted."

"And Strider figured this out," said Natsumi.

"All she did was double-check the contact information, confirming the business registrations, addresses and telephone numbers. It only took uncovering a half-dozen phantom borrowers to realize what was up. Once she isolated the special tag on each of the fake accounts, she had the whole thing."

I was doing the talking, but everyone was looking at Jersey, who seemed to be bursting at the seams to chime in. So I let him.

"Joselito labeled all these phony accounts to make it easy for the computer to go in there and scoop out all the embezzled money," he said. "It made it just as easy for Strider to write a command that transferred that same money into the accounts of legitimate borrowers, in equal amounts spread out across the entire program. With a friendly note that said, 'Please accept this one-time gift from the People of the United States of America, who wish you long life and prosperity.' "

We raised a toast to Strider, along with the heartfelt hope that she continue to evade capture, and if not, that she'd plundered enough bank accounts to afford a really good lawyer.

We gave Jersey and Desiree our big V berth and set ourselves up in the cockpit with pillows, quilts and the dubious attention of a small mutt. I was happier for it, to be in the warm air driven by the persistent trade winds that I'd thought about every day and night from the moment the mercenaries took it from me.

And that night, the gentle slap of the bay waves against the hull spoke to me as a whole man. Having lived in every world outside of the one I was born into, I knew with utter conviction that this was the one I would always long for.

Whether they let me stay here or not.